"My name's Mitch Ryan,"

he said softly, and held out his hand.

Tina took it, and knew instantly she shouldn't have. There was something about him that bothered her, and the feeling was immediately reinforced by his touch.

She looked down at her hand, engulfed within his. Jake's hands had been large, too, masculine and full of strength, yet they'd possessed the most tender touch she'd ever experienced.

Tina swallowed hard and found herself suddenly fighting to gain composure. Her reaction to him was totally ridiculous. She didn't know this man, and she didn't want to know him. He was just passing through.

Like Jake, she thought, reminding herself of a mistake she didn't need—or want—to repeat....

Dear Reader,

You'll be glad the kids are going back to school, leaving you time to read every one of this month's fabulous Silhouette Intimate Moments novels. And you'll want to start with *One Moment Past Midnight,* by multiaward-winning Emilie Richards. You'll be on the edge of your seat as Hannah Blackstone and her gorgeous neighbor, Quinn McDermott, go in search of Hannah's kidnapped daughter.

Elizabeth August makes a welcome return with *Logan's Bride,* a cop-meets-cop romance to make your heart beat just a little faster. With *The Marriage Protection Program,* Margaret Watson completes her CAMERON, UTAH miniseries, and a memorable finale it is. Historical author Lyn Stone has written her first contemporary romance, *Beauty and the Badge,* and you'll be glad to know she intends to keep setting stories in the present day. *Remembering Jake* is a twisty story of secrets and hidden identities from talented Cheryl Biggs. And finally, welcome Bonnie K. Winn, with *The Hijacked Wife,* a FAMILIES ARE FOREVER title.

And once you've finished these terrific novels, mark October on your calendar, because next month Rachel Lee is back, with the next installment of her top-selling CONARD COUNTY miniseries.

Enjoy!

Leslie Wainger

Leslie Wainger
Executive Senior Editor

Please address questions and book requests to:
Silhouette Reader Service
U.S.: 3010 Walden Ave., P.O. Box 1325, Buffalo, NY 14269
Canadian: P.O. Box 609, Fort Erie, Ont. L2A 5X3

REMEMBERING JAKE

CHERYL BIGGS

Silhouette®

INTIMATE™MOMENTS®

Published by Silhouette Books

America's Publisher of Contemporary Romance

SILHOUETTE BOOKS

ISBN 0-373-07953-2

REMEMBERING JAKE

Books by Cheryl Biggs

Silhouette Intimate Moments

The Return of the Cowboy #762
The Cowboy She Never Forgot #911
Remembering Jake #953

CHERYL BIGGS

was never really a reader while growing up, but got hooked on Gothics, then romances, when her three children were little. While they napped, she read. Finally she decided to write a romance. That manuscript went into the closet, with the next four or five. Years later, after selling her personnel agency, she pulled out her first manuscript and went to an RWA conference, which garnered her an agent and several good friends. A year later that first book was sold, and a dream came true.

Cheryl lives in the San Francisco Bay Area, in a sunny suburb at the foot of Mount Diablo with her husband, five cats and a blue-eyed dog. Her children are now grown, and in her spare time she loves to travel, shop, read and try to talk her husband, Jack, into adopting "just one more animal."

Readers can write to Cheryl at P.O. Box 6557, Concord, CA 94520.

This book is dedicated with lots of love to my mother, Dorothy Brassea, in appreciation for always being there with an encouraging word, among other things.

Chapter 1

Someone had wanted him dead. Someone had succeeded. Now he was going to find out who, and why.

He glanced at the road sign. Reimour Crossings, Georgia—ten miles. Memories came flooding back to him as he passed the weather-beaten marker. He bit down unconsciously on his bottom lip, and anxiety began to pound in his blood. Ten miles to hell. His left hand tightened its grip on the leather-encased steering wheel of the black Thunderbird the agency had arranged for him to use, while his right hand crushed the empty soda can he was holding. He shoved it into a trash bag that hung just below the passenger-side dashboard and cursed softly, thinking again about what had happened just off this road three years ago.

He didn't actually remember what had transpired that morning, at least not all of it, and the doctors said he should be thankful for that. The beating had been horribly savage, his survival a miracle. But he really didn't need to remember the actual attack; all he had to do was look into a mirror. His body showed the scars, and his face... He scoffed softly. His face wasn't even his face anymore.

He'd purposely taken a different route so that he wouldn't have to pass the spot where it had happened.

From behind the mirrored, aviator-style glasses that he wore, his gaze slid over the scenery as he sped past. Nothing good was going to come of this trip. The thought nagged at the back of his mind. Whether Tina was the one who had actually betrayed him or not, nothing good was going to come of going back. But then *good* wasn't what he was after. Revenge, justice, the truth; that was what he needed, to finally know who had stolen his life—who had murdered his brother—and why.

The late-morning sun shone brightly above the thick growth of oak and pine and cypress trees that grew on both sides of the road. But he knew that no matter how bright the light, it would never totally penetrate the tangled boughs and the deep shadows they created over the land below.

An edginess slipped quietly into his veins and he eased his foot off the accelerator slightly as he drew closer to the outskirts of town. Static suddenly overtook the music that had been playing on the radio. He glanced down at the dial and, frowning unconsciously, reached out to change it. Memory of a black pickup truck speeding up behind him and crashing into the bumper of his car flashed into his mind, unbidden and unwelcomed.

Tension seized him. Suddenly he could feel the fists beating on him, the flames licking at his legs, the excruciating heat searing into his flesh, the pain consuming him.

His gaze shot to the rearview mirror and his grip tightened around the steering wheel. Seeing nothing but empty road behind him, he let a long, slow sigh of relief escape his lips. Three years and it was still as if it had happened yesterday. He turned his gaze back to the road and his heart instantly jumped into his throat.

"Son of a…" He jerked on the wheel and slammed his foot down hard on the brake. The car's tires screeched loudly as the T-bird skidded, swerved and finally came to a stop, sideways, in the middle of the road. He glared through his window at the horse and rider who, barely a dozen feet from him now, had paused directly in the center of the road, obviously both in shock at nearly being hit.

The woman sitting astride the sleek, chestnut animal threw a quick glance over her shoulder at him. Sunlight glinted off the lenses of the dark glasses she wore, but before he could discern more, she turned her attention back to the horse, who was shuffling nervously about the road. Holding tight to the reins with one hand, the woman ran her other hand soothingly along the large equine's graceful neck while muttering words of comfort in an effort to calm him.

Music abruptly broke through the static on the radio.

She threw a glance toward the car, then turned back to the horse just as quickly.

He ignored the music as the breath that had stalled in his lungs broke free and rushed past his lips. As he waited for his heart to stop slamming against his rib cage, his gaze moved appraisingly over the mounted woman. Dressed in faded jeans and T-shirt, it was obvious she had a body that was all svelte curves and enticing lines. But that was about all he could see now as she leaned forward toward the animal's head, wavy strands of dark brown hair obscuring sight of her face from him as she continued to stroke the horse's neck and croon in his ear.

She could have gotten them all killed, riding into the road like that. He reached for the door handle. "Just a damned good thing there wasn't another car on the road," he grumbled to himself, throwing the door open and pushing to his feet, "or we'd probably all be roadkill right about now."

The horse jerked around to stare at him as he straightened behind the open car door. The sound of the animal's shod hooves connecting with the blacktop was an unchoreographed series of frantic clip-clops.

The woman drew the reins taut and pulled her attention from the horse to direct it at him.

"Don't move," she ordered, as he started to step around the door.

The animal's ears twitched frantically at the movement, and his brown eyes looked wilder than they had only a few seconds earlier, as if he was just waiting to be given the slightest reason to bolt.

"Stay still," she demanded again, raising a hand toward him, and holding tight to the reins with the other, but never taking her eyes from the horse. "Easy, boy," she crooned softly. The animal began to still, and she moved a hand up and down his neck, caressing away his panic. "It's okay, SunnyLad, no one's going to hurt you."

Time stopped, then sped wildly backward. The years he'd been gone, all the time he'd been "dead," suddenly disappeared. He froze, not because she'd told him to, but because he'd recognized her voice. He hadn't expected that. Holding tight to the door frame with one hand, his knuckles whitening from the pressure of his grip, he stared at the woman and silently willed her to look up at him.

"You could have gotten us both killed, you know," she said, looking directly at him finally, her tone edged with icy indignation. "Barreling around the curve like that. Didn't you see the sign back there that told you to watch out for animals and equestrians crossing the road?"

He couldn't answer. For months he'd thought of nothing

more than what he would say to her the first time he saw her again, and now he couldn't think of a thing.

As the horse finally began to quiet, the woman slid a gloved hand through her own dark hair and, glaring at him, yanked off her dark glasses.

Suddenly he found himself looking into the same blue eyes that had haunted his dreams and nightmares ever since he'd come out of the coma two years ago and learned his entire world had been destroyed. But before he could even begin to collect his thoughts and respond, she slid her glasses back on, and touched a rein to the horse's neck, a heel to his flank. The animal immediately swung around, jumped gracefully from the pavement, and horse and rider disappeared into the woods.

A bird chirped from somewhere in the trees. A car passed. Sunlight beat down on the back of his neck. He ignored it all, as if mesmerized, and stood next to his car, staring into the shadows in which Tina had disappeared.

"He could have killed us," Tina mumbled, dragging the grooming brush over SunnyLad's back. "The maniac." But she knew being nearly run down by a handsome man in a snazzy car wasn't what was really bothering her.

It wasn't the first close call she'd had while riding, and it most likely wouldn't be her last.

A fluttering wave of tremors swept through her, racing up her spine, down her arms, and through her fingers as she remembered the stranger, remembered that brief moment when she had taken off her sunglasses and they'd stared at each other. It was as if she could still feel his eyes moving over her. It didn't matter that she hadn't actually seen them, that his eyes had remained hidden behind the reflective silver lenses of his dark glasses. She had felt them roaming over every inch of her body.

Absently, she slid the brush over the horse's hip, then down his rear leg. No man had ever looked at her like that, as if assessing everything about her, probing and searching, and finally delving past all the barriers of her mind and heart in search of her most private thoughts and feelings. As if in search of her soul. No one except Jake. She tried to push the thought aside, then took several deep breaths and straightened, admonishing herself when her imagination wouldn't let go of the idea that had popped into her mind. That had been a long time ago and there was no connection between past and present, except maybe in her ridiculous fantasies.

Turning SunnyLad out to pasture, Tina left the barn. She had just enough time to get ready for work. The flowers in the pots hanging from the roof of the veranda that wrapped around the elegant old planter's-style house that had been in her family for generations, had opened to the morning sun while she'd been out riding. She paused and picked a few to take inside. The phone rang the moment she stepped past the back door and into the kitchen. Tina grabbed it from the wall. "Hello?"

"Hey, Sis, where've you been? I've been calling for an hour."

Tina recognized her younger sister's voice and instinctively braced for bad news—a trait that had become a habit she wished she could break. "Dee, is everything all right? The kids haven't—"

"Brought the city of Savannah to its knees?" Dee said, cutting Tina off and laughing. "No, well, not yet anyway. Your kids are fine."

Tina felt weak with relief. She knew she was overprotective, and she knew the children were safe with her sisters, but she couldn't help worrying. Too many things had happened in recent years to ever let her be complacent, or take life for granted again.

"Joey's on the floor playing with a truck set I bought him, and Jimmy's splashing around in the bathtub with a rubber duck that makes the most awful noises." Dee laughed. "Lily's keeping an eye on him, to answer the question I know you're about to ask."

"Thank you," Tina said, smiling as she remembered how her sisters had dubbed her the worrywart.

"Anyway, the beach was great, I'm just sorry you couldn't come, too."

"Well, until I can hire someone to replace Hilda and Ed to handle things at the café, neither Uncle Deano nor I can leave," she said, trying to sound cheerier than she felt. The older couple had worked for her father at the café for longer than she could remember, but upon her father's death they'd decided to retire. Tina had refused to sell the place, so her uncle had stepped in to help, but she still hadn't managed to hire anyone else. "But I have an ad in several neighboring papers for a waitress and another cook."

"Good, but listen. Some of the fabrics I ordered for Mrs. DeMille's redecorating job were delayed and won't be in until this afternoon, which as it turns out is okay because Lianne and I have been invited to a dinner tonight that could very well get us some new clients here in Savannah. But we don't want to make the drive home afterward, it'll be late, so—" her tone became slightly pleading "—would you mind terribly if we stayed over tonight and came home tomorrow?"

Another night in an empty house. Some people would relish it. Tina dreaded it. She forced a smile into her voice. "Fine. Have fun. I'll see you tomorrow." Twenty minutes later she was ready to leave for the café. As she grabbed her car keys from the small flower table set against one wall of the foyer, the mirror hanging above it caught her eye.

The stranger's face, his eyes hidden behind a pair of silver-lensed aviator glasses, filled her mind again. There had been something about him....

After sitting on the side of the highway for almost an hour after his encounter with Tina, he finally started his car and drove into town.

She hadn't recognized him. But then why should she?

The anger and frustration he'd lived with every waking moment of the past two years burned hot within him, but it was nothing compared to the loneliness and sense of loss that continually gnawed at him.

He'd loved her more than anything on earth. He would have given his life for her. But Raskin was right; she was the only one who'd known who and what he really was. Logic, past experience and his training pointed him in only one direction: purposely or unwittingly, she had to be the one who'd betrayed him.

He drove slowly down the narrow main street of Reimour Crossings, secure in the knowledge that behind the tinted windows of the black Thunderbird and the mirrored aviator glasses, no one could see him. Then he reminded himself that it wouldn't matter even if they did—no one would ever recognize him.

Jake Blaggette had died three years ago. A year later, when he'd finally come out of the coma to find his life had been destroyed, his brother had been murdered, and the woman he'd loved had married someone else, he had become Mitch Ryan.

His own grandmother, who'd raised him, wouldn't be able to pick him out of a lineup. Still, a nagging worry pulled incessantly at his thoughts. Maybe his grandmother wouldn't recognize him, but Tina was different. She had held his face while her lips passionately claimed his. She had pressed her body to his and explored his mouth with a tongue of fire, she had slid her hands over his naked body until he was nearly half-crazy with desire.

He dragged a hand over his face. No, there was no way anyone would recognize him now. Not even Tina. Twelve months in a coma had left his muscles weak and near emaciated. It had taken two years of mindless rehabilitation and grueling exercise to repair his body and get it back into shape. At the same time he'd endured seemingly endless and painful months of plastic surgery on his face. But rather than try to repair what had been almost totally demolished, the doctors had started anew.

There was very little about him now that was the same as it had been three years ago. His attackers' fists had broken his bones and torn his skin, then they'd set his car on fire and left him to die. But he hadn't died...and if it was the last thing he ever did, he would find them and make them wish they had never come after him, let alone left him in that clearing with even the slightest thread of life left in him.

His hair had grown back darker and coarser. His throat had been so damaged by the smoke he'd inhaled that his voice had a gravelly sound to it now, and the fire's heat had played havoc with his eyes, making it necessary that he constantly wear shaded contacts.

To further disguise any semblance of his old self, he'd chosen contacts that turned his blue eyes an almost depthless dark brown. His hands tightened on the steering wheel as memories, not quite discernible through the fog that swirled around them, drifted through his mind.

While he'd struggled to put himself back together, both mentally and physically, he had utilized every resource the

Agency had in order to learn everything he could about Tina, her family, her friends and Reimour Crossings, Georgia. But there was still so much he didn't know. He'd refused the Agency's suggestion of sending in an agent undercover. His brother had tried to find out what had happened, and he'd ended up dead. That was something he'd found almost impossible to live with, and he didn't want another man's death on his conscience. But without an agent in place undercover there were still many people in and around Reimour Crossings who remained mysteries, and incidents that went unexplained. Instead of easing his suspicions, the things he did learn and the horde of questions that remained unanswered only added to them.

But everything revolved around Tina. That had become an inescapable fact.

He let his gaze move over the old buildings that lined each side of the town's main street, most of which had been there since before the War Between the States, and had escaped Sherman's wrath.

No one paid him any real mind as he drove past. A few people sitting in front of the hardware store made gestures as if admiring his car, or commenting on what they assumed was a tourist who'd wandered off the main highway. But he knew no one suspected who it really was behind the stranger's face and tinted glass.

As he approached the opposite end of town, he neared the Magnolia Inn. Its tall, sloped roof was nearly hidden behind the sprawling, moss-laden limbs of the half dozen oak trees that lined the well-worn brick walkway leading to its porch. Several people sat on the gallery that ran the entire length of the nineteenth-century house. With green shutters adorning each glistening, tall window, and gingerbread woodwork edging its roofline, it seemed apparent the builder had been unable to make up his mind whether he was building an antebellum mansion or a Victorian town house. Like the rest of the town, though, the Magnolia Inn looked exactly the same as it had when he'd driven up to it and checked in three years ago.

His gaze moved to the half dozen cabins set off to one side of the house, tiny replicas of the main residence, and settled on the one nearest the creek.

They'd made love in that cabin the night he'd proposed to her.

Memories threatened to crash down on him and he swore softly. He jerked on the car's steering wheel and made an abrupt U-turn. Getting himself a place to stay could wait. He had somewhere else to go first. Anger churned through him now, blotting out every other thought and emotion. The last time he'd been in Reimour Crossings someone had stolen his life, then murdered his brother. Whoever it was thought they'd brought the situation to a close with Perry's death, thought that they were safe from whatever threat Jake Blaggette had posed to them, but they were wrong.

He moved his right leg slightly, feeling reassured as his calf muscle registered the touch of the lightweight Smith & Wesson strapped to his ankle. He pulled off the road and into the café's parking lot.

His gaze moved slowly over the familiar building, taking in every line and corner, every spot of light and shadow, as had become his habit since leaving the hospital. It was exactly the same as he remembered.

He flexed his hands, curling his fingers into hard, tight fists. Someone in Reimour Crossings had betrayed him. Someone had wanted him dead. Now he was back to find out who, and his prime suspect was the woman he'd once loved more than anything in life.

Chapter 2

Tina heard the sound of tires crunching on gravel and turned to look out the café's window. A ripple of unease slithered its way up her spine as her gaze came to rest on the same shiny black Thunderbird she'd encountered earlier that morning.

So, he hadn't just driven through.

She stared at the car's heavily tinted windows, trying to see past them, but they were too dark and the glare of the morning sun, dancing a near-blinding reflection off them, was too bright.

"Hey, Tina, how about another lemonade?"

She glanced over her shoulder at the two older men sitting at the counter. The tall, skinny retiree who'd spoken winked as he caught her eye.

"Another lemonade?" She forced her attention away from the car out front. "I don't know, Claude," she said, trying to sound cheerily flippant, "I make my brew kind of tart, you know, and I think you're already a pretty sour old sort, don't you?''

She heard a car door shut and tensed. He was coming into the café.

Claude's bushy gray brows shot up as his eyes widened. ''Sour? Me?'' He chuckled and slapped a gnarled hand on the counter. ''Hell, come on, Tina, you know blasted well I'm one of the sweetest guys around these here parts.''

Fred Gateau, owner of the hardware store, and sitting next to Claude, laughed. ''Yeah, sweet as a lemon, you womanizing old coot.''

In spite of the good-natured bickering that erupted between the two older men, Tina heard the sound of the screen door opening as it creaked on its old hinges. She tried not to look toward it, but she couldn't help herself.

He'd paused in the doorway, the bright light of the late-morning sun at his back combating the store's artificial light, so that his body was eclipsed by shadow, turning it to a black silhouette.

She couldn't see his face, couldn't distinguish his features, and that stirred a sense of annoyance through her she didn't understand.

He stepped forward then, just one step, and Tina felt the breath catch in her throat.

Darkness and light seemed to coalesce around him. The brilliance of the sun streaming in from the veranda and through the door and windows created a halo of light behind him, caressed the wide breadth of his shoulders and glistened off the black locks that curled raggedly over the collar of his white shirt. Yet for all the light streaming toward him, shadows still clung to him everywhere, obscuring sight of his eyes, lingering within the hollows of his cheeks and hovering about the folds of his shirt.

Tina told herself to stop staring, then continued to do so.

Finally, retrieving at least part of her senses, she nodded and forced herself to smile. "Hi," she said softly, pushing the lone word past a suddenly dry throat. Only then did she realize she was holding the curved handle of the lemonade pitcher in a death grip.

He took another step forward, as if her smile was all he'd been waiting for.

Her gaze met his, her own blue eyes locking with eyes so dark she wasn't certain if they were brown or black. She suddenly remembered how she'd always felt she could lose herself within the blue of Jake's eyes, but this man's eyes instantly threatened to devour her. Unable to look away, and not really wanting to, her gaze roamed his face, darting over features that were a blend of roughly cut lines and rugged contours.

Like the rest of him, there was intense strength in his features, along with unconcealed hardness. His jaw was square, like hewed granite, his cheekbones cut high, his nose straight. There seemed a barbaric handsomeness in that face that was at once intriguing and unnerving.

He was a stranger, yet something about him made Tina suddenly feel as if she'd met him before. Her eyes narrowed slightly as she studied him, trying to remember.

His lips, held tight at the moment, seemed neither full nor thin, but merely a slash of flesh above the faint cleft in his chin. Tiny lines curved about the outer corners of his mouth and eyes, like laugh lines, yet when she looked back into those inky dark eyes, Tina knew with a certainty beyond any doubt that this man didn't laugh all that much.

She also knew that, in spite of the sudden and intense sense of familiarity, a feeling that was unexplainable and unreasonable, but kept tugging at her as she stared at him, there was no way she would ever have forgotten if she had met him before.

"Well, I gotta be gettin' back to the store before that youngster I hired to help out sells everythin' at cost and leaves me sittin' in the poorhouse," Fred said, chuckling. He threw a few dollars on the counter, then slid off his stool and walked toward the door. He nodded at Mitch as he passed, gave him a curious once-over, and tossed a wave over his shoulder to Tina and Claude.

The screen door slammed soundly behind him.

Tina nearly dropped the pitcher of lemonade as the sound jerked her from the spell that had fallen over her. She cleared her throat and, setting the pitcher down, busied herself behind the counter. "Umm, can I get you something, sir?"

The truth, Mitch thought coldly. He moved toward the counter, his boots eerily silent upon the ancient plank floor.

She watched him approach, his steps long, easy, almost graceful. An aura of self-confidence seemed to exude from him in a barrage of masculine virility, stirring her senses and tossing her memories about, reminding her of another time, another man, who'd impressed her very much the same way upon their first meeting.

Tina tried to rearrange some glasses beneath the counter, keep her gaze averted from his, and ignore the fact her hands were trembling. But it was a useless effort, so she gave it up and straightened.

He smiled slightly, but in his eyes she saw something else, not warmth or welcome, but wariness. She wondered at it, and felt suddenly as if she were watching the approach of a hunter, cold-blooded and deliberate, his weapons well honed, his senses on full alert, his instincts directing him toward his quarry.

A shiver of apprehension quietly stole through her body. She felt an almost overwhelming need to escape, but found herself unable to even look away.

He slid onto one of the stools, never taking his gaze from hers. His lips curved into a smile, and the transformation of his features was almost shocking. Coldness turned to warmth, and the wariness Tina thought she had seen in him turned to friendliness.

"I'll have a piece of apple pie," he said, glancing at the large wooden menu sign her father had made and hung on the wall behind her only a few months before he'd died.

His voice was deep, but rather than velvet smooth, as she remembered Jake's had been, this man's voice had a harsh quality to it, as if having to force its way past a throat lined with sandpaper.

"Apple pie," Tina echoed, and turned away quickly, struggling to regain some sense of the composure she'd lost in the past few minutes. Something about him unnerved her. Something she didn't understand and couldn't explain. She cut a healthy piece of the pie he'd requested, slid it onto a plate, and placed it before him.

"Coffee too, please. Regular," he added, noting the sign also said "decaff, mocha and au lait." Strong, black and loaded with caffeine. It was all he needed in the morning to wake him up, and what had kept him going through endless days of rehab, and long nights of searching through the past for answers he hadn't found yet. He watched her move away from him. Emotion tied his insides into a knot. How could she have claimed she loved him, and then betrayed him so treacherously? Even if it had been unwitting, she must have realized what she'd done, and she hadn't warned him. Anger roiled through his blood, heating it, stoking his temper. How could she have set him up to be killed? Because unwitting or not, that was exactly what she'd done. He picked up his fork and stabbed at the pie she'd placed before him.

He remembered what his superior at the Agency had

tried to impress on him time and again over the past two years. The attempt on his life might have been the result of nothing more than her making a slip of the tongue to the wrong person. And his brother's murder could very well have come at the hands of someone from Perry's own past, someone not even connected to Tina Peychaud, Reimour Crossings or Jake Blaggette. But he'd shaken off those possibilities, because he had just never given much credence to coincidence.

And Ivor Raskin had agreed. Coincidence was not something they put much stock in at the Agency, and as his superior, and friend, Raskin also agreed. They had to proceed assuming the worst scenario was the right one.

The most logical conclusion was that Tina had betrayed him, and Perry had found evidence of it, or come too close to it for someone's comfort. For that he'd ended up dead, his body dumped in the middle of Savannah's Columbia Square.

Was Tina responsible for that too? Another *accident?* Another *slip of the tongue?* Or a plan well thought out and acted upon?

Mitch's free hand clenched into a fist as it rested on his thigh, and he watched her.

No one else had known the truth.

The need to grab her, accuse her, force her to tell him what had happened, why she'd given him away, almost overwhelmed him. Mitch gritted his teeth, rolled his shoulders slightly and struggled against the urge with the cold, hard resolve that had been his constant companion since the day he'd wakened from the coma and found his world had been utterly and forever destroyed.

As she retrieved a mug from under the counter and grabbed the coffeepot from its burner, he studied her face, finding both delicacy and strength in the temptingly curved lips, and nose that flared and turned up just slightly at the end. His gaze moved over the scoop-necked white blouse, lingered just a moment too long on the little red ribbon centered between and just above her breasts, then skimmed appreciatively over the subtle curve of her hips, accentuated by the snug fit of her faded blue jeans.

Without wanting to, he remembered how good it had felt to hold her in his arms, and how her body had fit so perfectly against his.

He'd made love to dozens of women before her, some more beautiful, more seductive or exotic, but none had affected him as she had. None had made him want to trust. None had made him feel love. None had made him think of endless tomorrows and promises of forever. Except her.

A knot of emotion Mitch hadn't expected to feel coiled itself, hot, burning and traitorous, in the pit of his stomach, while its twin lodged itself in his throat. He'd lived with nothing more than his memories for the past two years, and a picture of her the Agency had obtained from the Department of Motor Vehicles for the case file. But neither had done her justice. She was more beautiful than he remembered. Her long, dark hair appeared more luxurious, her blue eyes bluer, her gold-touched skin creamier. And he had forgotten how sensuous he'd always found her voice.

She set the mug of coffee down in front of him.

"Thanks." He raised the cup to his lips, letting the hot liquid burn his tongue, then scald his throat, the pain reminding him why he was there, and helping to dull the subversive thoughts and memories that had invaded his mind and body.

She looked up and their eyes met. Her breath nearly deserted her. Flushed, Tina turned quickly away, switched on an electric cooking pot beneath the counter, moved a glass, checked the ice cream freezer's temperature. It was only because she found him physically attractive, she told herself, and it had been a long time since that feeling had stirred to life in her. A long time since she'd allowed it to stir to life.

"Delicious," Mitch said, knowing he needed to draw her back to him and into conversation if he was going to get anywhere with his plan. "I think this is the best apple pie I've had in years."

She turned, forcing a bright smile to her lips. "Thanks. It's an old family recipe my uncle..." He was holding his fork with its prongs curved down, just the way Jake had always done. Tina swallowed hard, her gaze glued to the uncannily familiar sight. She never let herself think of Jake anymore, yet all of a sudden, with this stranger's appearance... She shook the thought aside. Lianne was right; she'd been working too hard lately.

He took another bite. "Peychaud Café," Mitch said, glancing at the wall menu again. "Is that you?"

Tina nodded and answered almost automatically. "My great-grandfather started the place. I took it over a few months ago when my dad passed away."

"Umm." Mitch nodded. "Sorry. Do you make everything you serve here?"

She found a thread of composure and laughed nervously. "Some, though my uncle does a lot of the cooking."

"Then I guess I'll have to come back for a real meal."

Warmth invaded her cheeks as he smiled, his eyes holding to hers. She was being ridiculous. Tina felt Claude watching her, but then that was what the people in Reimour Crossings did; watched each other, and watched *out* for each other. She forced a friendly smile to her lips. "So, what brings you to our little town, the fishing or the scenery?"

I need to know why you betrayed me. The words

screamed from Mitch's mind, but not his lips. "Actually, both," he said. "Got a little time off work so I decided to go somewhere my boss couldn't find me, do a bit of fishing and just kick back and relax a little."

Jake had come here on vacation, too, had said almost the same thing that first day, when he'd come into the café.

"Well, I don't know about your boss finding you, young fella," Claude said, spinning about on his stool and grinning at Mitch, "but you sure 'nough come to the right place to fish. If you want a guide, I'm just about the best one in the business around here."

Mitch nodded at the older man. "Yeah? Thanks, I'll keep that in mind if I decide I need a guide." He turned his gaze back to Tina. "Name's Mitch Ryan," he said softly, and held out his hand.

She took it, and knew instantly she shouldn't have. There was something about him that bothered her, and the feeling was immediately reinforced, deepened, by the touch of his hand to hers.

The moment his hand wrapped around hers Mitch felt an urge to let go of it, and at the same time he wanted nothing more than to hang on to it for the rest of his life. Memories of passion loomed up within him to war with suspicions of betrayal and the thin, fragile thread of hope he couldn't quite seem to get rid of. He forcefully shrugged them all aside except the one he needed the most...the deep, smoldering rage that would help him do what he had come here to do.

She looked down at her hand, nearly swallowed within his. Jake's hands had been large, too, masculine and full of strength, yet they'd possessed the most tender touch she'd ever experienced. She withdrew her hand from his, wishing her memories would go away as easily. "It's nice to meet you, Mr. Ryan. I'm Tina Dubois."

Dubois, not Peychaud. He'd known that, yet hearing her say it still set him back for a minute. He turned his attention to the apple pie and finished off the last bite before looking back up at her. Was it innocence he saw within those beautiful blue eyes? Or treachery? He felt as if he were being torn in two.

"Dubois." He looked at her left hand, even though he didn't have to. "Does that mean you're married?"

"Widowed," she said softly.

"Umm, sorry again." He let several seconds of silence pass, as if considering what he was about to say. "Would you have dinner with me tonight, Tina Dubois?"

Her heart hammered a thunderous beat in her breast. She swallowed hard and found herself suddenly fighting again for the composure she'd just barely managed to recapture a moment earlier. Her reaction to him was totally ridiculous. She didn't know this man, and frankly, she told herself, she didn't want to know him. He was just in town on vacation. Passing through. A handsome face on the way to somewhere else. Like Jake, she thought, reminding herself that had been a mistake she didn't need or want to repeat.

She opened her mouth to thank him for the invitation, and offer an excuse for declining it, when the sound of wheels rolling over the café's gravel parking lot drew her attention. She turned to glance out the window.

The instant she spotted the police patrol car, Tina tensed.

A few moments later, the screen door opened, its squeaky hinges screaming through the silence, and Sheriff Dack Brenaud stepped into the café. He practically filled the doorway as he paused there, meaty fists resting on his hips, mountainous shoulders stiffly poised, his Western-style sheriff's hat pulled low over his wide forehead, the shadows the hat created momentarily hiding his face.

Mitch glanced over his shoulder. The impression of a

menacing black shadow suddenly flashed through his mind. He wondered at it, then dismissed it. If there had been one man in Reimour Crossings he hadn't liked three years ago, it was Sheriff Dack Brenaud. Mitch allowed no recognition to register on his face.

"Hey, darlin'," Dack said, dismissing Mitch with a brief glance and smiling at Tina, "getting pretty hot out there this morning."

She'd always hated his casual endearments, but never more than when he'd used them in front of Jake...and now. But getting him to stop had proved a lost cause. "Would you like some lemonade, Dack?" she asked, forcing a cheeriness to her tone she was far from feeling.

"Sure, darlin', that would just hit the spot." He walked to the small counter, both hands resting on the thick gun belt at his waist, and slid onto one of the stools. Lazing an elbow on the counter, he turned his back to Claude, who had stuck his nose into a magazine upon the sheriff's appearance. Dack jammed a booted foot onto the stool next to his own, and stared at Mitch. "Well now." His gaze raked over Mitch. "Heard we had a stranger in town."

Mitch glanced over his shoulder at Dack, meeting the man's beady, hazel-eyed stare. "I guess you must mean me, Deputy."

Dack grinned. "Yep. But I'm the sheriff, stranger, not a deputy."

The door opened again just then, and a short, thin man in a uniform identical to Dack Brenaud's strode into the room.

Mitch looked back at the sheriff and nodded. "Sorry, but it's real nice of you to personally come welcome me to town, sheriff. Your deputy, too," he added, glancing at the man who sat at one of the tables nearby.

"Yeah, he's new to these parts, too, but he's learning."

"Well, it's a nice touch. Don't believe I've ever experienced that kind of hospitality before."

Dack smiled. "Then I take it you've never been south of the Mason-Dixon line before," he said easily, chuckling at his own remark.

Mitch shook his head and glanced over his shoulder again at the deputy he'd heard Claude call Harlon. The man grinned at him, and Mitch felt his insides instantly recoil.

Instinct told him the deputy was definitely deadly. The man's eyes told him he was cunning. The type who would strike with no warning, not wanting to give his opponent a chance to defend himself.

"You staying here in town?" Dack asked, with an air of importance.

Mitch nodded. "The Magnolia Inn." He glanced at Tina and saw her eyes widen, just slightly.

"Vacation?" Dack persisted.

Mitch turned to fully face the man. "I plan on doing a little fishing, a little relaxing, and getting a lot of peace and quiet," he said pointedly. He hadn't liked Dack Brenaud three years ago, had thought of him as too nosy and affable. The fact that he'd suspected the sheriff was more than a little interested in Tina hadn't helped either. Now, the few minutes the man had been in the café only confirmed there was no reason for Mitch to change that feeling.

They stared at each other for a long moment before Dack shrugged and glanced away. "Just like to know what folks are up to in my town, you know?" He took a long swig of the lemonade Tina placed before him. When the glass was empty, he pushed it across the counter and turned back to Mitch. "Especially strangers."

Mitch nodded again. "Sure. I understand. Nowadays you just can't be too sure of anyone." His gaze moved back to

Tina, but he felt the deputy's eyes riveted to his back. "Especially strangers."

"Would you like some more coffee?" she asked Mitch a moment later, breaking the brittle silence that had filled the air as the two men stared at her.

He rose. "No, thanks. I've got to get going." He tossed enough money on the counter to cover his check and a tip, and turned toward the door. Pushing open the screen, he paused and looked back.

The deputy was watching him. So was Tina, her brow furrowed slightly, a thoughtful expression in her eyes.

The sheriff was watching her.

"See you later, Tina," Mitch said.

Dack waited until he heard the screen door close. "What'd he mean, he'd see you later?"

She shrugged, trying to act blasé. But if it was working on the outside, it certainly wasn't working on the inside. Her heart was hammering so hard she thought it was going to explode, and her pulse was racing a mile a minute. An innocent comment that could hold so much meaning, or none at all. "I don't know. Probably that he'd be back sometime is all, I guess. We are a café, you know."

"He asked her to go to dinner with him," Claude said, and grinned like a lecherous old cat who'd just presented his master with a nice, fat mouse.

Tina felt like retrieving the pitcher of lemonade and throwing it at him.

"Dinner?" Dack echoed. His head whipped around and his eyes narrowed on her. "And you're going?"

"If I am," she said, giving both men a withering glance, "it's no one's concern but mine."

Dack's face suffused with color and one beefy hand closed into a fist as it lay upon the counter. He turned, his gaze following Mitch as he walked past the window and climbed into his car.

Several seconds passed. Claude watched Dack watch Mitch, while Tina dumped dirty dishes into a plastic bin beneath the counter and tried to ignore all three of them. She heard her uncle in the kitchen singing softly to himself as he began preparing various dishes for the lunch group that would begin arriving in a few hours.

"Well, you're right, darlin', of course," Dack said, turning back to her, his tone overly sweet and condescending, "it is none of our business." He threw a scowl at Claude, who immediately grabbed his magazine and buried his nose within its pages. "But, you know, it can be dangerous going out with someone you don't know nothing about these days."

Not as dangerous as going out with you, she thought to herself.

For years there had been rumors about Dack and a prostitute down in Savannah. No one in Reimour Crossings however, had cared, or gave the rumors much credence, even when, shortly after Dack returned from one of his trips to Savannah, her body was found in the river.

"Yeah," Claude quipped, smiling again, his eyes wide now. "This Ryan guy could be one of them killers on that television show, *America's Most Wanted.* A serial killer, or something like that."

She threw Claude a scathing glance. He wouldn't have said a word to Dack about anything if Mitch Ryan had hired him as a fishing guide.

Dack nodded thoughtfully. "You know, you might have something there, Claude."

The old man's eyes lit up.

Deputy Harlon Gates stood. "Yeah. Maybe I'll head

back to the station and check that out, Sheriff. Never know. Claude could be right.''

A few minutes later Dack got a call on his radio requesting him to return to the police station.

''Well, guess I'll be going too,'' Claude said, sliding off his stool.

Tina walked out onto the veranda after they left, feeling in need of some fresh air. The café was situated at the north end of town, the Magnolia Inn at the south end. She stared down Main Street, in the direction of the inn. What was there about Mitch Ryan that she found vaguely disturbing? That made her feel as if she'd met him somewhere—sometime before, when she was certain that she hadn't?

Disconcerted, she crossed her arms and thought back over their conversation. She remembered his eyes. Watchful, intense eyes, so dark and infinite, not quite black, but too dark to be brown. There was no way she could have forgotten a man with eyes like his.

Mitch looked around the cabin the inn's manager had shown him to. It wasn't the same one he'd had three years ago, but it wasn't much different. The fireplace was on the left wall instead of the right; the decor's accent color was burgundy instead of green; and there was a television. Three years ago there'd only been a radio.

A radio—softly playing one romantic tune after another. A fire—crackling in the grate, and sending its warm glow throughout the room. And Tina—lying naked in his arms, loving him.

Instantly annoyed by the traitorous bent of his thoughts, Mitch pushed them from his mind and tossed his suitcase on the bed. Too much time tripping down memory lane could very well get him killed. Especially if it was a lane bordered by treachery and lies. He set his laptop computer on the reproduction Louis Quatorze desk that sat near the door. Removing the computer from its travel bag, Mitch plugged it in and turned it on. A series of flashing lights and beeps followed as the screen colored.

Just before leaving the Agency's headquarters in Virginia, he'd requested some additional, up-to-date data be compiled on Reimour Crossings and its residents. He saw now, by the file names appearing on the screen, that some of it had been transmitted to him. He scanned the file headings quickly. Finances. Relatives. Travel. Taxes. There were a half dozen more listings, some new, some he already had. Nothing jumped out at him as suspicious, but he knew better than to discount anything.

He zeroed in on the largest file and opened it. A list of all the properties in Reimour Crossings, along with their parcel numbers and the names of their owners, came onto the screen. It was a file he'd gone over before, but this list seemed more complete than the previous. There was no Dubois, but Mitch already knew Tina's husband was dead. If they'd owned property, she'd sold it. Her father was gone, too, and Mitch had learned from the Agency's investigation that Tina and her children lived in her parents' old home.

The squawk of a bird in the trees beyond the cabin pulled at his subconscious and drew him back in time, to that moment just before the crash. He looked past the wide window that took up most of the cabin's front wall, but it wasn't the live oaks, their sprawling, gnarled limbs draped with long strands of prickly Spanish moss that he saw, or even the tiny black and white cat that darted out from the grove of dogwood beyond the oaks and sprinted toward the main house of the inn. It was the hood of his car, careening off the road—crashing into a tree—hands jerking him from his seat—pulling at him—pummeling him.

Silence devoured him. His body ached—his skin burned—his eyes stung—his lungs screamed for air.

Mitch jerked away from the nightmarish sensations that were the only memory he had of the attack, and forced his thoughts back to the present. His only hope of finding out who was behind the assault on him, and who had murdered his brother, was to find out why it had happened.

He turned his thoughts back to his recent visit to the café. He knew almost everything there was to know about Tina Peychaud Dubois. He knew when she'd been born, where she'd gone to school, the name of her first boyfriend and most of her relatives, dead and alive. He knew how she'd gotten the tiny scar on her left knee, that her favorite color was purple, her favorite flowers were violets, and she'd always had a passion for anything and everything chocolate. Regretfully, he also knew and remembered how it felt to hold her in his arms, what her kiss tasted like, where the most sensitive spots of her body were located, and the soft, throaty, almost purrlike sounds she made when overcome by desire. He knew everything about her, except what he really needed to know.

Had she betrayed him? Had she set him up to be killed, and a year later done the same to his brother?

The thought had given him no rest for two years. He'd trusted her. Perry, the only person outside of Reimour Crossings who'd known about his relationship with her, would have trusted her. That gave her opportunity. But the question that nagged at Mitch was why? Why would she have wanted Jake dead? She'd wanted him to leave the Agency. He hadn't wanted to, and they'd argued. She'd turned down his proposal then.

Mitch sighed, remembering that night.

Raskin insisted they couldn't ignore the possibility she'd given him away by accident and not realized it, but he'd been an agent for a long time, been hardened by some of what he'd seen and most of what he'd done. In his book, there was no such thing as an accident, an unintentional mistake or coincidence. And there was no way, in his mind, she could have given him away by accident, and not realized it.

And that didn't explain Perry's murder.

A movement beyond the cabin's window drew his attention again and he watched a heron break from the trees and take to the sky.

Tina had gotten married only two months after the attack on Jake. How could she have truly loved him as she'd claimed, and then married Ben Dubois? Mitch sighed and rubbed his eyes with thumb and forefinger, while his mind continued to go over every point it had gone over numerous times before since he'd roused from the coma. His brother's notes indicated he'd believed Tina was already several months pregnant when she'd married Dubois, an old friend. Perry had believed that she married him only to give her baby a name.

Mitch remembered the stab to his gut as he'd read Perry's almost illegible scribblings. Halfway through the notes he'd known what was coming, but it hadn't softened the blow any.

Perry had been certain the twins Tina had given birth to seven months after the assault on his brother were Jake's sons. When Mitch had read that, the pain of betrayal, the sense of loss, had sent his temper soaring to depths he'd never even imagined it could reach. He'd screamed out his rage, then slammed a fist into the wall, pushing through the thin plaster and reopening old wounds on his hand and arm. But the physical pain that followed his moment of rage was nothing compared to what had gone on inside of him—and was still there.

Mitch looked back at the computer and jabbed at one of its buttons. A second later the laptop's accompanying printer spit out a copy of the list. It was as good a place to start as any. Folding it, he slipped it into the pocket of his T-shirt and stood.

No matter how he looked at the situation, it inevitably came back to Tina. She was the only person in Reimour Crossings he'd confided in three years ago, the only one who'd known he was a federal agent, the only one who could have betrayed him.

Chapter 3

It was nearly seven o'clock when Mitch pulled his Thunderbird up in front of the café again. He'd made a half dozen requests to the Agency for additional information after looking over what they'd forwarded via e-mail, placed several phone calls, and done some hard thinking. The fact that he still desired Tina had taken him back slightly, thrown his focus off for a while and left his thoughts scattered, but no longer. He knew it was merely a physical attraction, and he could handle that.

After all, before her, that was all his affairs had ever been. No commitments, no emotional entanglements. Just a mutual, physical attraction.

But he'd have to be careful. He'd caught her more than once watching him, as if something about him puzzled her. He knew she couldn't recognize him, but he couldn't afford for her to be wary of him, or uneasy. For any reason.

Mitch looked around. There were no other cars in the café's small parking lot, which was barely illuminated by

the glow of light coming from the windows. A sign sat in
the one that faced the street, the word *Closed* printed across
its white face in large red letters. Shadows hovered about
the spacious veranda, and the faint sound of music drifted
out to him from inside.

He stepped from the car, closing its door softly. For several seconds he stood still and watched her. She was standing behind the café's counter, her back to him, but he knew
that she was aware he was there. It had been apparent, when
he'd been there earlier, that she could see and hear everyone who arrived and departed.

His gaze moved to the entry steps leading to the veranda
that surrounded the building. He'd leaned against the balustrade at the top of the steps and held Tina to him that
morning, just before he'd left for Savannah to buy her a
wedding ring, even though she'd rejected his proposal.

"Don't you be getting yourself lost now," Marcus Peychaud growled, his dark blues eyes dancing with both
amusement and challenge. *"Sic my hounds on you, I will,
and get my shotgun outta the closet, you hurt my little
girl."*

That had given him hope. She hadn't told her father
about the proposal, or at least that she'd refused to accept
it, and he'd figured then it was because she knew she'd
change her mind. When he brought her the ring, promised
to ease back on his assignments, she'd give in and marry
him.

Mitch wondered if Tina's father had sicced his hounds
on his trail when he didn't return that night—or if Marcus
had already known there was no reason. His mind turned
over the possibilities again. Could it have been Marcus
who'd betrayed him, and not Tina? It was not the first time
the thought had occurred to him. It was an unlikely pros-
pect, however. Marcus had been sick even then. He'd

wanted his daughters married, especially Tina, the oldest, and the only one of the three Peychaud sisters not bent on a career. And Marcus had seemed sincere about liking Jake. Why would he have wanted the man who wanted to marry Tina dead? For that matter, Mitch asked himself for what had to be the thousandth time, why would Tina have wanted him dead? That was exactly what he had come back to Reimour Crossings to find out.

He steeled himself against the feelings of physical desire he had no doubt now were going to assault him again when he was with her. It was a hindrance he hadn't expected, but he would handle it. Use it, if he had to.

"Show time," he mumbled, as he had at the start of every case he'd ever worked on. But this wasn't just another Agency case, this time it was personal, and most likely the most important thing he'd ever do.

Before moving toward the café's door, he looked up and down the street. Brenaud's patrol car wasn't in sight, but Mitch knew the man could be lurking in the shadows somewhere. It was what he was best at, and Mitch hadn't discounted the possibility that the affable sheriff had been behind the attack on him three years ago, even without knowing who he really was. It had been obvious even then that Dack Brenaud was more than mildly interested in Tina, and from what Mitch had seen in the café this morning, he still was.

He walked slowly up the café's entry stairs and crossed the gallery. In spite of the Closed sign hanging in the window, the entry door was ajar. He opened the screen door and stepped inside.

Tina tucked the adding machine into its drawer, then stared down at it. She'd been acutely aware of him from the moment he'd turned his car into the parking lot out front. Tension held her stiff. She'd heard him cut his engine. Heard him climb from his car and softly close its door. Felt his eyes watching her through the window. Mixed emotions surged through her now, as disquieting reflections filled her mind. She'd been afraid he would come back, and afraid that he wouldn't. Her thoughts hadn't made sense all day, and her feelings were even less rational.

Memories of Jake had been pounding at her all morning, memories she usually tried to keep stored away, locked in the farthest regions of her mind because they were still too painful to recall. Yet today, after meeting Mitch Ryan, her memories of Jake had refused to be ignored or banished, and had melded with her impressions of Mitch.

It made no sense, but then Tina had learned long ago that not everything in life did. She told herself not to turn around too quickly now, not to look up just yet. But, as it had been that morning when he'd entered the café, she couldn't help herself.

Mitch stood in the doorway, a cold knot of anxiety gripping his stomach as he stared at her. He'd spent the better part of the afternoon preparing himself for seeing her again. He had thought, before his arrival in Reimour Crossings, that the anger and hatred, the need for answers, and finally revenge, that he'd lived on for the past two years would be enough to see him through what he had to do. He'd been certain it had killed all the other feelings he'd had toward her…the desire, the want, the need. But he'd been wrong.

It was a painful and surprising awakener. It had struck him this morning, and it struck even harder now, but he knew he would handle it, because he had to—he had no choice. Mitch smiled through the fury that was suddenly churning through his blood. God, he had loved her more than anything. More than life. What had happened? How could he have been so stupid?

He drew on the cold, unfeeling mantle he'd always assumed when on an assignment. Leaving his emotions behind and operating only on intellect was the only way he would get through this. "I was hoping you'd still be here," he said, his voice smooth in spite of its raspy quality, his tone calm, giving away none of the turmoil churning about inside of him.

Tina stood near the café's cash register. She should have felt safe with the counter between them. She always did with Dack. But for some unfathomable reason, safe was the last thing she felt with Mitch Ryan, and the last thing she worried about when she looked into his eyes. The pile of receipts spread out on the counter before her, which she'd been sorting through, was instantly forgotten. "I was just closing up, tallying the receipts for the day."

"Will you go to dinner with me?"

Remembering Claude's speculations, and the way Mitch Ryan made her feel when he looked at her, Tina knew she should be more than merely cautious of him. He was a stranger, a man she knew nothing about. She'd made the mistake of ignoring that about a man once, and it was a mistake that had changed her life forever, and one she didn't intend to repeat.

She opened her mouth to say no. His gaze caught hers, and she instinctively, though unexplainably, felt certain there was no reason to fear him. Yet she still hesitated, unable to reconcile her desire to go out with a stranger with the extreme caution she'd lived with, invoked upon herself, for the past three years.

The only person who'd known the whole truth, everything, about what she'd hoped, what she thought, felt, and feared, had been her husband, Ben, and he was gone.

"I'm not dangerous," Mitch said softly, sensing her hesitation. He smiled teasingly, not realizing until he'd heard his own words what a lie they were. He was, in all probability, the most dangerous man she'd ever know.

Tina reluctantly returned his smile, reminding herself again that she had too much to lose now, too much to protect. She couldn't afford to make another mistake like she had with Jake. "Thank you, really, but…"

"Don't say no," Mitch said, before she could. "Please." He pulled the hand he'd been holding behind his back into view and held it out toward her. Clutched in his grasp was a small bouquet of red baby roses.

Tina's cheeks instantly stung with the warmth of a blush as she stared at the partially open blooms. No one had brought her flowers since… She swallowed hard, forcing the memories back.

Mitch watched her every reaction. He knew she loved flowers, and picking these up for her earlier this afternoon had been a calculated move, meant to sway her toward him. But he'd almost blown it, almost bought her violets.

Jake Blaggette would know violets were her favorite flower—Mitch Ryan wouldn't, and Mitch knew that coincidences could ruin a good plan, and sometimes prove fatal.

"They're beautiful," Tina said. "But you really shouldn't have."

In spite of her words, innocent pleasure shone from her eyes, intensifying the gall he felt at his well planned deceit. He slid casually onto one of the cafe's stools, and steeled himself against the rise of any emotional feelings by dredging up another memory from his past. It had been almost nine years since San Francisco, but he remembered everything about that assignment like it had happened yesterday.

The art world had been experiencing some very expensive losses, valuable works stolen, seemingly right from under their noses. But the authorities had been able to come up with nothing. And the Bureau hadn't done much better.

That's when they decided to send Jake, whose minor his first few years in college had been art, in undercover.

Erica Vandygrift, assistant curator of the Boston museum, became Jake's prime suspect. Like Tina, Erica had been beautiful, and seemingly innocent. She'd also been sensual, seductive, charming…and guilty. And in the end, very, very deadly.

Mitch smiled, and caressed Tina with his eyes, reassuring her, attempting to emotionally seduce her. "Then put them in water," he urged, and tossed her a devilish wink. "Think of me every time you look at them, and let me take you to dinner tonight."

She took the flowers. Her resolve against him was quickly waning. She reached under the counter for a vase, her gaze meeting his as she straightened. Something pulled at her as her eyes locked with his. That same something warmed her blood and banished the caution she'd been trying to draw around her since that morning. What could one dinner hurt?

The waiter cleared their dinner plates from the table, brought them coffee and, after being assured they did not want dessert, moved discreetly away.

"I'm sorry," Mitch said, looking at Tina when they were alone again, and resuming their interrupted conversation. "Losing your husband must have been very hard." His gaze melted into hers as he reached across the table and covered her fingers with his, a move meant to be nothing more than an innocent, sympathetic gesture.

He realized too late that touching her was a mistake. The moment his hand closed around hers, memories and old feelings assaulted him. He wanted to jerk his hand back, but knew that would only be another mistake. Instead, he swore to himself as his body's reaction to that simple and

innocent moment of physical contact with her threatened to
put all of his plans in jeopardy. Desire coiled in him like
fire, while want slammed into his gut, taunting him, urging
him to toss aside his caution and forget about the past.

Anger at himself singed the edges of his self-control. He
forced stiff cheeks to give way to a smile while softly biting
the inside of his lip in an attempt to use pain to quell the
mutinous hungers gnawing at his insides. It had always
worked before, but this time the effort failed him.

Beneath cover of the long, draping white tablecloth,
Mitch's other hand clenched tightly into a fist. He fought
to maintain his resolve, and his fury with her, by recalling
memories of his brother to mind, and what had happened
to him.

*"It was obvious Perry was tortured before he was
killed."*

*He stared at his superior, willing the man and his words
to be nothing more than a nightmare.*

*Ivor Raskin slid a hand through his thick, white hair.
"He was found in Columbia Park. In downtown Savannah.
By a beat cop on early-morning patrol." Ivor shrugged, as
if not knowing what else to say.*

Mitch's blood instantly began to cool; passion retreated
beneath a conquering flood of anger. Yet, as a result of his
long years of intense training and self-discipline, he managed to keep the fire of seduction in his eyes as he looked
at Tina, and a charming smile on his lips.

A rush of tingling gooseflesh swept over Tina's skin as
his hand lay atop hers. She felt its warmth, its strength and
its gentleness. Jake's hands had been strong, too, but his
touch had been the most tender she'd ever known. She
looked quickly and self-consciously around the nearly
empty restaurant. The few other patrons, and the staff moving about, didn't seem to be paying any attention to them,

but that didn't mean anything. Rumors had a way of starting in Reimour Crossings over a lot less than two people momentarily touching each other's hands. "Thank you."

She smiled, though he thought he detected a hint of sadness in the curve of her lips.

Tina slid her hand from beneath his as casually as she could.

Regret swept through Mitch, but even stronger was his relief, though he was careful not to let it show. Touching her had shaken him more than he'd expected.

"Losing Ben was one of the hardest things I've ever had to face," Tina said.

Losing Ben, not Jake. Hurt sliced through him, sudden and unexpected.

"He was a wonderful man," Tina said. "I still miss him very much."

The wistful smile on her face cut through Mitch as deeply as her words had, but he quickly pulled himself back together. What she felt or hadn't felt didn't matter now. It was what she'd done that mattered.

"You must have loved him very much...." The words nearly stuck in his throat.

Tina smiled as memories of Ben skipped through her mind. She nodded. "Yes, I did."

So much for his brother's theory she'd only married Dubois because she was pregnant and wanted a name for her child. Jealousy flared in Mitch, sweeping through him, instant and hot.

The information Perry and the Agency had managed to gather on Ben Dubois had failed to give Mitch much of a feel for the man. He'd grown up in Reimour Crossings. His parents had been killed in an auto accident and he stayed with a neighbor until he graduated high school, a month later. Then he left town, eloping with his girlfriend and settling in upstate New York. She'd died within the year in childbirth, leaving him with an infant daughter. Ben had eventually become a photojournalist, freelance assignments mostly, until six months before marrying Tina. Then he'd suddenly quit working altogether—seemingly for no reason that anyone could ascertain.

That fact intrigued Mitch. Had Ben Dubois known when he married Tina that he was dying? The answer had so far eluded him, and her statement now, that she'd loved him, and still missed him, made it a moot point.

"But I have my sons," Tina said, interrupting Mitch's thoughts, "and my stepdaughter." Her smile had turned bright, and her eyes glistened with the mention of her children.

The light tone that had come into her voice at reference to the children grated on Mitch's senses. *Her sons.* Born seven months after her marriage, and nine months after the attack.

Her sons.

His sons.

Their sons.

Tina sipped at her coffee and watched him furtively from behind partially lowered lashes. Something about him reminded her of Jake. She'd been trying to deny it all evening, maybe even from the first moment she'd seen Mitch Ryan. Maybe it was the way he walked, maybe it was the way he carried himself. Or maybe it was the way he looked at her. The idea bothered her. There was something, but it wasn't any of those things exactly, and yet it could be any one of them. She didn't know. Nor did she know whether or not she liked the feeling.

She was attracted to him, but was it only because he reminded her of the man she'd once loved with all of her heart?

Physically Mitch and Jake looked nothing alike, except both were about six feet tall. Jake's features had been classically handsome, as if sculpted by a master from the most perfect marble the world had to offer. Whereas Mitch's face had a rougher, almost savagely rugged quality to it, seemingly slashed from granite by the knife of an amateur, his features blunt and bold. Jake had been handsome. So was Mitch, but in a very different, almost opposite way.

Mitch's eyes were nearly black, whereas Jake's had been the most mesmerizing midnight-blue Tina had ever seen, and accentuated with tiny specks of silver. She remembered how she used to love staring into his eyes, as if she were looking into the endless regions of a star-strewn universe. Their universe, she'd secretly called it. Tina sighed softly, remembering. She used to love to run her fingers through Jake's hair, luxurious and silky brown, touched by highlights of gold that seemed always to be shimmering with light, even when there was none to reflect. She glanced at Mitch's hair now, so coarse and dark as to be almost as black as the darkest of winter nights.

Even their voices were different. The raspiness of Mitch Ryan's was nothing like the deep, soothing drawl that had been so naturally and uniquely Jake Blaggette.

"Sons and a stepdaughter?" Mitch said finally, smiling and pulling Tina from her musings. "I'm sure they must keep you pretty busy."

Tina nodded. "Usually. They're off on a trip with my sisters at the moment. Sort of a little vacation mixed with business. But they'll be home tomorrow."

He nodded. "How old are they?"

"Lily's twelve going on thirty." Tina smiled. "Jimmy and Joey are two and a half."

He pretended surprise. "Jimmy and Joey? I take it they're twins?"

Her eyes shone with pride. "Yes."

"Too bad their father isn't still around to see them grow up." He studied her for reaction, but she merely nodded and glanced away, the look in her eyes telling him louder than words that her thoughts had drifted to another time, maybe even to another man.

Was it memory of Ben Dubois that filled her mind? Jake Blaggette? Or someone entirely different? The thought threatened to send his mood spiraling even further into the black pit of anger and frustration he'd been dealing with since waking from the coma, so he shrugged it aside. He needed to remain cool and in control.

The Agency had come up with nothing that pointed to another man in her life, yet it was the logical conclusion to come to in regards to why she'd betrayed him. If it had been done willfully.

Mitch cursed silently, an old habit whenever he was frustrated or angry. Whom she was thinking about didn't matter, he told himself. Unless it led him to the truth. "I'm glad you came to dinner with me tonight, Tina Dubois," he said, attempting to draw her back to him.

She smiled, her eyes met his, and she shook off her memories. "So am I," she said, realizing it was the truth. His gaze seemed to suddenly search her face, as if trying to reach into her thoughts, and she looked away.

"You know, this afternoon at the café I thought, maybe you and the sheriff were...?" Mitch shrugged, leaving the rest of the comment unspoken and feigning a hesitancy to go on.

Tina's eyes instantly shot back to meet his again and she shook her head, irked that anyone would even think there was something between herself and Dack Brenaud. "No."

He responded with a mock cringe. "Sorry. It was just, I don't know, the way he looked at you, I guess."

She waved a hand at him, and shook her head. "No, I apologize. I didn't mean to snap at you like that. Dack Brenaud and I grew up together. He's an old friend, but that definitely is all he is."

"My suspicion is that he would like to be a lot more than that," Mitch said.

"Well, that's not my concern. Anyway, people don't always get everything they want in life," Tina retorted, her tone cool.

Mitch smiled. "Very true. But sometimes it's fun trying."

One gracefully arched dark brow rose slightly as she looked at him, realizing suddenly that she had become much too comfortable with him. She was enjoying this evening with him way too much, and she didn't know him. The safest thing she could do would be to get up and go home. Right now. This very minute. Instead, she accepted the refill of coffee the waiter poured into her cup. When he left, Tina folded her arms on the table and looked at Mitch. This was just a casual dinner date, nothing to worry about, and most likely there wouldn't be a second one. After all, he was just here on vacation, and would be gone before she knew it.

She ran a finger absently around the warm rim of her coffee cup. "The sheriff's a nice man," she said, her tone warmer now. "And I'm sure someday he'll find the right woman."

"It's just not you," Mitch said.

"No, it's not me."

He nodded.

Tina smiled, crossed her arms, and laid them on the edge of the table. "Okay, so, what about you? All we've done this evening is talk about me and my family and Reimour

Crossings. But you haven't told me one thing about yourself." She laughed. "So, c'mon, start telling."

He shrugged casually, ignoring the sense of pleasure that slid through him at the soft sound of her laughter, the interest in her eyes. A pang of longing sliced through him, sudden and wholly unexpected, surprising him. There were so many things he'd missed about her. He pushed the thought aside, coldly reminding himself she'd married Ben Dubois only two months after the man she'd supposedly loved disappeared from the face of the earth. "There really isn't much to tell. I've led a rather boring, nondescript life, until I came here and met you."

It was happening all over again. A chill touched the warmth of her blood as Tina felt a shiver of déjà vu sweep through her, and an image of Jake's face flashed, unbidden, into her mind. She had asked him about his life too, on their first date, and he had said exactly the same thing. *There really isn't much to tell.* Her hands began to tremble. She quickly shoved them into her lap, clasped them together and struggled to smile and push aside her uneasiness.

Coincidence. It was only a coincidence. Jake was gone. This was Mitch Ryan.

"Tina?" Mitch studied the suddenly pensive look on her face. "Is something wrong?"

She shook herself free of the momentary panic. She was being ridiculous. "Oh, I was…just thinking of something. Sorry." She forced a smile to her lips. "So, you want me to believe you were born yesterday, is that it?" she quipped, hoping her tone sounded light and casual. "You came into this world fully grown, with no known parents, and became instantly and totally self-sufficient."

His smile turned to laughter. "Okay. But I warn you, it's boring. I grew up in Kentucky," Mitch said, figuring it wasn't really a lie since the little Virginia town he had grown up in was situated right on the border and he'd spent as much time on one side as the other. "I'm an only child of only children. My parents died in an auto accident, my grandparents have also gone on to the great beyond. I've got a few second cousins scattered across the country—we're not close, obviously—and a couple of second aunts, one back home, one down in Florida." He deleted any reference to having had a brother, or the fact that his maternal grandmother, who'd raised him and Perry after their parents' deaths, was still very much alive and well.

"Sounds lonely," Tina proffered.

Mitch shrugged again, and his eyes met hers. "Only the past couple of years."

They left the restaurant and walked into the night. It was the last month of summer. The air was warm, and filled with the heady scents of the carefully manicured flowers that lined the walkway.

Tina turned toward Mitch as they neared the parking lot. "I had a nice time tonight, Mitch. Thank you."

She had insisted on driving separately to the restaurant, saying it was on her way home.

He would have preferred to drive her, to get close to her, so that she'd open up to him, but he'd suspected she wasn't quite ready to be alone in a car with a stranger, so he'd let it go and said nothing. The last thing he wanted to do was push her too far, too fast. There was a wariness about her that he'd picked up on almost immediately that morning. She seemed to be more cautious than he remembered, almost uncertain. Or maybe she just felt that way about him.

The thought bothered and puzzled him, but then, maybe wariness was what happened to a person when they betrayed a lover and became responsible for cold-blooded murder.

Mitch reached out and wrapped one of his hands around hers, then drew it up and pressed his lips to the delicate curve of her knuckles. "I enjoyed tonight, too," he said huskily. "Very much."

The touch of his lips to her skin sent a fluttering sensation racing through Tina's veins, and stalled the breath in her lungs. It was the kind of feeling she'd thought she would never feel again, and didn't want to feel now. Not for anyone. She pulled her hand free, afraid of what might happen if she didn't, and shoved it into her purse in search of her car keys. "Well, I, ah, really have to go. Work tomorrow, you know. Thank you again for dinner, Mitch. And a lovely evening." She took a step away from him, then turned toward her car.

He moved with her. "I don't usually have more than coffee for breakfast, but if you serve pancakes, and they're as good as your apple pie, and you promise to serve them to me yourself, I just might change that habit."

Jake had rarely eaten breakfast—but he'd loved pancakes. The thought flew at Tina out of nowhere as she stared up at Mitch.

Mitch hadn't driven more than a few blocks when he noticed the car behind him, just far enough back so that he couldn't make out anything but two headlights. Every muscle in his body tensed instantly.

An image of a black pickup truck flashed through his mind. He'd told himself it couldn't happen again, yet now he knew he'd been expecting it all the same. A parade of ugly curses sped through his mind. Three years ago he hadn't been prepared for them. This time he was.

He pushed down on the accelerator and the Thunderbird cruised down the street, pushing at the speed limit.

The car behind him kept pace.

The sensation of fists and flames and searing pain filled his mind, all he could remember of the attack. All he needed to remember. He held on to the steering wheel with one hand while he felt under his seat with the other for the small gun he'd placed there earlier. His fingers touched its grip as he turned the car to the right.

The car behind stayed with him.

Mitch was just about to slam his foot all the way down on the accelerator when a sudden flash of red light filled his rear window. A split second later the unmistakable wail of a police siren pierced the night's silence.

He groaned, instantly relieved and angry at the same time. There was no question in his mind who was in the patrol car behind him. He glanced down at the speedometer, as if to confirm his suspicion. He hadn't yet gone over the posted speed limit.

Cursing softly beneath his breath, Mitch began to slow down, having no doubt it was the sheriff behind him in the patrol car. There was no legal reason for Dack Brenaud to pull him over, which probably meant the sheriff had seen him with Tina. She might think there was nothing between her and Brenaud, but the man obviously didn't share that opinion now any more than he had three years ago. That suspicion had put the sheriff real high on Mitch's suspect list for a while, but a late-night computer-hacking job into the department's duty reports had shown that the sheriff had been making an arrest in town at the time Jake was being attacked out on the highway. Mitch steered the Thunderbird to the side of the road and stopped, then rolled down his window and waited.

Dack pulled up directly behind Mitch's car, cut his engine and flicked off the radio.

Mitch glanced into the mirror on his door as the wail of

the siren died and the sheriff climbed from his car and sauntered toward him, leaving his roof lights flashing.

"Hey there, Mr. Ryan, isn't it?" Dack said, pausing beside Mitch's door, legs spread wide, arms crossed over his barrel-shaped chest, a wide smile on his face.

"Yes. Can I help you, Sheriff?"

"Well, sorry to have to stop you like this, but I just noticed one of your taillights was broken." Dack pulled a ticket book from where he'd tucked it under one arm and flipped it open.

"My taillight?" Mitch echoed. He pushed open his door, climbed out and walked to the rear of the car. At least half of the red plastic covering of the car's large right taillight was missing, and what remained was only a few ragged shards.

He looked back at the sheriff, who was now in the process of writing him a ticket. There had been nothing wrong with the Thunderbird's taillight when Mitch had driven away from the Magnolia Inn earlier this evening, but he'd bet there were more than a few shards of red plastic lying in the parking lot back at the restaurant.

"Yeah, we just like to make sure everyone around here stays nice and safe, even our tourists, you know what I mean, Mr. Ryan?" Dack said. "Want you all to have a good time and come back."

Mitch suppressed his anger behind his own smile. "Sure thing, Sheriff."

"Wouldn't want someone to go running into the back of this fancy car of yours, now would we?" Dack said. "A person could get real hurt that way."

Mitch's eyes narrowed as he contemplated what could be a lightly veiled threat. Was Brenaud actually saying *What happened before, could happen again?* Mitch stared long and hard at the man, then shook the thought aside. I' couldn't be. There was no way Brenaud could recognize him.

Mitch signed the ticket.

"Nice ring," Dack said. "Unusual."

Mitch looked at Perry's ring. Did the sheriff recognize it? He handed back the ticket book.

Dack ripped the ticket from his book and held it out. "I'd recommend you get that taillight fixed down at the local garage tomorrow," he said. "Although, come to think of it, Quattman might have to order it up from Savannah. Don't see too many of these kinda cars up here. Could take a few days. Maybe you ought to just drive on down there and get it fixed."

Mitch shoved the ticket into his pocket. If he'd ever heard a more unsubtle way of being told to leave town, he couldn't remember it. "Thanks," he mumbled, and climbed back into the car.

Dack laid an arm on the roof over Mitch's window and leaned down toward him. "Saw you having dinner at the Lamp Post with Tina Dubois."

Mitch looked up. Fury, instant and unreasonable, rolled over and through him, and the urge to put his fist into Brenaud's nose was almost irresistible. He didn't like to be watched, and he didn't like other people minding his business. But most of all, he didn't like the idea of the sheriff paying attention to what Tina did.

His dark eyes met Brenaud's. "Is my having dinner with Miss Dubois a problem, Sheriff?" he asked, struggling to keep his tone cordial.

"Nope. Seeing you two together just got me to thinking, that's all. Tina's had a bit of trouble in the past," Dack said, "and with you only being here for a while on vacation and all, well…" He smiled again. "She's a nice lady, Mr.

Ryan. I just wouldn't want to see her get hurt again, you know what I mean?''

''Well, I'm sure she appreciates your concern, Sheriff. But I hadn't planned on hurting her,'' Mitch said, knowing that was exactly what he'd do if it meant getting to the truth he sought.

Chapter 4

Tina pushed away from the old trunk and sat back on the floor, the framed photograph she'd been searching for held tightly between her hands. She stared down at it intently, but could find no real resemblance between the man in the photo and Mitch Ryan.

"Why did you leave me, Jake?" she whispered, her eyes meeting the midnight-blue ones of the man in the picture. "Why?" She traced the line of his jaw with the tips of her fingers, then ran them over the outline of his hair, tossed by the wind that had been blowing the day she'd taken the photograph.

They had been on a picnic, down by the river. She pressed the photograph to her breast and closed her eyes, remembering. Several hours after she'd snapped the photograph, he'd asked her to marry him. And she'd said no. It had been the hardest thing she'd ever done, but he'd refused to leave the FBI, and she couldn't accept that.

Tina opened her eyes and held out the picture again,

looking at the image she didn't really need a picture to
remember.

At first when he hadn't returned she'd been terrified, and
unable to stop crying. No one had been able to console her.

Dack and his deputies claimed they'd searched the roads
for any sign of Jake or his car, but there had been no sign
of him, or of an accident. The state troopers verified that,
and so did the Savannah police. But Tina had refused to
believe Jake had just walked out on her. She'd called the
FBI, even the police department of the town where he
claimed he'd grown up. No one had ever heard of Jake
Blaggette. Eventually her tears dried and gave way to anger. Hot, burning, all-consuming anger. Resentment had
followed. Finally, she'd put her memories aside, accepted
it as fate and forced herself to get on with the job of living.

Now, whether Jake Blaggette was dead or alive, she
could only feel sorry for him—because he had two wonderful little boys and didn't know what he was missing.

Tina sighed deeply. She hadn't taken Jake's photograph
from the old trunk in the attic since the day before she'd
married Ben, but this morning the urge had been too strong
to resist. Something about Mitch Ryan reminded her of
Jake, and she needed to know what. She'd thought she
would see it if she looked at Jake's picture, some kind of
resemblance, but she'd been wrong. There was no resemblance.

Yet... She looked closer at the cut of Jake's jawline, the
tilt of his lips as he'd smiled, the gleam that seemed to
reflect out of his eyes. There was nothing of Mitch Ryan
there and yet...

"Oh, for mercy's sake, Christina Marie, you're really
losing it this time," she snapped at herself, her words echoing through the musty attic, which was filled with more
than one hundred years' worth of her family's treasures,

keepsakes and, in some cases, junk. She pushed to her knees and shoved the photograph back into the trunk as frustration overwhelmed her. Tall, dark and handsome. That was what the two men had in common. Period.

And she was just lonely. Obviously way too lonely if she was imagining that Mitch Ryan reminded her of Jake Blaggette. She reached out to close the old trunk. The soft gold of the picture frame caught her eye. Tina paused, looking down at the picture, then grabbed it, slammed the trunk lid closed, pushed to her feet, and hurried toward the door leading downstairs.

The café was crowded with regulars, but Tina knew the instant Mitch walked into the room. She set a cup of coffee on the counter in front of one of the customers, and looked up.

His mercurial dark eyes, hard, cold and intensely probing, impaled hers.

Tina felt a chill sweep up her spine and mentally recoiled, yet found herself unable to look away.

He made no attempt to hide the fact from the others in the café that his gaze had captured hers, and intended to keep it. Her pulse skittered alarmingly as she watched him cross the room, toward her.

"Hey, Tina, can I have that orange juice I ordered?" the man beside her at the counter asked.

The sound of his voice, and her name, allowed her to grasp back her senses and escape the spell in which Mitch's appearance had momentarily imprisoned her. She turned toward the refrigerator.

Mitch slid onto one of the stools at the end of the counter.

Tina took her time waiting on others, refilling coffee cups, taking orders and money, and listening to tidbits of gossip. She knew she was stalling, but she couldn't help it. Finally, she forced herself to turn toward him.

His gaze caught hers again, but the cold cynicism she'd seen there only seconds earlier was gone. Now his eyes seemed full of warmth and sparkle, and instantly threatened to drag her toward a place she wasn't certain she was ready to go. She paused and grabbed a cup and saucer from beneath the counter. "You're up early this morning," she said, trying to sound casual as she set the cup down and poured his coffee. His presence affected her more than she wanted it to, and she didn't know what that meant. What she did know was that she liked it, and she hated it.

Mitch took a long swallow before answering. "Had a date for breakfast, remember?" He smiled, and Tina felt an unwelcome surge of excitement. She found it suddenly too easy to get lost in the way he was looking at her, as if his eyes were saying the rest of the world could disappear, he didn't care, she was all that mattered to him.

An image of Jake's face suddenly flashed through her mind. She blinked, startled and confused, then hurriedly shook herself mentally. "One order of pancakes coming up," she said, trying desperately to sound calm. She hurried into the kitchen, practically threw the order tag at her uncle and leaned her back against the wall. What was the matter with her? Why did Mitch Ryan make her think of Jake?

"Anything wrong, Princess?" her uncle asked, as he poured pancake batter onto the griddle.

"Nothing dropping my brain into the washing machine wouldn't cure," she mumbled, suddenly angry with herself. Jake had been gone for almost three years. But something about Mitch reminded her of him. He'd come to Reimour Crossings for a vacation, like Jake had. In a few days he'd be gone and she'd never see him again. Like Jake. Only she wasn't going to make the same mistake and lose her heart to Mitch Ryan the way she'd foolishly done with Jake Blaggette. That was never going to happen to her again.

She inhaled deeply, stiffened her shoulders and gritted her teeth. There would be no more dates with Mitch Ryan, no whirlwind romance and no promises of tomorrow and forever. End of story.

Five minutes later, her resolve set, she placed a plate piled high with six large buttermilk pancakes in front of him. A ball of butter sat on top of them like a crown, quickly melting and dripping over the sides.

"Wow." His eyes widened at the mountain of food, then he smiled and looked up at her. "I had a good time last night," he said softly, before she could turn away.

"I did too. Thanks."

"Do it again tonight?"

No, a faint voice in the back of her mind screamed. She stared into his eyes, searching, and not knowing what she was searching for.

"Hey, Tina, how about some more coffee down here?" someone yelled from the other end of the counter.

She whirled and grabbed a coffeepot from the burner.

Mitch silently cursed the old coot who yelled for her, then spread the butter over his pancakes and reached for the basket of syrup containers she'd placed on the counter.

Tina, who'd paused and looked back, turned away to talk to someone, suddenly realizing she'd been waiting for Mitch to grab the blueberry syrup—as Jake would have done.

The door of the café crashed open. "Mommy! Mommy!"

Mitch turned.

Two little boys ran across the room, arms waving, hair flying, a young girl of about eleven following them.

"Auntie Lee took us to the beach."

"Auntie Dee bought me a truck."

The chunk of pancake threatened to lodge in Mitch's throat. His air passage tried to close. His heart nearly stopped, then felt a tug so emotionally charged he nearly doubled over from the impact. He watched the children run behind the counter. The girl demurely kissed Tina's cheek, then disappeared into the kitchen, while the boys threw themselves excitedly at their mother, their little arms wrapping around her legs as they jumped up and down and chattered nonstop. But their words weren't what Mitch's attention was riveted upon.

"The mob is home," Lianne Peychaud called out, entering the café carrying suitcases and bags, while their younger sister followed, her arms filled with toys.

Tina laughed happily and hugged both children close, then knelt and spoke to each in a soft whisper. She looked up at her sisters, carbon copies of herself. They'd dropped their parcels behind the counter and were both getting something to drink. "Everything okay?"

"If you mean, did your little terrors finally bring the city of Savannah to its knees? Yes," Lianne said, and laughed. "But we managed to save most of it."

His sons. The words repeated endlessly through Mitch's mind. His sons. He knew, without any doubt now, that he was looking at his sons. Their silky brown hair, their midnight-blue eyes. It was like looking at himself and Perry when they'd been children. The urge to reach out to them, to drag them into his arms, tell them who he was, was so overwhelming Mitch had to ball his hands into fists and call on every ounce of willpower he had to keep himself rooted to his stool, and silent.

But as quickly as he'd become engulfed in the realization that he truly was a father, as swiftly as he'd felt a tide of love sweep over him, it was overshadowed and devoured by a rush of fury.

Someone had robbed him of three years of his life—three years of his sons' lives. He tore his gaze from the two boys and looked back at Tina. Was she responsible for what had happened?

Find the why of what happened, Raskin had insisted and you'll find the who that was responsible.

Mitch ordered himself to calm down. Every step he took in search of the truth had to be a slow and careful one if he hoped to survive. And he had to survive. Now, more than ever.

But someone was going to pay.

Tina looked up to find that Mitch was gone. Her gaze darted toward the door as the twins continued to wrestle about her legs, describing their trip in excited chatter.

Unease mixed with confusion as she stared past the window where his car had been parked in the lot. A sense of disappointment filled her, yet it was an emotion she couldn't explain, even to herself.

"Tina?"

She blinked and looked up, her gaze meeting Dack's. She hadn't noticed him enter.

"That newcomer, Ryan, he's not giving you any problems, is he?"

"Joey, Jimmy," she said, bending down and talking to the twins, "why don't you go into the back room and say hello to your Uncle Deano. He's missed you, and I think he's got some treats back there." Charging like two little bulls, the boys ran toward the swinging door at one end of the counter, yelling for their Unkie. Tina straightened and turned to Dack, her shoulders as stiff as her mood. "No, Dack, Mr. Ryan hasn't given me any problems. Why would he?" she asked, trying not to be impatient.

Dack shrugged. "Who knows? Harlon ran his name through the computer, but didn't come up with anything. No wants or warrants out on him that we know of yet, though the check ain't done. But DMV claims the plates on his car are registered to some little old lady in Kentucky."

Tina shrugged. "So? He said he was from Kentucky. Maybe it's his mother's car." Except his parents were dead, she remembered he'd said, a split second after she'd made the comment. He'd said his aunt was alive though, so it was probably her car. She pictured the sleek, black Thunderbird in her mind. It wasn't exactly a sedately auntie-type car—but then maybe his aunt wasn't sedate.

"Yeah, maybe," Dack said. "But you can't be too trusting of strangers nowadays, you know. Too many crazies out there. Anyway, I've got someone checking on this little old lady, making sure she's okay, it is her car, and he's got it legit."

You can't be too trusting of strangers. His words hit too close to what Tina had been telling herself for hours, but she wasn't going to let Dack know that. She shook her head and laughed softly, the sound ringing so false even to her own ears that her cheeks burned in reaction. "You almost sound like you hope Mitch Ryan's an escaped serial killer or something, Dack."

He grabbed her hand as she set a cup of coffee down on the counter in front of him. "No, I don't, but I am worried about you, not him. You need to be more careful."

Tina pulled her hand from his, and smiled. Would he ever realize she couldn't love him? He had a good heart, she knew that, but he needed to find someone who would love him back. She didn't want to hurt him, but she had to try to make him see he didn't need to "worry" about her.

"I'm a big girl now, Dack. Believe it or not, I can take care of myself."

"You don't have to, you know." His voice became rough with emotion. "I could..."

She knew what was coming—and she didn't want to hear it. Not again. "I'd better see what the kids are up to," she said, cutting him off. As if on cue, the sound of the boys' laughter and a giggle from Lily suddenly echoed from the back room and Tina felt a rush of relief. "They're probably driving Uncle Deano nuts by now."

"Tina."

She'd turned to hurry toward the door, but stopped at the sudden sharpness in his voice.

"Be careful around that guy. I've got a feeling he's not what he claims."

"Maybe none of us are," Tina said softly, and turned away.

Mitch stared out the cabin's window. He needed to make friends with some of the locals and get them talking. Reaching into his pocket, he retrieved the piece of paper he'd taken from the café's bulletin board and dialed Claude Hannidoe's number.

Within five minutes he'd arranged for Claude to guide him to some of the better fishing spots along the Ogeechee River that afternoon. The old man seemed to like to talk, Mitch told himself, so why not find out how much he knew, if anything.

He'd requested a background check of Claude, not that he expected much to come of it, but it was the overlooked tidbits that could get an agent in trouble. And he'd requested the research guys dig deeper into the sheriff's background, and that of Deputy Harlon Gates. After encountering them in the café the previous morning, he wanted to know everything there was to know about both of them, starting with the day they'd crawled out of their first holes.

He glanced at the fishing gear sitting in a corner of the cabin. He'd been fishing all of two times in his life. Once with Perry, who'd loved the sport he'd claimed was the most relaxing in the world, and once with a kingpin drug dealer who'd had no clue the affable ''Texan'' who had promised to buy his entire next shipment was an FBI agent.

Patience had never been one of Mitch's virtues, so sitting for what could be hours, doing nothing more than waiting for a fish to bite down on his hook, was not his idea of a great way to pass the time.

He glanced down at the open file on his desk. Tina looked back up at him from the photograph pasted to one corner of his case folder.

Mitch absently reached into his shirt pocket again, not realizing until his fingers came out empty that he'd been seeking a cigarette. He'd given them up after coming out of the coma and realizing he hadn't had one in a year, but every once in a while the urge was still there.

Once, the thought of suspecting Tina of anything more heinous than killing a fly would have been unthinkable to him. But he was no longer the man who'd loved her more than life. That man had died three years ago.

Mitch swore beneath his breath and slapped the folder closed, not wanting to look at her face anymore. But then he didn't need her picture for that. Her image was ingrained upon his memory for all time.

He moved to stand at the window. He'd thought he could just come back here, do whatever he had to do to get at the truth and satisfy the need for revenge that had been burning inside of him for the past two years, and leave. Never, not for one minute, had he let himself consider that he might still be attracted to Tina.

His thoughts spiraled back in time—to that day. He'd trusted her, and that had been his downfall. His fatal mistake. He'd broken the one rule that had always kept him alive as he'd moved from one deadly situation to the next. He'd given another person his trust—the one thing he'd sworn never to do—and he'd paid the price. But it wasn't going to happen again. It was never going to happen again.

He grabbed the fishing gear and stalked from the cabin. Before coming back to Reimour Crossings his suspicions on the matter had been colder, harder and more calculating. Now that he'd seen her again, felt the warmth of the fire that still burned between them, it was proving more difficult to keep his suspicions focused on Tina, and keep himself convinced that she could have betrayed him. But he had to. Who else could have given him away? Who else had known he was an FBI agent? Who else had known he'd be going to Savannah that morning—alone?

He'd gone over all the alternatives, examined both his professional and personal lives. Every case he'd ever worked on had been pulled from the files and examined, looking for someone who might be after revenge, or someone who wanted to keep him from testifying in an upcoming case. But all of the possibilities he came up with lacked the one thing that would make them ring true: they were the type of people who wouldn't have walked away without being sure he'd taken his last breath. They would have made certain he was dead. And most likely, never found.

The fact that whoever was responsible had left his brother's body in a public park in the middle of downtown Savannah bothered him though. It was a definite warning, but to whom? The Agency? Or did the men who'd attacked Jake three years ago know he was still alive? Were they warning him not to come back?

Mitch threw his gear into the car. No matter how he

looked at things, it always came back to the same question. Why?

The afternoon turned out as miserable as Mitch had expected. Claude caught himself several good dinner prospects. Mitch caught a shoe, tangled his line in the underwater roots of a dead tree, nearly fell overboard and into a gator's lap and learned more than he'd ever wanted to know about Claude and Fred Gateau's days as young studs in Reimour Crossings. According to Claude, whose face reminded Mitch of a road map of downtown L.A. freeways, there hadn't been a woman in town, regardless of age, who hadn't wanted him at one time or another.

Mitch figured Claude either had one fanciful imagination, or he actually been Reimour Crossings's answer to Rhett Butler. Either way, he left him his stories and kept trying to veer the conversation to more recent gossip, but that didn't seem to interest the older man. Either that, or he just had no intention of passing any of it on to an outsider.

By five Mitch was back at the cabin. He took a long shower, ridding himself of the smell of swamp, bait and fish, then pulled on a clean pair of jeans and polo shirt. An hour later he was on his way to the café. Hopefully, to have dinner with Tina again. She hadn't exactly said yes to his invitation, but then, he told himself, she hadn't exactly said no either.

There were five cars in the parking lot. He didn't see her red Chevy Malibu, but concluded it was probably parked around back. Mitch walked into the café and stopped short, staring at the young woman leaning over the counter and talking to one of the men sitting there.

"Hey," she said, smiling as she spotted him. "Welcome

to Peychaud's. What can I get you?'' Her gaze traveled over him curiously.

"I was, um, looking for Tina," he said, recognizing her younger sister immediately, as well as the cloud of suspicion that darkened her eyes.

"Why?" she asked.

"He's sweet on her."

Mitch glanced toward the end of the counter and saw Claude sitting on a stool. The old man grinned and waved at him. Mitch nodded and looked back at Dee. "I was hoping to take her to dinner."

"Oh. Well, hey!" she instantly smiled and held out a hand. "I'm Dee, Tina's sister. She wanted to go home early today, so I took over for her for a while."

Mitch felt something like apprehension seize him. "Is anything wrong?"

Dee laughed. "No. She had to..."

The phone rang, interrupting her, and she turned to answer it.

Mitch walked back outside. Nothing was wrong, he told himself. She'd merely decided to take off early. But the explanation didn't satisfy the sudden need to see for himself.

Mitch pulled his car to the side of the road a short distance from Tina's house, and turned off both his lights and ignition.

The old Peychaud house sat by itself on fifty acres of land that had been cleared more than two hundred years ago, when the old planter's cottage-style house had been built. He remembered Tina telling him there had originally been more than five hundred acres, but some hard times through the years, especially after the Civil War and during the Great Depression, had forced her ancestors to sell off

most of it. Now only the immediate acre surrounding the
house remained cleared. Ancient live oaks and cypress trees
grew thick upon most of the rest of the property, like a wall
of greenery, the trees' limbs dripping with Spanish moss,
tall fronds of ferns covering the ground at their bases.

Light, flowing out through the windows of the house,
shone softly upon the gallery and illuminated bits of the
well-tended yard, but failed to break into the inky darkness
that had engulfed the old trees.

Mitch settled back in his seat, not quite certain what he
was watching for, or why he wasn't just going up to the
house and knocking on the door.

Over the past two years he'd had a lot of time to think.
Not only about what had happened, but also about whether
he wanted to continue with the Agency. It was a question
he'd never thought he would ask himself, but the unexpected attack, Perry's death and the Agency's apparent in-
ability to find the answers had changed all of that.

He began playing with the ring he'd started to wear on
his right hand. Perry's ring.

His brother had been murdered while trying to find out
what happened to Jake. He had to remember that, keep it
uppermost in his mind whenever he was around Tina. *Especially* when he was around Tina.

The front door of the house suddenly opened.

Mitch straightened instantly, alert.

Tina stepped out onto the gallery and walked to the mailbox, at the end of the drive.

Mitch watched her, remembering another night just like
this one—the sky a rich blanket of ebony, strewn with a
spray of stars that twinkled as bright as diamonds, the day's
warmth still clinging to the night air, the tiny creatures of
the swamp offering up a faint serenade.

They'd picnicked down by the river that day, and gone

to the Lamp Post for dinner that night. She'd wanted to freshen up before they went to dinner, so he'd dropped her at the house, gone back to the cabin to clean up himself, then come back here to pick her up. He had arrived early, so he'd parked almost in this same spot. It was that night, sitting here alone, that he'd finally admitted to himself that he was in love with her. A shocking turn of events for a man who'd decided love was a fantasy only other people believed in, and that the only person he could truly trust a hundred percent was himself.

He'd known then, if there was a future for them together, that the time would come when he'd have to tell her that he was an FBI agent. But in spite of his growing feelings for her, black clouds loomed over the relationship. She hadn't told him about her brother, but from what she'd said he'd known whatever trouble Mace Peychaud was in, she blamed the authorities. So he'd checked, and discovered the FBI had played an integral part in nearly getting Mace killed, and had practically destroyed his life.

He'd known then that she'd never accept that he was with the Bureau, and he didn't know how he felt about that.

His parents had said "I love you" to each other a lot, but their constant fighting and dissatisfaction with each other had made a lie of the words, and Jake had done his best to keep himself and Perry out of their way. After their deaths, the two boys started to come out of their shells with their grandfather, but then he'd died too.

On the surface neither incident seemed enough to warp a young boy's mind against the kind of emotions that most people thought made the world go round. But most people, including his grandmother, didn't know that Blake and Melinda Blaggette had been fighting over the other woman in Blake's life the night of the car crash that took their lives, but spared their children.

Nor did his grandmother know about the other woman who had come to the hospital to say goodbye to Jake's grandfather as he lay dying.

Love and trust were highly overrated, and brought a person nothing but trouble as far as he was concerned. But obviously he'd forgotten those well-learned lessons when he'd met Tina. Another mistake.

He watched her retrieve several envelopes from the mailbox and walk slowly back toward the house while looking through them. Suddenly she paused and looked over her shoulder in his direction. Mitch stiffened, knowing there was no excuse he could offer that would sound believable if she saw him sitting there, watching her.

Mitch sighed in relief when she turned and continued toward the house. When he'd been in the hospital in Virginia, recuperating, he'd been able to distance his mind from her, had been able to look at the situation coldly, rationally, and accept the fact that she was his prime suspect. She was the most logical suspect. But now it was becoming difficult to imagine her purposely betraying him to someone who'd wanted him dead.

He slammed a clenched fist down on the seat beside him, an ugly curse ripping from his lips.

Maybe Raskin was right. Maybe he wasn't ready for this, but he had no choice now. He'd started this thing, and he had to finish it—and sitting here in the dark dwelling on the past and arguing with himself wasn't going to get him any answers.

Chapter 5

Tina flipped the hamburgers on the grill and checked the boiling noodles for the macaroni and cheese. Not exactly a gourmet meal, but it was Jimmy and Joey's favorite. She also made chocolate brownies for dessert, which Lily adored.

A soft knock on the front door drew her attention as she stirred the noodles. She looked toward the foyer and frowned, not having been expecting anyone. Then her pulse sped up as she thought of Mitch. But most likely it was Dack, ''stopping by'' to check on them again. The first few times he'd done it, right after Ben died, she'd thought it was nice of him. His checkups had become more frequent after the death of her father, and lately she'd begun to find them increasingly annoying, mainly because once in the house, he never seemed to want to leave.

Joey raced across the foyer toward the door. ''Cumpkany,'' he screeched.

''No!'' Tina yelled, but it was too late. He was already

turning the knob. Teaching him that he wasn't supposed to open the front door, or talk to strangers, was proving to be an impossible feat.

Lily suddenly appeared and grabbed Joey just as the door swung open.

Tina set down her spoon and hurried into the foyer, wiping her hands on her apron while her mind raced in search of some excuse she could offer to keep from asking Dack to come in and join them for dinner.

"Your sister told me you left early," Mitch said.

Her pulse skittered as their eyes met and Tina suddenly felt like a young girl again, staring at her first date and too nervous to even greet him.

"I just wanted to made sure everything was all right," Mitch said. "I mean..." He shrugged, and a boyish smile pulled at his lips. "It was an excuse."

Tina smiled, the mystery reflecting from somewhere deep in his dark eyes pulling her. "Everything's fine," she said finally. Convictions of caution deserted her before she could even remember them. "And friends don't need an excuse to visit."

"Is that what we are?" he asked softly, the deep timbre of his voice wrapping around her like warm silk, as his eyes melted into hers.

"Barney!" Joey suddenly yelled, racing toward the living room as a big, purple dinosaur who resembled a stuffed animal came onto the TV screen and began singing and dancing.

Tina laughed. "We were just about to have dinner."

Don't invite him, a voice whispered in the back of her mind.

"It's only hamburgers and macaroni and cheese," Tina said, "but you're welcome to join us."

Mitch glanced past her shoulder, to the two little boys

sitting on the living room floor and singing along with the dinosaur. "I don't want to intrude."

There was some kind of magnetism between them. Though it frightened Tina, and she knew she should ignore it, she found herself reluctant to let it go. "You wouldn't be," she said softly. "Anyway, I could use the help. The kids are still pretty keyed up from the trip."

Mitch's gaze swept over both living and dining rooms as he entered. They were comfortably furnished. Distressed pine, soft blue gingham fabrics, plush rugs and lots of plants and flowers. Rooms to live in, rather than show off. He smiled. It reminded him of his grandmother's place. "I would have brought wine."

"I don't usually drink, but you can set the table while Lily fights the battle of getting hands washed."

He followed her into the kitchen.

"So, how did you find my house?" Tina asked.

Mitch's hand paused on the pile of napkins he'd been about to grab for the table, her question throwing him. Three years ago, if he'd been operating undercover, he would have been prepared for any question. Especially one that basic. "Claude," he said quickly, hoping she wouldn't say anything to the old man and find out Mitch had just lied.

Tina nodded. "One of the town's worst gossips. Figures. If there's anything about anyone in Reimour Crossings worth telling, Claude will tell it."

Mitch frowned. If Claude was one of the town's gossips, he'd certainly kept things to himself that afternoon. Or maybe the old man just liked to start with the good old days and work himself up through the years. Mitch felt like groaning just thinking of how many afternoons of fishing that could take. "Don't get after him about it," he said, and forced a mocking grimace to his face. "Please. Or the next time he takes me fishing I might end up gator feed."

"Well, I certainly wouldn't want to be responsible for that," Tina said, and laughed. "So, I guess my lips are sealed."

Mitch hurriedly set the table while she prepared the macaroni and cheese, then transferred the hamburgers from the grill to a plate.

"Let me take that," he said, stepping in front of her and reaching for the plate of hamburgers as she turned from the grill.

They stood staring at each other for several long seconds, his hand covering hers.

Without thinking about what he was doing, Mitch leaned forward and brushed his lips lightly across hers.

It was a touch as light as the gentlest of breezes that riffled through the swamp on a sweltering summer afternoon. Yet it turned her lips to fire. Its burning heat quivered through her veins, then settled in the pit of her stomach.

When he pulled away, it was with reluctance, yet at the same time Mitch silently and instantly cursed himself as a fool. He hadn't meant to do that.

Tina turned away, not wanting him to see the hot flush she could feel covering her cheeks, or the tears that were filling her eyes. The blush was reasonable, but the tears were not, and she couldn't explain them, not even to herself. She grabbed the bowl of noodles and pitcher of milk and turned toward the dining room. "We'd better eat before it gets cold," she said, her voice feeling almost as fragile as her nerves.

He touched her arm as she started to pass him, and she paused. "That was merely to say thank-you," he said, "and that I think you're very beautiful tonight."

Tina looked down. She was wearing her oldest pair of

jeans, a baggy T-shirt, a Mickey Mouse apron, and tennis shoes with purple tassels, one of six sets Lily had made in school and presented Tina for her birthday. Plus she most likely had macaroni cheese on her face, and smelled liked grilled hamburger and onion.

She nodded, but remained silent, not expelling the breath she wasn't even aware she was holding until he released her arm and walked into the dining room. "Damn, I'm pathetic," she cursed under her breath. Her reactions to him were ridiculous. He hadn't meant anything by that kiss other than what he'd said. But it didn't matter, she realized. In only two days and a few hours together, he'd managed to push his way past the barriers she'd built around her emotions in recent years. And he'd done it with such ease she hadn't even seen it coming.

In spite of her nervousness, dinner was an enjoyable experience. The boys seemed to thoroughly enjoy Mitch's stories of growing up in the city, and Lily kept staring at him as if she thought he was the next best thing to her movie star idol, whose name at the moment escaped Tina. But then, the object of Lily's young affections seemed to change every week.

"You have great kids," Mitch said, after Tina had shooed the boys off to bed and Lily had retreated to her room to read.

Tina handed him a cup of coffee and settled into the overstuffed chair, set opposite the sofa, where Mitch sat. "Thanks, I think they're pretty great too."

"Do they look like their father?"

Tina smiled to herself as her thoughts spun to another time. Did they look like their father? His midnight-blue eyes swam through her memory. "Yes. The boys have Jake's eyes, and hair, and sometimes I think..." She suddenly stopped, realizing what she'd said.

Mitch frowned. "I thought you said your late husband's name was Ben."

The shock of what she'd just done left her momentarily dumbstruck. That had never happened before. Why had she mentioned Jake? She hadn't spoken to anyone about him since her father died. Not even her sisters knew the entire truth. "I...I'm sorry. I guess my thoughts were somewhere else for a moment."

"Looked to me like that somewhere else was pretty far away."

She nodded. "Far away and long ago," she said, and smiled. "And thoughts better left forgotten."

"I always believed no one should ever be forgotten," Mitch said.

She stared down into her coffee, unable to look at him any longer. His eyes were the wrong color, his hair too coarse and dark, his features were all wrong, even the way he walked was different, yet he'd never reminded her of Jake more than at this moment.

Or was it just that her mind had betrayed her, let her think of Jake while talking to Mitch?

"Mommy, I want water."

Tina looked up to see Jimmy standing in the doorway. She glanced at Mitch as she rose and found him staring at her son, a wistful look on his face. Then he looked up at her. A chill swept up Tina's spine at the hard, cold look she saw suddenly shade Mitch's eyes.

"Mommy," Jimmy said again, drawing the word out into a whine.

She grabbed his hand and hurried him into the kitchen. Her imagination was getting the better of her. Why would Mitch look at her that way? Almost as if... She shuddered, unable to really define the look. Cynical. Calculating. Accusing. She wasn't sure, but she knew it was the same look she'd thought she had seen in his eyes that morning when he'd come into the café. She gave Jimmy his water, then escorted him back to his room and tucked him in bed.

Maybe it was just her imagination. She was upset after having foolishly mentioning Jake, and she'd merely imagined that look in Mitch's eyes.

He watched her walk back into the room and knew instantly that she was shaken, and it was his fault. He'd have to be more careful. It had been a long time since he'd worked to hide his emotions, and he was finding it even more difficult to do around Tina. But his life could very well depend on him doing just that.

"The other one should be out any minute," Tina said, smiling to cover the uneasiness still churning about inside of her.

"Joey?"

She nodded. "What one has, or gets, the other is always right behind for his. But if I'd taken it in to him, he'd find another reason for coming out."

"Mommy?"

She gave Mitch a knowing look and rose. "Told you so."

He watched her leave the room again, and balled his hand into a fist, pressing it into the arm of the sofa. When she'd mentioned Jake, he had nearly come out of his seat with anxiety. He'd wanted to keep her talking. Now he was back to square one.

"Okay, that should do it for tonight," Tina said, slipping back into the room and taking her seat across from him. "Lily's old enough to get her own water."

He watched her lips move, and remembered what it had felt like, just a few hours ago, when he'd touched them with his own. Hot, soft, sweet, inviting. He didn't want to believe that lies—so treacherous that they could get a man killed—could purposely pass those lips.

"Do you want some more coffee?"

"Sure." He handed her his cup as she rose. What he wanted was this whole damned thing over with. He wanted answers to the questions that had been haunting him for two years, and he wanted to know that she hadn't had anything to do with the attack on him, or Perry's death.

He pushed off the sofa and walked to the window and stared into the night. God, he hated this. He moved around the room, pausing to look at the pictures she had situated on an end table. The kids. Her. A man he knew from the photo in his case file was Ben Dubois. Her sisters, Lianne and Dee, each of them born almost exactly two years apart. Her father, Marcus. Mother, Selena. Pictures of all her family, but none of Jake Blaggette. They hadn't been together long, back then, but long enough for her to have taken several photos...at the fair...down by the river. But none were here.

It was the same with the arrangement of photographs sitting on an antique étagère set in the corner.

"Here we are." Tina walked back into the room, two cups of coffee in her hands.

Mitch looked at her. God help him, in spite of everything, in spite of his anger, his frustrations and resentment, even his suspicions, he wanted her. Desire had been gnawing at his insides from the moment he'd walked into her house. What was there about Tina Peychaud that made him forget everything he was ever taught in order to survive? That made him want to drag her into his arms and make love to her until they were both too exhausted to take even one more breath?

Tina sat down, setting the cups on the coffee table. "Mitch?"

He was losing it again. His concentration. His drive. He shook himself mentally and glanced back at the photos. "I was just admiring your gallery of family photos." He picked up the one of Ben Dubois. "Was this your husband?"

She moved to stand beside him and looked down at the photo he held. A sad smile touched her lips. "Yes, that was Ben."

The way she said his name, the look that came into her eyes, sparked Mitch's temper again. Disgust swelled within him. He was jealous of a dead man. Mitch knew he should leave, get out of there before he said something that gave him away. He set the picture back on the étagère, then looked at Tina while his mind sought the resolve of the agent who could pull off this charade with cold objectivity. He'd gone over and over every scrap of information, every note Perry had made, every bit of evidence and conjecture that had been gathered in the past three years. None of it proved she was responsible, or even involved with what had happened. But none of it proved she wasn't either.

"You know," he said finally, "it's getting pretty late. I probably should leave."

Surprised, Tina glanced at the refilled coffee cups sitting on the table, ignored, then looked up at Mitch. "I've enjoyed your company tonight," she said, knowing it was all too true, and something in her wishing it wasn't. She walked beside him to the front door.

As he stepped onto the gallery, Mitch turned and looked back at her. Moonlight touched the long strands of her dark hair, while shadows darkened the curls of each wave and the redolence of her perfume—the same scent of gardenia she'd always worn—seemed to fill his senses. She was so close he could almost feel the warmth of her skin. For one brief second he was tempted to tell her the truth. He looked deep into her eyes. What would her reaction be? Fear or joy? Would she deny knowing anything about what had happened, or confess to it all?

But the second passed, and with it the temptation. Nothing had ever been that simple, and there was too much at stake for him to play that kind of foolish game.

If she was responsible for setting him up and getting his brother murdered, whether intentional or not, then it was also possible that other agents were also at risk. It was a point he and Raskin had agreed was probably the most important of all.

Looking into her eyes, gut instinct tried to convince him she was innocent. That had been something he'd always trusted in the past: his own hunches and feelings. They'd taken him down the right path and kept him alive more times than he could remember. But his instincts had let him down three years ago, and he wasn't about to take the risk of trusting them now. Evidence, hard and irrefutable, that was all he could rely on now. "Thanks again," he said, pulling his car keys from his pocket and moving across the porch before he did something he'd regret—like pull her into his arms and kiss her again.

That had been a stupid mistake.

She knew Jake too well. Mannerisms, speech patterns, looks, habits. *And kisses.* He was walking a tightrope, and if he didn't keep his balance he was going to fall. Then where would he be?

Most likely where you were supposed to be three years ago, a little voice in the back of his mind whispered—dead.

When he'd pulled out of her driveway, something, like the flash of a reflection off chrome, had caught Mitch's eye. He'd stared into the darkness for a minute, but he hadn't been able to make anything out. About half a mile from

Tina's house he pulled his car off the road and doused the lights. He was either paranoid as hell, or there had been a car parked off the road just beyond her house.

The minutes ticked by.

He stared into the rearview mirror.

The road remained deserted.

Mitch could hear as well as feel the heavy pounding of his heart. He reached into the console between the seats and drew out his gun, setting it on the passenger seat, within easy reach. Tension settled into his shoulders and wrapped around his spine as he waited.

Something moved in the bushes to the right of the car.

Mitch snatched up the gun and whirled around in his seat.

A bird, sitting on a tree branch several yards from the car, looked back at him curiously.

Mitch sank back against his seat, momentarily overcome with relief.

Spanish moss swayed softly from the boughs of the trees lining the road. An owl hooted. A frog croaked.

If anyone was sneaking around, the night's creatures would have scurried for cover and remained silent. Or so Mitch told himself, remaining unconvinced and on edge. Was this the way it was going to be from now on, he wondered? Had he thoroughly lost his nerve? Grabbing his gun and jumping at the slightest of sounds? He cursed softly beneath his breath. He didn't trust his instincts anymore, and he'd most likely lost his nerve. Great attributes for an agent. He started the car and pulled back onto the road. Obviously he was also developing a fanciful imagination.

As he pulled the T-bird past the Magnolia Inn and parked next to his cabin, he suddenly wished fervently that this whole mess was over with.

Mitch locked the cabin's door behind him, closed the drapes over the large window and, kicking off his boots, collapsed on the bed. He hadn't expected that seeing Tina again was going to be so hard. A long sigh slipped from his throat and he closed his eyes, but just as quickly opened them. He had a few things to do before he could catch some sleep, so he rose, poured himself a finger of whiskey from the flask he'd brought and sat down at the desk by the window. Turning on his laptop, he went directly to his e-mail site. It indicated he had a message from Raskin.

Have to be out of the office for a few days. Don't talk to anyone else at the Agency until I contact you. IR

Mitch stared at the message, a cold shiver of unease snaking its way up his spine as he wondered what in the hell Raskin was up to. The man was never gone from the office for more time than it took to sleep, and that included weekends.

Something was wrong. The thought nagged at him. Something had happened to make Raskin leave the office, and someone had been tailing Mitch tonight. Could the two incidents be connected? He didn't see how.

The phone rang.

Mitch shot up off the bed and dived for the gun he'd laid on the nightstand, his jangled nerves nearly standing on end. At the phone's second ring, relief nearly buckled his knees. He yanked the receiver from its cradle. Disgusted that the mere ringing of a telephone could rattle him so thoroughly, the greeting came out more like a growl ripped from his throat. "Hello?"

"Mitch?"

He recognized Tina's voice instantly, and frowned, alarm and puzzlement seizing him. "Tina? What's wrong?"

"Nothing, I..."

"Tina." The edginess in his voice grated across her already overly sensitized nerves as he listened to her speak. Several minutes after closing the front door, she'd heard the cat scratching at it and had gone back to let him in. That was when she'd seen the rear of a car moving slowly down the road in the same direction Mitch had taken. She'd stood and watched it, not realizing why at first, and then, as her uneasiness grew, thoughts of Jake filled her mind. She'd known then why the sight of a car moving almost stealthily down the road and disappearing into the darkness after Mitch bothered her.

Fear, unreasonable and unwelcome, had filled her. She'd thought of calling the sheriff—but facing Dack Brenaud with her fears was more than she could contemplate. She had thought of getting in her own car and speeding down the road after Mitch—but she couldn't leave the children.

For one brief second Mitch felt a rise of spirit such as he hadn't felt since before the attack. But just as briefly as it swept over him, the black cloud of another thought pushed it aside. Was she really worried about him—really calling to make certain he was all right? Or was she checking to see if he'd escaped the trap again?

After mumbling an embarrassed and almost incoherent good-night, Tina quickly hung up the phone. Her heart was beating rapidly and her hands were shaking. Why had she done that? She sat back against the headboard of her bed, wrapped her arms around her drawn-up legs and rested her head on her knees. Long-ago fears, deep-rooted and all-possessive had crept up to overtake her earlier, and they'd prodded her into acting like an idiot. It was the only excuse for the impulsive call.

Mitch Ryan was probably in his cabin now, laughing at

her, and convinced he'd shown too much interest in a woman who watched too many spooky shows on television.

She opened the drawer of her nightstand and pulled out the photograph of Jake she'd put there after taking it from the trunk in the attic. She cradled it between her hands and stared into his eyes. He had walked out on her. It was as simple as that. Just because he'd claimed to be an agent for the FBI, which might or might not have been the truth, it didn't make him a stand-up, nice guy, and it certainly didn't mean that there was some dark, mysterious reason he'd never come back. He'd decided he didn't want to marry her, and he'd left. End of story.

So why hadn't she ever been able to really believe that? Sighing deeply, she set the picture down, let her head fall back against the headboard and closed her eyes.

Mitch wasn't an FBI agent. He owned an electrical security company in Richmond. They'd only had one date. Two, if she counted his having dinner at her house that night. Who would be sneaking around and following the owner of an electrical security company? Tina sighed. Maybe she had been watching too many television shows. She'd seen a car and jumped to a ludicrous conclusion. More than likely, it had been one of her elderly neighbors going somewhere and driving slowly because it was dark and they couldn't see all that well.

The more she thought about it, the more foolish she felt. She shouldn't have called him. He probably thought she was crazy. Yet, when she saw the outline of that car moving slowly down the road behind him, its lights not going on until it was away from her house, the fear she'd felt had nearly turned the blood in her veins to ice.

Three hours later, Mitch gave up the quest for sleep and turned his laptop back on. If he kept this up much longer he'd become a zombie, or at least look like one. But, if he was going to be awake—and after that phone call from Tina he was definitely awake—he might as well try to get something accomplished besides staring through the darkness toward the ceiling. The computer beeped, signaling it was ready. He punched in the classified code that would connect him with the Agency's mainframe at Quantico. The connection went through instantly, but he found no information on where Ivor Raskin had gone. It listed him as on vacation. Mitch stared at the words in disbelief. Raskin was on vacation like polar bears were in Florida.

He tried several different approaches to the file, and failed to get any more information with any of them. Raskin was either being extremely careful about where he'd gone, and why, or someone in the Agency had erased his file after he'd filled it in.

Mitch's frustration level neared the max and he swore for several seconds, then cut the connection with Quantico and went into the files Raskin had sent him earlier. He pulled up the list of properties in Reimour Crossings and began scanning the listings, paying particular attention to the ones along the road Tina lived on.

Chapter 6

Tina reined SunnyLad up near the barn and slid to the ground. She loved riding early in the morning, when the sun had barely made its way over the treetops and the coolness of night's wee hours still clung to the air. It was when time stood still, when imagination could turn back the clock, and she could envision herself in an era much simpler, much more elegant and much more innocent than the one in which she actually lived.

After giving the horse a good brushing and turning him out in the pasture, Tina turned toward the house and caught sight of Lianne's dark blue Trans Am parked in the drive.

"Hey, what's up?" she asked, stepping into the kitchen and seeing both Lianne and Dee sitting at the table. She could hear Lily and the boys playing in the living room. Tina poured herself some coffee and joined her sisters.

Lianne shrugged. "We don't have to look over the Claymores' house until noon, though I'm dreading it—the place hasn't been redecorated since Georgia seceded from the

Union. Anyway, Dee and I figured, since you don't open the café until noon today, and we haven't had a chance to chat since we got back from Savannah, we could have ourselves a little visit."

"Really?" Tina said, eyeing them both with good-natured suspicion. "You just want to chat—or is it that one of the town gossips has already told you I've been out to dinner at the Lamp Post with a man recently, and you're both dying of curiosity?"

"No!" Lianne gasped, slapping a hand to her chest dramatically. "You had a date? Well, miracle of miracles, I had no idea."

"But since you brought it up," Dee said, making no effort to hide her interest, "tell us everything about him, starting with who he is, what he does, where he comes from, et cetera, et cetera."

After the passing of an hour, Tina had told them everything she knew to tell about Mitch Ryan, except that he made her think of Jake. Lianne and Dee hated Jake for walking out on Tina, and any man who reminded her of him was mostly likely a good target for their wrath.

"Look, I have a favor to ask," Lianne said, breaking into Tina's thoughts. "My car is scheduled for the shop—it's nearing 200,000 miles and started making weird noises on our way back from Savannah. We've got an appointment this afternoon with a prospective client—he just bought the old DeMoray place—and, well, I rather doubt we'd look like successful decorators worthy of his contract if we arrived driving Mel's primer-painted Chevy. Can we borrow your car?"

An hour later the coffee was gone, as were the half dozen doughnuts Dee had brought.

"Okay, you two," Tina said, "you've got what you really came for, and I've probably gained two pounds. So, now I've got to get to work before Uncle Deano opens the café without me and gives everything away."

"So, when do we get to meet the new man in your life?" Lianne asked.

Tina grimaced. "We've had one date, and he came to dinner at the house once. I don't exactly call that 'being in my life.'"

"Counting the amount of dates you go on, I would," Dee said teasingly, running a hand absently through her short mass of dark curls.

"Okay, enough," Tina said, laughing. "Mrs. Stimple will be here to watch the kids in a few minutes, so I'm going to grab a quick shower."

Lianne scrunched up her nose mockingly. "Good. You do smell kind of horsey."

"Thank you," Tina said, tossing her a derisive grin. "You two can drop me at the café and take my car, but don't forget to come back and get me."

"You sure you wouldn't rather hitch a ride home from Mitch Ryan?" Dee asked, smiling slyly.

Mitch stared at the sign on the café's door. She didn't open until noon on Saturday, which he hadn't known until just that moment. That meant he had almost an hour and a half before she'd be in. Her phone call had haunted him long after they'd hung up last night. He wanted to believe she'd been worried about him, but he couldn't help but suspect there had been a darker motive to her call.

He walked back to his car, climbed in and sat staring at the café. There were things he should be doing, yet all he could think about was Tina. He wanted—no, he needed—to see her, to look into her eyes when he asked her why she'd called him last night.

Mitch started the car and pulled out of the parking lot.

There were at least two addresses on the property list the Agency had provided that had aroused his curiosity. One was an old plantation house that had been the issue of a lawsuit over ownership for the past five years. Another was listed as condemned.

On the surface of it, they meant nothing. But to Mitch, they could mean the answers he sought. It wouldn't be the first time the law was used to hide illegal activities, or that an old building, supposedly uninhabitable, hid a smooth-operating drug factory. He'd put in a request for a deeper check on both properties this morning, but he also intended to take a look for himself.

Mitch grabbed a cup of coffee from the little hamburger stand a few blocks down from the café, and talked for a while with two old gents sitting on the porch of Gateau's Hardware Store. A while later he helped a little old lady, who introduced herself as Miss Liddy Cosselmeyer, carry her packages from Landry's Market to her 1935 Ford, parked next to his T-bird. She'd tossed the Bird an appreciative glance and informed Mitch she'd received her car brand-new from her daddy on her twenty-first birthday and she hadn't had a lick of trouble with it in all those years.

With another forty minutes left before Tina would open the café, Mitch climbed back into his car. The condemned building turned out to be empty, so he headed toward the old plantation having ownership problems. It was probably a long shot, but he couldn't overlook anything. According to his map, it was located about ten miles north of town.

Fifteen miles north of town he pulled the car to the side of the road and, cursing soundly, grabbed the map again. How hard could it be to locate a plantation? Weren't these old monstrosities supposed to be huge? He threw the map back onto the passenger seat and climbed out of the car to have a look around.

The old two-lane road was deserted as far as he could see in both directions. He'd passed numerous side roads, entry drives without mailboxes or address signs, and what had looked like old roads or drives nearly obscured by overgrown brush. Mitch looked around. The sun was blazing overhead, humidity hung so heavy in the air the well-worn, cracked blacktop seemed to be rolling in the distance, and everything seemed so silent it was eerie.

Suddenly a vehicle appeared in the distance.

Mitch started to step into the road as it approached, intending to wave the driver down and ask him if he knew where Hickory Hill plantation was located. Sunlight sparked off the black hood of the pickup and Mitch stopped, his hand raised in midair, the breath abruptly stalled in his lungs.

The truck drew nearer.

Mitch felt a cold sweat break out over his skin. His heartbeat accelerated, his pulses raced. Time stopped, then sped backward as memory of another spot along the side of the road, another pickup, another time, mercilessly took over his mind. He glanced toward his car, and toward the console where his gun lay safely tucked away, out of sight—out of reach. His eyes turned back to the truck, drawing nearer. He could hear the roar of its engine, see the shadow of two men sitting in the cab. His mouth went dry.

Flames—heat—fists—pain. The sensations that were memories, but not memories, flashed through his mind. Spinning on his heel, Mitch jerked open the car's door and lunged toward the console, yanking it open and grabbing his gun.

The truck pulled up beside him just as his fingers wrapped around the weapon's handle. He jerked the gun from the leather holster it lay in.

"You okay there, young fella?"

Mitch spun around and straightened, shock stealing his thoughts as he stared into the eyes of one of the old men he'd been talking to in front of the hardware store earlier. His gaze moved to the truck, seeing now that it was dark blue, not black, old, not new.

"You ain't sick or anything, are you?" the man behind the steering wheel asked, leaning forward to look over his passenger's shoulder. "Look kinda green around the gills."

It was the other old man from the store.

Mitch shook his head and finally found his voice, feeling somewhat foolish for his attack of near panic. "I'm fine," he said. "Thanks. But I could use your help. I'm looking for an old plantation that supposed to be around here someplace. Called Hickory Hill."

The old men looked at each other, then back at Mitch, both frowning now. "What for?"

What for? He hadn't planned an answer to that one. Why wasn't he prepared? He'd had two years to get himself ready for this case, to plan every detail. So why did he find himself scrambling for the answers to the simplest questions? His mind raced in search of something they'd believe. "The, uh, families have been fighting over ownership of the place for quite a while now, you know, and, um, I'm a friend of the Taylors...." He remembered one of the family's names from the list. "They asked me to look in on the place if I could, since I was passing through this way." He shrugged. "You know, make sure it was still even standing."

"Damned Yankees," the driver spit.

"Well, tarnation, course it's still standing," the man in the passenger seat snapped at the same time, his tone laced with outrage. He glared at Mitch. "I suppose they're thinking of moving down here now and throwing her out, right?"

Mitch frowned, confused. "Throwing who out?" he asked, wishing now he'd never asked for directions.

"Miss Liddy, that's who. Darn place belongs to her just as much as to them no-goods who been squabbling over it ever since their pappy died."

"More," the driver said, putting in his two cents. "She's always lived here. They ain't, thank the powers that be."

Mitch looked from one man to the other, thoroughly confused now. "Miss Liddy?" he echoed, remembering the little old lady with the groceries.

The two old men looked at him suspiciously. "Thought you said the Taylors from up north asked you to look in on the place?"

"They did."

"And that pipsqueak Fred Taylor didn't tell you about Miss Liddy Cosselmeyer?

"No," Mitch said, wondering how any of this played into his theory of illegal activities going on in an old, secluded mansion. He instantly came to the conclusion that it didn't.

"Hickory's been Miss Liddy's home since right after she married ol' Judge Taylor, or at least thought she did, some what, sixty years ago?"

The passenger nodded. "Just 'cause that old coot never made sure his divorce from that woman up in Richmond was final before he married Miss Liddy ain't no reason to say she wasn't his wife and take her house away from her. He built it for her, not them."

After another ten minutes of listening to them harangue "those damned Yankees," Mitch learned the directions to Hickory Hill, which he was no longer interested in finding, and watched the two old men drive away. He climbed back into his car, tucked his gun into the console and headed toward town. He'd stop by the café and invite Tina to dinner, then check on his e-mail and see if the Agency had gotten back to him with anything new. Then if he was lucky, maybe he could catch some sleep.

Five miles later, he was zooming down the winding, two-lane road at about sixty miles per hour, deep in thought, when he was startled by a sudden clunking sound. His gaze jumped to the rearview mirror, expecting to see someone behind him, but the road was deserted for as far as he could see. The sound came again, and this time his attention was drawn to the hood of the car. He pulled over quickly and killed the engine, then climbed out and popped the hood.

Steam rose up to greet him, along with a sight that brought a groan to his lips. The water pump's drive belt had gone slack and one of the pulleys was jutting out at a forty-degree angle, the wrong way.

Mitch cursed soundly. There was no way he could jury-rig the belt, which meant he wasn't driving himself anywhere. He drew back from beneath the raised hood and, stepping around the car, looked up and down the road.

Nothing.

A long, deep sigh of frustration rumbled from his throat. It was at least ten miles back to town, maybe a bit more, and ninety degrees in the shade, of which there was little on the road.

The day had gotten off to a not-so-wonderful start, and seemed to be progressing downhill at runaway speed. He walked to the rear of the car and popped the trunk. Jake had favored baseball caps. Mitch retrieved the black cowboy hat he'd bought while refurbishing his wardrobe before the trip.

He hadn't purchased anything even remotely similar to the styles he used to wear—mainly expensive polo-style shirts and khakis. Now he favored T-shirts and jeans, and actually hadn't wanted the Stetson, but figured it was better than nothing.

He settled it on his head, not feeling any more comfortable with it than the one and only other time he'd tried wearing it, but welcoming the shade its brim threw over his face. With another soft curse, and a silent prayer that the two old men would come back by and give him a lift, Mitch clipped his gun to his belt—figuring he'd say he always traveled with protection, if anyone asked—and started walking toward town.

After an hour of walking alongside the road, Mitch knew why cowboys didn't do any long-distance hiking in their boots, and was cursing the sun for not giving him a break. The hat felt like a blanket on his head, his gun seemed like a ten-pound weight on his hip, and his mood was turning blacker with each passing second.

By the time he made it back to the outskirts of Reimour Crossings the sun had finally relented and was merely a soft glow of reflected gold on the horizon. Mitch was so exhausted and out of sorts it was a toss-up whether his most fervent wish was to drop onto a bed and sleep for a week, or kill somebody.

He kept walking, but stopped abruptly when he saw what he thought was Tina's car approaching. It was hard to tell, with a streetlight bouncing a reflection off the windshield. As it neared he looked at the right front fender. When she'd left the restaurant the other night after they'd had dinner he'd noticed the dented fender. Mitch started to step into the street and wave so she'd see him, then stopped when the car turned into a drive several hundred yards from where he was standing.

Tall brick pillars framed the drive, and a wrought-iron fence fronted the property. A set of ornate gates silently opened upon her approach.

Mitch moved along the fence until he came to a spot where he could see beyond the heavy growth of brush and trees growing up against it. Several cars, including Tina's, were parked in the circular drive that swept gracefully past a very majestic, antebellum mansion.

For a split second his mind wandered and he wondered if every old southerner before the Civil War had used the same floor plans and design. Then he snapped back to the moment at hand, and frowned. Except for the attack on him three years ago, he'd never forgotten a thing, his memory being about as photographic as it could get without actually being there. He mentally reviewed the property list the Agency had provided. There were eleven old mansions in the area, but most, like Hickory Hill, were well out of town. None, that he remembered, were listed as being almost within the city limits of Reimour Crossings.

So had this house been built later? And why wasn't it on the Agency's list? He looked around for a mailbox, hoping to see something with a name on it, but found nothing. He looked back at the house again. New or old, it should be on the list, and it wasn't. He might be making something over nothing more than a government clerical error, but it bothered him, almost as much as having seen Tina go to the house.

He turned to go, then stopped as Sheriff Dack Brenaud's patrol car turned into the drive.

Tina smiled at her Aunt Marge as she slipped another movie into the VCR for the kids to watch. It was getting late, and she would rather have just gone home after closing the café, but her sisters still had her car and her Uncle Deano had insisted she come to his house instead.

Feeling restless now, Tina turned to look at the tall grandfather clock that stood in a corner of the room. They'd finished dinner, and it was nearly ten. Her sisters should arrive soon. In spite of the fact the café had only been open half a day today, she felt exhausted.

Why hadn't Mitch come to the café? The thought seemed to come to her out of nowhere, but she knew it hadn't really. He'd been on her mind all day. Was he gone? Had he left Reimour Crossings without saying goodbye—as Jake had done? Was that why she hadn't seen him?

"You got everything ready for the festival tomorrow?" Deano asked.

Tina shrugged away the thoughts that tried to pull her into a despondent mood and turned back to her aunt and uncle, forcing herself to smile, her tone to be cheerful. "Well, let's see. Lunch is all ready to be packed, blankets are folded and in the trunk of the car, our donation for the raffle of a week's free lunches at the café is typed up and in my purse. I'm signed up to do an hour of manning the information booth, and the chili and spareribs you cooked for the competition are packed and ready to be put in the cooler." Tina laughed. "Did I forget anything?"

"I made cupcakes today, and a potato salad and fried chicken," Marge said, smiling. "So I'd say we're ready." She got up to refill the coffee carafe, while Deano took the kids some cookies.

Tina stared down into her empty coffee cup. The last time she'd been to the town's annual summer festival, she'd been with Jake. She had refused to go since, first saying she didn't want to take newborns into a crowd. The next year she'd used her grief over Ben's death, and last year Joey and Jimmy had both come down with colds and saved her from having to think up another excuse. This year however, she couldn't decline. She was officially the new owner of Peychaud Café, and that meant she was expected to participate. But she wasn't looking forward to it.

Jake had proposed to her at the festival.

Tina's memories surged forth and she felt a deep tug of emotion that drew her back to that day. They'd spent the whole afternoon at the festival, then had decided to stay for the evening's fireworks. It had been an unusually warm day, and the park's flowers had been in full bloom, scenting the air heavily with their sweet fragrance.

But it was what he'd said to her just before proposing that she remembered now.

"Before we go any further, Tina, there's something about me you have to know, something I should have already told you," Jake said, holding both her hands in his. *"I'm an agent with a secret branch of the FBI."*

She saw the anxious look in his eyes, heard the rush of her pulse in her ears, felt the slamming of her heart against her breast in reaction to his confession. He knew about her brother's problems with the FBI, knew how she felt about them. Tina closed her eyes for one long second, struggling with her emotions. She hated that agency, and she loved Jake with all of her heart. But she couldn't live a lie.

"Why didn't you tell me?" she asked, already knowing the answer. *If she'd known, she never would have had anything to do with him. Her heart threatened to shatter into a million pieces as she looked into his eyes.*

He shook his head. "I didn't know how to tell you before, and kept putting it off, telling myself this thing might not work between us and then it wouldn't matter. But it is working." His eyes begged her to understand. *"And it does matter."*

She nodded.

"Marry me, Tina," he said. *"Marry me and make me the happiest man in the world."*

"So," Marge said, coming back into the room, "your uncle told me you went out to dinner with a nice young man the other night."

Chapter 7

Mitch had forgotten about the festival. He shouldn't have, there were signs about it all over town. But he just hadn't paid attention to the date. Maybe subconsciously he just hadn't wanted to remember. Now he stared at the sign taped to the café's door—Gone to the Festival. He turned and walked back to his car. Main Street was practically deserted. Like a ghost town.

He should have come back a month sooner, or waited a few weeks. Cursing himself for not planning better, he climbed into his car and headed for Beauregard Park. If that was where Tina was, then that was where he needed to be today, if for no other reason than to get an answer to the two questions that had been nagging at him all night and stirring his suspicions to new heights.

The Agency had finally gotten back to him just before he'd left the cabin, though not Raskin, who was still "on vacation." But his assistants were having a hard time getting much information on the house that Mitch had seen

Tina enter the night before. They did confirm that it was old, having been built just before the Civil War by some general. Since then it had been passed from one descendant to the next over the years. Ownership now, however, was still an unanswered question, as the proprietor was listed as a Florida corporation the Agency hadn't been able to gather any information on yet.

His second question, and the one uppermost in Mitch's mind, was why had Tina gone there?

He took a narrow road that led toward the river. Within minutes the entry to the park came into view. The last time he'd been there was the only time in his life he'd completely trusted someone. A few hours later that trust, and his life, had been viciously destroyed.

He got out of his car and entered the park. It seemed the whole town was there, but he didn't have any trouble spotting Tina. Her long, dark hair glistened richly beneath the sun, while the white shirt and shorts she wore complemented both the tantalizing curves of her body, and the golden hue of her skin. She was on the grass, playing what looked to him like ring-around-a-rosy with Lily and the twins.

Mitch paused by an old oak tree and, leaning a shoulder against its massive trunk, watched her with the children. The heat of resentment built slowly within him. He should have been in that circle with them, holding his sons' hands from the moment they'd been born, and he would have been if someone hadn't betrayed him. He forced the thoughts aside that only promised to send his mood spiraling into the depths of hell, where it had so often been over the past two years. This was neither the time nor place.

A horn blared across the park, announcing the finish of the three-legged race. The sound broke the momentary spell that had swept over Mitch. For a split second, while watch-

ing Tina, he'd felt as if the past few years hadn't existed.
As if all the pain had never happened. He shook himself
mentally, bringing his thoughts back to reality. But it did
happen, and Perry was dead.

Mitch walked slowly toward Tina and the children. Three
years ago she and he had spent the day together in this
same park, during this same festival. That evening he'd told
her everything and asked her to marry him, and she'd said
no. For the rest of the night he'd done nothing but try to
figure out how to change her mind. The next day, with the
foolish notion that if he went to Savannah and bought her
an engagement ring she'd change her mind, he'd left, and
someone had tried to make certain he never completed that
trip, and never came back.

He caught sight of Dack Brenaud sauntering across the
grass toward Tina and the kids. Mitch stopped.

Dack grabbed Tina's arm, stopping her in midstep and
making her nearly lose her balance. The kids stood, staring
up at him. "Sorry. I didn't mean that, but we need to talk."

"I'm busy, Dack," she said, and pulled away from him.
Long before she'd met Jake, Tina had dated Dack for a few
months. For a while she was charmed by his attentiveness,
then it had started to become a bit possessive. When he'd
begun making suggestions about who should and should
not be her friends, and subtly attempting to make decisions
for her, she'd known it would never work between them.
Unfortunately, Dack had never given up, not when she was
seeing Jake, or even when she was married to Ben.

"I haven't been able to find out anything on that Ryan
fella."

"So?"

"So I just thought I'd tell you. I think you should stay
away from him, Tina. He could be dangerous. You should
think of the kids too."

"Dack, I really think I can…"

"Look, Mom, there's Mr. Ryan," Lily said.

Tina instantly glanced in the direction Lily had indicated. Her gaze met Mitch's, and the warmth of a blush swept over Tina's cheeks. He was here. He hadn't left. A spurt of joy that she tried to deny, and couldn't, filled her. She watched him close the distance between them, but as he drew closer a chill raced down Tina's back at the cold anger she saw darken his eyes as they moved to rest on Dack. She'd seen a look like that once in Jake's eyes when Dack had tried to kiss her. She had tried to think of it as an innocent gesture of friendship, but Jake hadn't. Tina shivered. That had been exactly three years ago, at the festival.

"Hey, Sheriff," Mitch said, pausing before Tina and Dack, "pretty nice festival. Peaceful too."

"Yes," Tina said, feeling suddenly deliciously warm as his gaze moved over her approvingly. "Sheriff Brenaud was just reminding us to be careful on our way home later, in case some of my neighbors have a little too much to drink."

"Good advice." He looked at Dack. "But don't worry, Sheriff. I'll be happy to see that Tina and her family get home safely."

Dack ignored him and continued to look at Tina. "I'll come by later. Maybe the kids'll get a kick outta riding in a patrol car."

Mitch watched him walk away.

"I thought maybe you'd left town," Tina said, then instantly wished she hadn't. The last thing she needed to do was to let him think she'd been waiting for him to come around.

"No. I had some car trouble yesterday."

"Nothing serious, I hope." She didn't really care, she

only cared that he was here, even though she knew she shouldn't.

He shook his head. "Your local mechanic managed to fix it last night. Luckily he had the right parts."

"Good, but I hope Quattman didn't charge you a fortune. He does that sometimes to strangers, when he figures they're in a hurry."

Mitch smiled. "I wasn't, and he didn't."

The energy of attraction between them seemed even stronger today. "Would you like to join us for lunch? We were just about to eat."

"I'd like that, if I'm not imposing."

"She wouldn't have invited you if you were imposing," Lily said.

Tina frowned down at the girl. "Mind your manners," she said softly, and Lily blushed. "Sorry," Tina said, looking back at Mitch as Lily ushered the twins toward the blanket laid out under a tree. "She has a habit of sometimes saying whatever pops into her head."

"She's young. I think we all did that, but she'll learn."

As they neared the blanket, Mitch felt a swell of apprehension at seeing her sisters there. He drew in a deep breath, telling himself that he'd fooled Tina and her uncle, so there was no reason to get jumpy about her sisters. But he remembered Lianne as an extremely astute person. Nothing got past her. And Dee, the youngest, had been so enthralled by the fact that Jake had come from "up north," she'd asked him every question imaginable.

"Welcome to Reimour Crossings, Mitch," Lianne said, when Tina introduced them.

Dee leaned close to Tina. "Another northerner?" she whispered, frowning in concern.

"He's a friend," Tina said softly, nudging Dee's arm. "Don't make more of it than it is."

Mitch watched Lianne and Dee for any hint of recognition, listened for any sign of sarcasm in their tones. But there was nothing.

"So, Mr. Ryan," Marge Peychaud said, "tell us about yourself. Where's your family from?"

He quickly thought over the details of his cover story, and what he'd already told Tina. "Actually, Mrs. Peychaud, my family history is so boring I nearly put your niece to sleep the other night while relating it."

They all laughed, but the older woman wasn't about to let him escape the question so easily, and Mitch found himself relating the details of his cover story, as well as adding to it, over the next hour.

"It's time for my volunteer job," Tina said, getting to her feet. She looked at Mitch. "Every business owner has to donate at least one hour's volunteer work at the festival."

"And I have a pie contest to enter," Marge said, grabbing her entry and hurrying away.

Mitch nodded and looked at Tina. "Need help?"

"I'm manning the information and carnival ticket booth," Tina said, looking at him in amusement. "I really doubt you'd be much help since you don't know where anything is."

"I could keep you company," he said, grinning, "and buy all your tickets."

His eyes sent her a private message, and Tina felt herself begin to blush. Warning bells went off deep in the back of her mind. "Thanks, but why don't you just enjoy the festival, and I'll see you in a while." She turned to Lianne and Dee, who were cleaning up the family's lunch remains and repacking dishes in their aunt's large picnic basket. "Lily's off with her friends. Watch the boys, okay, Lianne?"

"Actually," Lianne replied, "Dee and I just spotted one of our prospective clients, and I think another little nudge just might push him into offering a contract. And it could be a lucrative one. So, if he doesn't mind, I thought maybe Mitch could…"

Tina looked at Lianne, reproach in her eyes. They'd agreed on this weeks ago, and Mitch Ryan was not a baby-sitter. "Never mind. I'm sure Uncle Deano will…"

The old man's snoring suddenly cut through Tina's words.

"Hey, I'd love to watch the kids. " Mitch looked at his sons, then glanced back at Tina. "If it's all right?"

Ten minutes later Mitch, Jimmy and Joey, the toddlers babbling nonstop, found a spot on the river's edge and sat down. "Hey guys, how about building a sand castle?" Mitch suggested. Before he had more than a couple of squares of sandy dirt patted out, Jimmy had positioned his toy cars around the mounds and Joey's plastic spiders immediately began their attack on civilization.

Mitch grabbed Jimmy's miniature fire truck and sent it racing to the rescue of the poor humans trapped in their cars by the spiders.

Snatching a nearby twig, Joey called it the "tree monster," and attacked.

Tina could hear them laughing long before she found them. At the edge of the park's meadow, which sloped down toward the river, she paused and leaned against the thick trunk of an oak tree, watching them and momentarily overcome by melancholia.

The boys need a man in their lives.

Dack's words echoed through her mind. It was a conversation they'd had more than once, and one she didn't want to have again. It was true, they did need a man in their lives, but it wasn't going to be Dack Brenaud.

For a while her father had filled that void, but now he was dead, and Uncle Deano didn't have the time, since he'd come out of retirement to help her with the café. She'd known Ben was dying when she married him. He had been her brother's best friend since kindergarten, and almost like another brother to her for years.

Tina sighed, remembering her late husband. What she'd told Mitch had been the truth, she had loved Ben, and she did miss him. He'd been the kindest, gentlest, most giving person she'd ever known. The marriage had been a favor each had done for the other. Lianne had told him about Tina's situation, and he'd called instantly. He had no one to take care of Lily after he was gone, and Tina had needed a husband before her pregnancy really started showing.

Reimour Crossings was still an old-fashioned town, with old-fashioned values, and one of them was that women didn't have children without the benefit of marriage.

An unexpected rush of anger swept through Tina, overriding her warm, comfortable memories of Ben. Jake had not only walked out on her, he'd walked out on his own children, and if she ever saw him again... All the vengeful things she'd dreamed of saying and doing to him three years ago flashed through her mind, but almost as quickly as they were there, she rejected them. If she ever saw Jake Blaggette again she wouldn't do or say anything, because he didn't deserve to even know he had sons.

Tina shook herself slightly, as if ridding herself of thoughts she didn't want to have anymore, and smiled. "Dessert's ready, guys," she said, walking up to them and kneeling. Her eyes met Mitch's, and the breath momentarily caught in her lungs.

"Cake! Cake!" Joey yelled, jumping up and racing

across the beach. He was halfway up the hill toward their picnic site by the time Jimmy had finished methodically picking up his toys and started toddling after him.

"I think Joey left us in charge of his spider army," Mitch said softly, his eyes never leaving Tina's.

His words meant nothing. It was the message in his eyes that made her heartbeat flutter.

"Cake, ice cream and candy take priority over everything," she replied, her voice barely above a whisper, the words automatic. She had never thought a man's eyes could speak to her that way again. Her fingers tingled with a warmth that began to rapidly spread through her veins, while a hot, delicious heat swept over her skin. The corners of his mouth began to deepen into a slow smile and the light in his eyes intensified, like a softly burning flame far back within the dark depths of those black pools. It pulled at her, and Tina was suddenly aware of the masculine force of the man before her. His will and purpose were nearly overwhelming, his aura of strength beyond anything she'd ever experienced.

"For the moment, I'm glad," Mitch said. Invitation smoldered within the midnight blackness of his eyes.

Tina found herself unable to move, to tear her gaze from his or even to breathe, and totally unable to respond to his comment. Things were moving too fast between them, yet they were moving too slowly. Her heart and her mind were at war. She tried to exert control, and failed.

Her gaze moved over his face, unconsciously searching for Jake. The late-afternoon sun shone blue-black off each wave of his dark hair, and played about the strong features of his face, lending shadows to the rugged lines and curves, and painting his skin a burnished hue.

Mitch was fully aware that the game plan was getting away from him again. He was also aware that, at the moment, there wasn't anything he could, or wanted to, do about it. He reached out to her, skimming his fingertips lightly over her cheek, down one side of her neck. Then his hands slid beneath the long tumble of her hair to her nape.

Fighting her own growing desires, Tina made no effort to move away from him. She knew what he was going to do, knew she should pull away from him...but it was too late. She had neither the will nor the strength.

He drew her near as he began to lean toward her, ever so slowly, almost hesitantly.

She was acutely aware of the hand at her neck, the other that had moved to settle upon her waist. The faint scent of his aftershave surrounded her, reminding Tina of freshly fallen pine needles, warmed upon the forest floor by the soft caress of the hot afternoon sun. She felt his breath gently caress her cheek, the pressure of his hands upon her deepen slightly, saw the look in his eyes darken with desire.

With tormenting slowness Mitch lowered his head, then brushed his lips over hers lightly, tenderly.

It was nearly her undoing. She felt a rending, deep down inside of her, as if all the barriers, all the walls of caution and fear she'd enforced upon herself were cracking and falling away.

His mouth returned to claim hers, and this time his kiss was deeper, less hesitant and more demanding as his arms tightened around her, crushing her body against his— curves and lines coming together, leaving no space between them.

Passions that had lain dormant suddenly threatened to rise up and overwhelm Tina.

His nearness, his kiss and the feelings igniting within her consumed her until she was barely aware of her surroundings. The crowds of people only a few yards away became merely a blur of reality, their laughter and conversation a soft hum to her ears, and the merry little song of a bird sitting on a branch overhead seemed to match the song her heart had suddenly began to play.

Jake, her heart sang. She had missed him so much, waited so long for him to come back.

His hand moved to bury itself in the thick waves of her hair as his tongue entered her mouth, probing and hot. A delicious languor instantly invaded her body. Tina slid her hands across his shoulders and embraced him tightly, never wanting to let go again, never intending to let go again.

The loneliness of the past three years disappeared from Tina's blood as if it had never been there. He had come back to her, and that was all that mattered.

He stood beneath one of the gnarled old oak trees that bordered the edge of the park near the river, casually leaning a shoulder against its massive trunk as if he didn't have a care in the world. So far from the truth. To anyone glancing toward him it would look as if he was just standing there thinking, or getting a moment's respite from all the day's activities. That was what it would look like, but what he was doing was watching them. He inhaled deeply, struggling to control his fury, then reached up to reposition the dark glasses that sat on the bridge of his nose. He'd been right, it was happening all over again. He wanted to yell at her to stop, but the rage churning in his chest choked him and held him immobile.

His thoughts weren't immobile though. Someone had to make Mitch Ryan stop, had to make Tina see that what she was doing was wrong, just like last time.

"Mommy, Mommy!" Joey ran across the riverbank. Sanity and reality slammed into Tina and she jerked away from Mitch. She swallowed hard as her heart banged wildly against her breast, and her pulse raced so rapidly she felt momentarily faint. My God, what had she just done? She looked at Mitch. Mitch, her mind repeated, over and over. Mitch, not Jake. Mitch.

"Unkie said we c'n wide t'ponies if you say okay." He crashed into Tina, little arms flying about her neck, and nearly knocked her over.

Tina held her son and fought for composure.

Mitch saw the fear that seemed to draw Tina's face and veil the color of her eyes, and frowned. Was she comparing him to Jake? Then panic struck. Could she possible know now, had his kiss just told her the truth?

"Pease, Mommie, pease, pease, pease," Joey yelled, jumping up and down beside Tina.

She laughed finally, but held on to her son as she tried to gather her composure. For some reason she still hadn't figured out, Mitch Ryan reminded her of Jake, so, she decided, it was only natural when Mitch kissed her, she would think of the man she'd once loved. She looked past Joey to Mitch, taking his frown for puzzlement over Joey's words.

"Their Uncle Deano said they could ride the ponies if I say it's okay," she explained.

"Pease, Mommy," Joey wailed again, flailing his hands excitely.

"Okay," Tina cried, in an effort to escape his pummeling. "Go."

No sooner had the words left her lips, then Joey was up and running back in the direction he'd come.

Tina looked at Mitch, his gaze taking hers willing captive. "Mitch, I think we're moving too fast. I'm not sure I'm..."

He smiled and touched the tip of his index finger lightly to her lips. "I know."

Her world suddenly tilted, and for a millisecond of time Jake was back, kneeling before her, touching his finger to her lips as he'd done so many times after he'd kissed her.

The blood in her veins turned from a scorching heat to nearly ice cold, while a knot gripped her stomach in its vise and squeezed tightly.

Mitch looked back up at the others in the park, as if suddenly aware once again of their presence. "We'd probably better get back up there," he said softly.

Tina nodded. "Yes," she said weakly, pushing to her feet. It was just coincidence that he'd done that, she told herself. Just coincidence.

Mitch dredged up every curse and pithy oath he'd ever heard and ran them through his mind like a bulldozer repaving a street and repeating the task, over and over. He'd blown it. Like a first-class, rookie, untrained fool, he'd blown it. He hadn't been thinking—but then, when he was around Tina, he was finding that harder and harder to do. Touching his finger to her lips had been a purely instinctive move, one he'd done dozens of times before. But that had been three years ago, in another lifetime. The minute he'd done it, the minute he'd seen the look that came into her eyes, he'd known he had just made another mistake, and possibly one that could cost him everything.

He followed her back to where her family sat talking and laughing, as he sought ways to correct what he'd just done. Time, he finally decided, he'd just have to give it time. If he didn't do it again, didn't make any more mistakes, maybe she'd just assume it was a coincidence. After all, what else could she assume?

He was just about to sit down when he glanced up and caught Tina looking at him as if deep in thought.

Mitch, Tina said to herself again, and smiled quickly at being caught looking at him. Mitch Ryan. Not Jake. "I think I'll go with Deano and the boys to the pony rides," she said, hurriedly turning and walking away.

Marge and Lily decided to join her.

Mitch watched Tina, wanting to get up and follow her, and knowing that was the wrong thing to do. He'd made a mistake; now he needed to let some time and space try to heal it over. He turned to Tina's sisters. "So, did you reel in that client?"

"I think so," Lianne said, looking satisfied. She grabbed a cola from the cooler, handed one to Dee, then held another up in offering to Mitch. He accepted it and she settled back on the blanket and looked at him for a long moment, as if studying him. Finally, she spoke. "Dee and I have been wondering about something, Mr. Ryan."

"Call me Mitch," he said, and smiled to cover the wariness that had instantly come over him at her words.

"Fine. What are your intentions toward our sister, Mitch?"

The cola threatened to explode in his throat, and Mitch jerked the can from his mouth, coughing slightly.

Lianne laughed. "Sorry. Guess you weren't expecting that."

Mitch shook his head and wiped bubbles of dark liquid off the front of his shirt. "No, not quite."

She gazed past him and across the grassy field to where Tina was skipping alongside Jimmy, who was sitting astride a black and white pony. Her expression turned somber when she looked back at Mitch. "My sister's known too much hurt already," she said softly.

He nodded. "Watching someone you love die is rough," Mitch said. There was an edge to his tone he hadn't intended, but then his own words had taken him somewhere he didn't want to be. He hadn't actually watched Perry die, but his imagination had done the job for him, and the hurt was as bad as if he'd been there.

"It was more than that," Dee said.

Lianne looked at her sharply, and Dee mumbled a barely audible "Sorry." She looked up at Mitch and shrugged.

Lianne turned her gaze back to Mitch. "Ben was our brother's best friend. His folks had a place out near ours and we all kind of grew up together. After Ben's folks died, he was at our house so much it was like we'd adopted him. I guess emotionally we did. Anyway, Zach, our brother, left home abruptly and after that we all kind of leaned on Ben as our big brother." She smiled, as if her thoughts had spiraled back to another time. "I dreamed about marrying Ben for a while, but then I was only sixteen. I dreamed about marrying Sonny on *Miami Vice*, too." She laughed.

"Yeah. I always wanted David Cassidy," Dee offered.

"Dee used to use Ben to make her boyfriends jealous," Lianne went on, as if Dee hadn't spoken, "but Tina and Ben became best friends, closer even, I think, than Ben had been with my brother. She always knew that if she was ever in trouble, she could count on Ben." She turned to Mitch then, the dreamy tone of her voice gone, replaced by a look in her eyes like anger, or challenge. "She doesn't have a white knight to rescue her again, Mitch."

"Rescue her?" he repeated softly, his gaze locking with hers.

Lianne pushed to her feet. "I think I'll go see how the ponies are holding up against my nephews." She glanced down at Dee. "Coming, Sis?"

He watched them walk away, Lianne's words echoing through his mind. *If she was ever in trouble, she could count on Ben.... Doesn't have a white knight to rescue her again.*

Was Lianne telling him Tina had married Ben Dubois only because she was in trouble—the kind of trouble that could be a young woman pregnant with another man's child—a man who had left her? Was she confirming his own suspicions? Or was he only hearing what he wanted to hear?

He turned and stared at Tina, but instead of his suspicions disappearing, they began to darken. He didn't want to believe Tina had betrayed him. He'd *never* really wanted to believe that. Or that she could have had something to do with Perry's death. But he knew from hard-won, ugly experience that what he wanted to believe and what was fact were not always the same thing.

Now another thought lodged itself in his mind, one so heinous he didn't want to even consider it, yet he knew, as an agent, he had to. She'd married Ben Dubois, but she hadn't been in love with him. Was there any possibility she'd killed him too, once she'd gotten what she wanted from him?

The mere idea sent Mitch's thoughts and emotions reeling. It was ridiculous, he told himself. A suspicion totally without basis. More ludicrous than anything he'd thought so far. But it had happened before. Other women, just as innocent-seeming as Tina, had murdered their husbands and lovers, and Ben Dubois had died before he and Tina had reached their first anniversary.

Mitch felt as if he were suddenly two people at war with each other, yet both inside the same body. The man against the agent. Every cell in the man's body, in his heart, screamed denial of a speculation he couldn't help but deem absurd. But the agent in him, that cold, hard and calculating side of his personality, knew he had to follow up the suspicion, no matter how improbable, no matter where it led.

Fury with himself roiled wildly. Finally, getting to his

feet, Mitch walked down to the pony corral, then fell into step beside Tina as she came around beside Joey. "I've got to go," he said.

She looked up at him.

"This was supposed to be a vacation," Mitch said, trying to sound light and shrugging, "but I made the mistake of calling my assistant last night and, well, I've got some work I have to see to tonight. It's either that, or Ryan Security could lose out on a job we've been counting on."

Tina smiled. "Too bad. You're going to miss the fireworks. But I hope you get your problems worked out okay."

Mitch felt the fist that had hold of his insides twist cruelly. He hadn't watched fireworks since the night he'd sat in this same park with Tina cradled in his arms, trying to find the words to tell her the truth about his job and ask her to marry him, all the while his imagination spinning out pictures of what their life together was going to be like.

"Giddap," Joey yelled, kicking the sides of the pony's saddle.

Tina held one arm around her son, the other hand holding tight to the animal's reins so he couldn't bolt.

"I'll try to make it back," Mitch said, knowing full well he was lying. That was one piece of nostalgia he didn't need to experience again.

Chapter 8

Soft radio music filled the momentary silence in the café. The early-bird breakfast rush was over, and they had at least an hour before the church-goers would be coming in for Sunday brunch. Tina yawned. Her sleep had been so restless and filled with dreams she might as well not have bothered.

Steps on the porch drew her attention and she turned to look at the entry door. It opened. The bell above it jingled merrily, but it was Fred Gateau who entered, not Mitch. Tina felt a wave of disappointment, then admonished herself. The best thing she could do was just forget about him. In a few days he'd have been gone anyway.

It was a good speech, but it didn't work, because she couldn't quite forget his kiss. A kiss that had made her think for a moment that she was kissing Jake. And then he'd touched his finger to her lips.

That had left her so shaken she hadn't been able to think of anything else all evening. She hadn't been able to sleep, eat breakfast or carry on a decent conversation with any of her early-morning regulars.

"I think I'm coming down with something," she said that morning to several of them when they'd asked her point-blank what was wrong.

No matter how many times she told herself she was being ridiculous, that it had just been an innocent gesture, a coincidence, and she was making something out of nothing, that simple, innocent-seeming gesture haunted her thoughts.

The door opened, and Tina looked up expectantly again.

Dack filled the doorway for a split second, pausing there and surveying the room, as he always did before entering.

Tina felt her spirits plunge further, but put a bright smile on her face.

He walked directly toward the end of the counter where she stood. "Hi, darlin'."

She nodded and set a cup of coffee down in front of him. "So, what'll it be this morning, Dack?"

"Well, I'll have me one of those sugar doughnuts, and I thought maybe you'd have dinner with me tonight. Heard about a new little place up the road."

She shook her head. "I'm sorry, but I didn't sleep well last night. All the excitement of the festival kept the kids up late and..." She shrugged. "Another time."

Dack took a drink of his coffee, but his eyes never left her.

Tina knew he suspected she was lying. He just kept on asking, and she wished he'd stop. She hated the hurt look that always came into his eyes. But it wasn't enough to make her accept.

Two hours later, the brunch crowd was thinning out and Tina couldn't stop wondering why Mitch hadn't come by.

He's gone, a little voice of fear whispered cruelly.

She sighed. Maybe he was gone. After all, they'd only

had a couple of dates together. He'd kissed her, but she was the one who'd said they were moving too fast. He had probably taken that as a brush-off, and anyway, it wasn't as if there was anything real between them. And she didn't want there to be.

Liar, the voice whispered again.

She stared past the window at the road that led out of town. Three years ago she'd been at the café, standing almost in this same spot, when she'd watched Jake drive away. Some men didn't like to say goodbye. Or maybe they just didn't know how.

Tina turned away and began to refill the ketchup bottles she'd gathered from the tables and counter, in an effort to keep busy and not think. But each time she heard a car outside, she'd tell herself not to look up, then she would, hoping to see a sleek, black Thunderbird pulling into the café's parking lot.

It was almost one. The brunch-lunch crowd had left and, since they didn't serve dinner on Sunday and were closed on Monday, Tina was almost finished setting the tables for the next day's business, and ready for her off time.

The sound of tires upon gravel caught her attention and she turned. A genuine smile curved her lips for the first time that morning, yet at the same time Tina felt a sense of apprehension fall over her as she instantly remembered what had kept her up and on edge most of the night.

"Umm," Deano said as he strode into the dining room and saw Mitch's car, "guess we're not quite ready to close after all."

Ignoring her uncle's knowing glance, Tina hurried into the back room and checked her hair and lipstick in the small mirror that hung on the office wall. Straightening her white blouse and yellow cotton slacks, she examined herself for food stains and said a silent prayer of thanks that by some

miracle she'd passed the morning without getting anything
on herself. She reentered the café just as Mitch walked
through the front door.

"Guess it's time for me to clean the stove," Deano said
softly, then winked as he passed Tina and retreated into the
kitchen.

Mitch slid onto a stool at the counter.

"Hi," Tina said. "Coffee?" She turned and grabbed a
cup before he answered, then realized she'd already
dumped what was left of the coffee.

He smiled when she turned back to him, but it seemed
to her a halfhearted gesture, as if his mind was preoccupied
with something else. A sense of unease rippled through her,
but Tina shrugged it aside. Her mind had played a trick on
her last night, and his innocent gesture had merely reinforced it. That was all.

"Hi, yourself," he said, noticing the empty coffeepot.
"How about some orange juice?"

She nodded and reached into the small refrigerator under
the counter, then set a glass of juice in front of him. "You
missed some great fireworks last night. How'd your work
go?"

"Not great. Problems at the office kept me on the phone
half the night." He glanced toward the bakery cupboard.
"Got any bear claws left?"

She stared at him for a moment, waiting to see Jake's
image overtake his. When it didn't, she almost sighed in
relief.

"Tina?" Mitch said, noticing she suddenly seemed very
far away.

"Oh, sorry," she said, and laughed self-consciously. She
retrieved the pastry and set it down in front of him. "Everything okay now? With your business, I mean?"

"I've still got some work to do." He watched her take

a straw from a glass beneath the counter and start twisting it about her fingers. "But I think things will work out."

What he wasn't saying was that he planned to use the Internet to do a little on-line digging into a few things. He'd already gone over all his own old cases and Perry's, looking for a link or a tie to Reimour Crossings or Tina, and had found none. But that didn't mean he hadn't missed something. Now he'd received an e-mail message from Raskin, who had returned, telling him the house was owned by the Brigand Corporation and Laren McAllreaux, who had "no history." And though he knew he shouldn't, he also intended to confirm that Ivor Raskin had done nothing more while he'd been gone than fly out to California to visit his sister, who he claimed was in the hospital in serious condition after being struck by a cable car.

Tina nodded. "Good. I was worried you might have to cancel the rest of your vacation." The minute she heard her own words, she cringed, realizing they sounded like a very blatant come-on.

But they brought a smile to Mitch's lips. "Well, I'm glad you were worried about me. Does that mean you'll have dinner with me tonight?"

She met his eyes and felt a sense of familiarity, but quickly dismissed it, as well as the barriers of caution she'd been unconsciously reerecting around her heart all morning. "I'd love to." A tug of guilt pulled at her as she remembered turning down Dack's invitation. "It's Sunday, so we close early," Tina said. "In fact, my uncle and I were just doing that, but I've still got receipts to do, then an afternoon full of errands. How about picking me up about six?"

Mitch stood. "Great." He reached out to touch his finger to her lips.

Deano came through the swinging doors that led to the kitchen, and Mitch suddenly realized what he'd been about to do. He hurriedly withdrew his hand as Tina glanced toward her uncle.

"Hey," Deano said, smiling broadly as he strolled toward them, a wicked gleam in his eyes. "Couldn't help overhear you two out here. You taking my niece out, you gotta remember one thing, Mitch." He smiled broadly. "I got me a shotgun out in the kitchen, and I ain't afraid to use it if you stand my niece up, you hear?"

Mitch stared at the man, feeling a sense of déjà vu that nearly robbed him of breath. Marcus Peychaud had said nearly the same thing to him that last day, just before he'd climbed into his car and driven away.

Everything was perfect. Or at least as perfect as things could be under the circumstances. Mitch looked across the table at Tina. She was staring past the restaurant's wall of windows at the slowly moving, black waters of the Ogeechee River, its dark surface glistening silver beneath the moon's glow. He turned his gaze in the same direction as hers, putting off what he knew he had to say to her. It would ruin the sensuous, easy mood of the evening, maybe even destroy the tentative thread of a relationship that had begun to develop between them. But that couldn't matter, he told himself. He had no choice but to do what he had to do. He was getting nowhere fast and his investigation was basically at a standstill. The Agency had come up with nothing new, and all his on-line digging that afternoon had turned up a series of dead ends.

"I love looking out at the river at night," Tina said, her soft voice breaking into Mitch's thoughts.

He turned to look at her. For two years the anger and pain of betrayal, and his brother's death, had allowed him to consider her his prime suspect. In all that time he'd found nothing to give him a reason to change his mind. He still hadn't found one, but he wanted to. Unfortunately, he had more suspicions now than when he'd started the investigation, which made him wonder if Raskin hadn't been right. Maybe he was just too close to the situation to see things for what they really were, or weren't.

"It is beautiful," he said finally, breaking the silence that had descended between them again. It wasn't what he'd intended to say, wasn't what he needed to say, but he was loath to ruin the fragile intimacy of the evening.

Tina nodded, but didn't take her gaze from the ragged silhouette of trees growing dense upon the opposite shore of the river. She'd been telling herself since last night, when he'd kissed her at the festival, that this feeling of familiarity she felt toward him was just in her imagination. Maybe, subconsciously, she wanted to feel it, to think he reminded her of Jake.

Nothing like a little self-torture, a faint voice in the back of her mind whispered.

Tina smiled absently in agreement. If she didn't stop doing this to herself she could go as crazy as she had after Jake had left and she'd found out she was pregnant. She'd had her father and Ben to lean on then. Now they were both gone, and she had people depending on her. Falling apart, for whatever reason, was not an option.

But Mitch wasn't Jake, she reminded herself adamantly. She wasn't in love with him, or he with her, and they hadn't made any commitments to each other. Sighing deeply, she turned toward him, about to tell him how much she'd enjoyed the evening, when their eyes locked and her breath caught in her throat.

In the reflection of the crystal-ensconced candle that flickered merrily upon their table, his eyes took on a rich, whiskey hue. Shadows entrenched themselves about his eyes, within the curves of his cheeks, and along the strong slash of his jaw, giving him a darkly sinister yet almost irresistibly seductive look.

Memory of his kiss and the feelings it had stirred within her engulfed Tina, bringing a blush to her cheeks and a heat to her veins that left her feeling as if on fire. But was it because she was truly attracted to him, or because for some reason she still couldn't understand, he reminded her of Jake?

"It's almost as if time has stood still out there for aeons," Mitch said, suddenly wishing that were true, and that time had stood still for them. "The rest of the world seems to continue on, but the bayous remain untouched, primitive and exotic."

The underlying sensuality of his words touched something deep down inside her. "Ben and I used to come here," Tina said, both the look on her face and the tone of her voice wistful, as if her mind were reliving those times. "He loved the peacefulness of this place, the river being so near, the sight of the sun settling beyond the horizon, how the tips of the Spanish moss hanging from the trees touched the slowly moving water and fanned out like billowing shreds of gray lace."

Jealousy, hot and swift, rushed through Mitch as she talked so lovingly about Ben Dubois. Within seconds his mood had plunged into the depths of darkness, and all of his suspicions about her, warranted, wanted or not, welled up to taunt him.

He played with the stem of his wineglass, his thumb and index finger moving slowly up and down the narrow shaft as he fought to control the feelings churning inside of him. Focus, he ordered himself. He needed to do what he'd come here to do, and stop letting his feelings and memories get in the way. "I saw you pull into the drive of a mansion on the edge of town the other day," Mitch said.

Startled by his tone, Tina looked at him and was surprised to see what she thought was anger blazing in his eyes.

"The sheriff pulled in right after you."

His words seemed impassively cold. Tina shook her head, not having the faintest idea what he was talking about, or why his mood had changed. She felt suddenly wary, instinctively cautious and uncertain why.

"Old-looking, majestic place," Mitch went on, when she frowned, as if not understanding him.

Tina shook her head. "I'm sorry, I don't know..."

He cursed his own uncontrolled emotions and purposely softened his tone when he realized her reaction to his curt words was one of unease. The last thing he wanted was for her to pull away from him. "Beautiful old plantation-style house. Surrounded by tall oak trees, a wrought-iron fence and gates. Just off the main street of town."

She smiled. "Oh, you must mean Chancellor Oaks. I was there once, years ago. My high school senior party was held on the grounds. It still belonged to Marie Chancellor then, but I haven't been there since."

Mitch held her gaze, probing, looking for proof that her words were a lie. But if they were, he had to admit, she was good. There had been no hesitation in her words, no flicker of unease in her eyes, no uncertainty in her tone. "Well, then obviously I wanted to see you so badly I saw someone else in a car like yours and assumed it was you."

She watched as featherlike lines crinkled around his eyes when the corners of his mouth turned upward. "I'm flattered." She returned his smile. "As long as it wasn't Gladys the pig lady you mistook for me."

Mitch laughed. "Gladys the pig lady?"

"Gladys Tufonte. She drives a red car too, but she prefers pigs over people. Says they're smarter, and never goes anywhere without at least one by her side, or sitting in the passenger seat of her car.''

"You've got some real characters in this town," Mitch said, shaking his head. He was enjoying himself with her too much, too easily forgetting what he was supposed to be doing, which meant it was time to get back to business. And this time he needed to keep himself on it. "When I was at the garage having my car fixed, the mechanic didn't stop talking for an hour. I think he told me just about every rumor and old story that ever took root in Reimour Crossings."

Tina nodded. "Quatt does like to gossip. His wife brings it home, and he spreads it around."

"He asked me if I'd had some of your apple pie. You have a fan there, by the way."

She smiled.

"Anyway, once he found out I had, and his assistant mentioned seeing me having lunch with you and your family at the festival, well..." Mitch shrugged. "He just kept talking."

"Oh, no," Tina said, feigning a look of horror, but it was only half pretense. She'd generated enough gossip about herself over the years, starting with being involved in a couple of high school pranks, then being nearly jilted at the altar by Jake, followed by her hasty marriage to Ben, and his death soon after. She'd hoped people would have forgotten about those incidents by now, but obviously they hadn't. "And you just had to listen, right?" she said, trying to sound teasing.

Mitch grinned sheepishly. "Guilty." He asked her about the high school prank.

Tina laughed, relieved, and explained. If that was the worst of what Quattman had said, she just might go down and kiss the old coot.

"He also said before you got married you were engaged to someone who disappeared." Mitch tried to look sympathetic rather than nosy. "Sounds rough."

She had been staring out at the river again, but his words brought her reeling around. Blood pounded in her ears. Apprehension coursed through her as she stared at him for several long seconds, searching his face for some hidden meaning behind his words. Finally, she dropped her gaze from his and found her voice. "That was a time I'd rather forget."

Her words stung him deeper than he'd imagined possible. "Understandable. But did you ever find out what happened to him?" he pressed, suddenly needing desperately to hear her say something, anything, that would confirm she'd loved him once. "I mean, I've heard stories about how on some of these lonely southern back roads people get attacked, you know? Arrested and sent off to prison farms, and…"

She looked back up at him, and the rest of his words caught in his throat. The flicker of hurt in her eyes tore at him, made him feel like the rottenest of heels, but he knew he couldn't back down now. One way or the other he had to find the truth about what happened, and about Tina.

He wanted to reach out to her, but refrained. Instead, his gaze delved into hers. Could she really sit across from him, look into his eyes, kiss him, and not know who he was? He knew he had to hope that was the case, but for some reason found himself not liking it.

But it didn't matter what he liked, he told himself coldly. He had to find the truth. That was what he was here for. He owed it to Perry, if not to himself. And to his sons, he reminded himself. He owed the truth to his sons.

Tina's thoughts swirled as Mitch's question seemed to echo repeatedly through her mind, taunting and merciless.

What happened to him? How many times had she asked herself that question, trying to deny that Jake would just leave her? But in the end, it had become the only thing she could think, the only thing that made any sense. There had been no accidents in the area, fatal or otherwise, reported to the authorities, no unidentified bodies in the morgues, no mysterious men checking into the hospitals or clinics, or found wandering about with amnesia. Jake Blaggette had merely left her. "No," she said finally, the lone word filled with as much anguish as a person could instill in such a short reply. "I don't know what happened to him."

He watched her mentally and physically shake off her memories of the past and force a smile to her face.

"He had a dangerous job," Tina said, "and one that took him all over the country." She shrugged nonchalantly. "I didn't know that until just before he...proposed. But, obviously, he just had a change of heart."

"Pretty strong change of heart," Mitch said.

She smiled, but he noticed the sadness that seemed to touch her lips, and reflect from somewhere deep within her eyes. "I guess not everyone's totally committed to the idea of marriage, picket fences and the pitter-patter of little feet." The moment the words left her mouth, she cursed herself. The last thing she'd wanted to do was sound as if she felt sorry for herself. "I imagine it would be hard for a man who's used to traveling a lot to put down roots and stay in one place forever."

"But he proposed."

She shrugged. "I couldn't accept his job, and he obviously didn't want to leave it." She forced a smile. "Can we change the subject now?"

Mitch felt an invisible hand jerk at his guts. Was she telling the truth? Was that what she really believed? That he'd just left her because he wasn't committed? That he'd just changed his mind? "That's crazy," he said, reaching across the table without thinking and taking one of her hands in his. "Any man who would choose his job over you is obviously missing more than a few gray cells."

But Jake hadn't intended to quit the Agency, he remembered. Merely cut back for a while, until she learned to accept it.

Mitch's eyes bored into hers and he found himself momentarily lost within those fathomless blue depths, with no desire to find his way back.

She was silent as he drove her home, and Mitch couldn't help but wonder what, or who, she was thinking about. Him? Ben Dubois? Jake Blaggette? Or someone else? The question threatened to tie him in knots, and restoked the jealousy he'd experienced earlier. He pulled the car to the curb in front of her house, but before he could push the gearshift into Park, he saw Tina tuck her purse under her arm. Mitch reached across her quickly, putting his hand over hers as it settled on the door handle, preventing her from opening the door.

"Tina, I'm sorry I brought that up earlier, about the guy who disappeared. I had no right and it ruined your evening."

She inhaled deeply, and sighed. "No. It was a long time ago and—" she shook her head slightly, her thoughts momentarily moving back to that day again "—and something I try not to think about much anymore."

"The café is closed tomorrow, isn't it?" he asked, trying to change the subject.

She nodded.

"Have breakfast with me? We could drive down to Savannah for the day and..."

Tina shook her head. "No, I can't. I planned to take inventory tomorrow, and the kids..."

Mitch climbed from the car before she could finish, not wanting to hear her rejection, and hurried around to open her door. He reached for her hand, but she pulled away from him the moment she got to her feet.

"I'll help with the inventory, and then we could go. We could take the kids," Mitch offered as he walked beside her on the pathway to her front porch. "Maybe to the beach."

At her door, Tina turned toward him. "Thank you for a lovely evening, Mitch, and for the invitation to the beach," she said, a slight coolness to her tone. "But I don't think so." To avoid prolonging what she felt was an awkward moment, Tina turned and started to insert her key into the front door's lock.

He knew he couldn't let it go like that. If she turned away from him now, everything could be lost. He might never find out the truth, and he was determined that wasn't going to happen, even if he had to jeopardize his cover, his life, he was going to get to the truth. Mitch reached for her, knowing he was turning the game in a deadly direction, and one he'd sworn only that afternoon he would avoid.

She looked back at him as his hand touched her arm.

"Don't shut me out because I was a fool," Mitch said softly. His arms slipped around her waist, and he pulled her to him.

"Mitch, I don't think this is a good idea," Tina whispered huskily, her hands on his arms. She knew she should push him away, yet even as she spoke the words she knew she had to speak, she felt her willpower, her resistance to him, deserting her.

"I know," he said.

His deep voice wrapped around her, invaded every cell of her body, ignited it with the fire of desire she'd been so desperately trying to ignore and deny even existed.

"People can get hurt."

His warm breath caressed her cheek.

"But I can't deny what's happening between us." His eyes bore into hers. "Can you?"

She swallowed, hard. "No."

His arms crushed her to him, and his mouth descended upon hers, impressing it with his passion, and stopping any further words of hesitation she might have uttered.

The instant Mitch's lips claimed hers, Tina knew there was no resistance left within her. An explosion of desire ignited in her veins and burned through her, conquering the essence of her soul. She melted against him, knowing she shouldn't, and unable to stop herself. His mouth was so hard upon hers, so demanding and savage, yet it was exactly the kind of kiss she'd unknowingly needed from him. Without her asking, without her even being consciously aware of it, his lips upon hers, ravaging, taking everything she had and demanding more, answered all of her dreams.

Mitch drew her closer, nearly crushing the breath from her lungs, but she didn't care as she clung to him. Her tongue met his, each twining about the other, as their hips ground together, seeking release of the mounting passion threatening to overwhelm them both.

The moment seemed to go on forever, an endless foray into eternity during which Tina found herself wanting never to return. This was what she had wanted from the very first time she'd seen him on the road that day, on his way into town. The fears of familiarity, the caution and hurt she'd lived with for so long, were suddenly gone. Sanity played little part in her desire, reality no longer existed. She was oblivious of everything—the sounds of the television on the other side of the door, the faint cry of a bird somewhere in the trees, even the warmth of the night's lingering humidity upon her skin. Nothing mattered anymore except this tall, dark man who held her in his arms, whose mouth was inciting passion within her such as she hadn't felt in years.

Mitch tore his lips from hers and trailed them down the side of her throat, drawing the scent of her perfume into his lungs, the taste of her flesh onto his tongue. "God, I've missed you," he groaned softly, all but lost to the heat of desire that had engulfed him.

Suddenly it was as if someone had doused her with a bucket of ice water. Tina instantly stilled, the passion that had only seconds before threatened to sweep her mindlessly away on a tide of pleasure disappearing as abruptly as it had come over her. For the briefest of seconds her heartbeat stopped, the breath in her lungs stalled, and the rush of blood through her veins stilled. The caress of the night air on her skin turned as cold as the fear that suddenly invaded every cell in her body. *He'd missed her?*

Mitch felt the change in her, heard his own words ringing in his ears. It took a few seconds for their meaning, and possible consequence, to make it through the passion that had overtaken his senses and fired his blood. He cursed silently. What the hell was the matter with him? He knew he was still physically attracted to her, that had been un-deniable. But he'd been physically attracted to dozens of women, some his sworn enemies, and he'd never made the kind of mistakes he was making now. He pulled away from her, not wanting to meet her eyes, and knowing he had no choice.

The color had drained from her face. "You missed me?" she said, fear edging her words, the terror of uncertainty and confusion widening her eyes. Tina stared at him as if she didn't know him, and as if she knew everything there was to know about him.

Mitch's arms fell away from her and he stepped back,

struggling against the fury he was feeling with himself, against the unreasonable urge to tell her the truth so that he could pull her back into his embrace. His mind sought an excuse, a reason for the foolish words. "Since the other night, by the river," he said finally, trying to sound light and casual. He brushed his lips lightly across her cheek.

"I'll call you in the morning," he said, knowing he had to leave before the situation got any worse, and he made any more mistakes. "Good night."

She watched him walk away. Once he got to his car he paused and looked back at her. He was a bigger fool than he'd ever realized. The last thing he wanted to do was leave her. His body ached for her. The touch of her lips still heated his blood, the feel of her body pressed to his remained imprinted upon his length. And she might be responsible for his supposed death and Perry's death, he told himself coldly, trying to cool the ardor that he knew he shouldn't be feeling. There would be no sleep for him tonight. She'd haunt his thoughts and dreams, and give neither his imagination or body rest. He watched her turn away and disappear within the house.

It was getting harder and harder to think of her as being responsible for what had happened to him and Perry.

Mitch sighed, and stared at the closed door for several long seconds, willing it to reopen, willing her to come back outside to him. But she didn't, and the night seemed suddenly darker, the air cooler, his loneliness more intense than he'd ever felt it.

He slid behind the steering wheel and started the car. The soft purr of the engine failed to interrupt his thoughts. If he was smart, he told himself when halfway back to the inn, he would just pack up right now and get the hell out of town. He should have taken Raskin's advice and let someone else come in undercover and investigate. Someone who could be totally objective, who wouldn't have old feelings, old prejudices and a need for revenge under his skin to interfere. But Mitch had been adamant that he had to do this himself. The fire that had been in his gut since the moment he'd wakened from the coma had demanded answers, demanded he avenge Perry's death, himself. But now he knew it had been more than that. It had been Tina. He'd needed to see her again, to look into her eyes and determine for himself whether she had really been the one who betrayed him.

Mitch drove through town, the streets dark except for the soft glow of light coming from the old-fashioned street lamps on each corner.

His thoughts remained centered on Tina. He had looked into her eyes. He'd held her in his arms. He'd tasted her kiss, and for a few brief moments he had let himself forget why he was really back in Reimour Crossings. He'd almost blown it with her several times already, and it was a risk to continue. If she suspected who he was, or somehow found out, he knew she would never forgive him for not contacting her the moment he'd come out of the coma. But mostly, for not telling her the truth about himself now. But that didn't really matter.

He pulled into the parking space beside his cabin. What if he operated on the assumption that Tina was innocent, rather than guilty? Maybe if he began looking at things from that angle, he'd find the answers he sought.

It wasn't the way he was trained to operate, and it wasn't a way Raskin would approve. The silence of the night pressed upon him as he sat in the car for several minutes after switching off its engine.

Tina had been the only one in Reimour Crossings who'd known Jake Blaggette was an FBI agent. If she was innocent, then there was someone else in Reimour Crossings who'd wanted him dead, someone she had trusted enough to confide in.

Mitch's first thought was Tina's father. Marcus was dead, but that didn't make him innocent. Then he thought of Ben Dubois. He'd lived up in Charlotte until just before marrying Tina, but it wasn't that long a drive from Reimour Crossings. On the surface, the background check he'd received on Dubois had been innocent enough, but maybe the Agency just hadn't dug deep enough. He had been a war correspondent for a while. Maybe there had been more to Ben Dubois than anyone realized.

Mitch reached for the door handle, but hesitated as he thought of Tina's sisters. Who had they been involved with three years ago? Who were they involved with now? He sighed. They were all good questions, and ones he couldn't just come out and ask Tina about.

With her kiss still warm upon his lips, and suspicion roiling about in his mind, he felt as if he'd dug himself a hole so deep he couldn't even see light anymore. Last night, for a brief instant, he'd actually considered telling her the truth. He scoffed at himself now. Agent's rule number one: how not to commit suicide.

But someone had wanted him dead three years ago, and most likely was still out there. If they knew he had survived, he had no doubt they'd come back to try to finish the job.

He sighed in frustration. If that happened, he at least wanted to know *who* was coming after him.

Mitch locked the car after climbing out, and walked to the cabin. This time, before he went to bed, he'd make certain to pull the drapes across the window.

He knew the moment he opened the door that something was wrong. There was a feeling in the air...a sense of unsettledness. His hand dived beneath his sports coat, seeking the gun clipped to the back of his belt. The moment his fingers wrapped around the grip, he jerked the weapon from its holster, crouched and flipped the wall switch.

The room's two lamps, one on the desk, the other on the nightstand beside the bed, instantly went on, flooding the room with light. His gaze raced around the room, diving past furniture and shadows, his hand and gun jerking toward each direction his gaze darted.

Nothing seemed out of place or disturbed, but the feeling that it had been persisted, and he'd never been wrong about that yet. But then he'd been out of the game for almost three years. Maybe he was just being paranoid. He moved cautiously into the room, gun gripped tightly between his hands, his finger secure on the trigger, senses alert to the slightest sound or movement.

The very air about him was as still and silent as death.

He pulled open the drawers of the desk, then of the night stand, and finally of the dresser. Everything was there, including the extra clip to his gun. To anyone else, it might appear nothing had been disturbed at all, but Mitch knew better. He moved one of his folded T-shirts, confirming the conclusion he'd already reached. The thin piece of invisible, two-sided tape he'd pressed between the bottom of the drawer and the shirt was loose. The rolled pair of black dress socks he'd left in the corner of one drawer, surrounded by several pairs of white boot socks, was no longer resting in the corner, but sat nearly in the center of the shallow drawer.

Mitch moved to the closet, noticing similar changes there. Finally, reassured he was alone in the room, he moved hurriedly around the desk and pulled it away from the wall. His laptop sat exactly where he'd left it. But Mitch knew appearances could be deceiving. He placed it on the desk and turned it on, then waited until his e-mail appeared on the screen, cut the screen in half, then showed the files he had saved on his hard drive.

Whoever had searched his room wasn't a professional. If they had been, they wouldn't have missed the computer. Though even if they'd discovered it, they would never have figured out the security codes needed to get into the files.

He turned and glanced around the room again, his trained eye seeking anything that would give him a clue to who it had been who'd searched the place. It hadn't been someone intent on robbery, because nothing was missing, not even the extra cash he'd left in one of the drawers. But it hadn't been Tina, either. He knew that, because she'd been with him when this happened. But she could have had someone else do it while she'd kept him busy all evening. She could have sent one of her sisters.

Unless someone had discovered who he really was. The thought sent a chill up his back. Or had known from the moment he'd arrived in Reimour Crossings.

Mitch slid his gun under his pillow, removed his dress clothes, slid into a pair of jeans and lay on the bed. He wasn't going to get any sleep. That was a given. But he had to rest. At least his body did. He began mulling over the facts of the case—what few there were—in his mind, trying to concentrate on each point, pull it into perspective and make it fit any scenario other than the one he'd been convinced of for the past two years. If Tina wasn't the one who'd betrayed him, then who was it?

There was no ready answer, because the circle of people he'd known in Reimour Crossings then could be counted on one hand. Tina, her sisters and her father. Her aunt and uncle had been in New Orleans, he didn't even remember the waitress who'd helped out in the café then, and the woman at the front desk of the Magnolia Inn seemed about as dangerous as a fly. And she hadn't known anything about him anyway.

Unless she'd searched his cabin.

The thought flew at Mitch out of nowhere. She would have had access, and would have known when he was gone. But why would she do it?

The answer to that evaded him, even the question turned fuzzy, as erotic images of Tina kept infiltrating his thoughts. They pulled at his body, taunting him, until all Mitch could think of was how badly he wanted her in his arms...and in his bed.

Chapter 9

"*I*'ve missed you." Tina leaned her back against the door as the words echoed endlessly through her mind. Her insides were quivering uncontrollably, his words having brought her as close to hysteria as she'd ever come. She closed her eyes, and a flood of memories tore through her.

"*Marry me, Tina,*" Jake said. "*Marry me and make me the happiest man in the world.*" He held her tightly pressed against his body, her breasts crushed to his chest.

Suddenly the image of Jake turned to Mitch.

"*I've missed you,*" he whispered softly, bending to press his lips to her throat.

Tina's eyes shot open as a bone-chilling shudder raced through her. Why was this happening? Why did she feel Jake so strongly sometimes when she was with Mitch? She pushed away from the door, anger boiling up inside of her, chasing away even the remotest thoughts of sleep. Ignoring Dee, obviously exhausted from baby-sitting and asleep on the couch, Tina stalked to her bedroom, threw her bag onto the bed and began to pace.

Jake had been gone for almost three years, and so many things had changed in her life since then. She'd gotten married, given birth to two sons and adopted a daughter. She'd watched her husband and her father die. Now she was a widow, a single mother, and she had a business to run. Tears of resentment, anger and loneliness fell from her eyes as the feelings knotted within her breast.

The café had been in her family for more than one hundred years, and Marcus had left it to her because she loved it, cherished its sense of history, and he'd known Lianne and Dee weren't interested. Tina would keep it going and hand it down to her children.

She paused before the fireplace and stared at the small inlaid mahogany and lemonwood box that her mother had given her when she was ten, and that had sat on the mantel ever since, holding her treasures. More memories assaulted her, more pain and confusion swirled through her mind. Finally, grabbing the box, she opened it and took out the photo of Jake she'd placed in it only a few days earlier.

"Why are you haunting me?" she asked softly, gazing upon the face of the man she'd once loved more than life itself. Moving to sit on the window seat, she never took her eyes from the picture. Why now, when someone else had finally come into her life that she might be able to care about, might even be able to love, was Jake constantly in her thoughts?

A fleeting image of Mitch swept through her mind and she touched her fingertips tentatively to her passion-bruised lips. The feelings that kiss had stirred in her had been dormant a long time. Was that why they were so forceful now? Because she hadn't been with anyone else since Jake?

She let her hands, and the picture, drop to her lap and

turned to stare past the window, ignoring both the reflection of the room that glistened in the silvery pane, and the shadows of the gardens beyond the house. She had never thought she could experience real desire again, never thought she could even think of loving someone like that again. Jake had been her world, the man she'd waited all of her life to love. But now there was Mitch Ryan. When he'd kissed her on the beach the other night, she had felt overwhelmed by the sensations that rushed through her body. But since then she had just about decided it was only her memories playing with her mind and emotions. Until tonight. When he'd pulled her into his arms on the porch the feral heat of his kiss had shaken her to the core, and awakened a primitive surge of desire within her. Heaven only knew what would have happened if his softly whispered words hadn't shocked her dumb.

"I've missed you."

They echoed through her mind, and Tina wrapped her arms tightly about herself. Thinking of them now, and what she'd thought they meant, just for a split second after he'd muttered them, sent a cold shiver skipping up her spine.

Tina saw Deano's car in the café's parking lot when she arrived the next morning. The kids tumbled out of the car and ran for the play area she'd had built behind the building. Tina waved to Lianne as she drove off, borrowing her car again, then turned and walked inside. "What are you doing here?" she asked, when Deano came out from the kitchen.

"Well now, if that isn't a real nice greeting," he said, giving her a mock scowl. "Good morning to you, too, Mary Sunshine."

"Sorry." She threw her bag down behind the counter and grabbed an apron. "Good morning, Uncle Deano, but

the café's closed today. You should be home with Aunt
Marge. Doing something fun. Going somewhere together.''

"She's at her quilting club this morning, and the fish,
they ain't biting, so I figured I'd come on down here.
You're gonna take inventory today, right?''

She nodded, not looking forward to the job. They only
did it once a year, but once a year was enough.

"Good." The ever-teasing glint in his eyes offset the
smug smile that creased his heavily jowled face. "'Cause
I already started.''

An hour later Tina dropped a can of olives. She glared
down at it as it rolled across the floor and settled itself
against the refrigerator.

Mitch hadn't called or come by the café, and she couldn't
help but look out at the road every time she heard a car go
by, in spite of the fact they were closed and she knew he
knew it. Was it happening again? Had she started to fall
for a man, only for history to repeat itself?

"Hey, Princess," Deano Peychaud said, a mock scowl
on his face as he looked at her, "you getting like your ol'
uncle and turning into a klutz?''

Tina looked up from the can she was still glaring at. She
made an effort to smile, though she knew she didn't wholly
succeed. "Just daydreaming for a minute, that's all.''

"Yeah?" Deano tucked his big, burly hands into the
waistband of the white apron wrapped around his hefty
midriff and leaned against the counter. "Sounds interesting,
though I'm not too sure we can afford much more of it.
What's your dream about?''

Biting her lip, she looked away. His tone had been one
of friendly joviality, but she could see in his eyes that he
was concerned. Her uncle had always been the only one
she could really talk to about Jake, and she knew, without
doubt, he would understand if she told him about Mitch

and the feelings and memories he stirred within her. Nevertheless, she hesitated.

"C'mon, Princess," he said. "Tell your old Uncle Deano what's on your mind. Maybe then you give the things around here a little break, huh?" he said, laughing at his own pun.

Tina threw him a weak smile. She'd been Princess to him for as long as she could remember. Lianne was the Duchess, and Dee was Amour Petit, Little Love.

Half an hour later he was frowning and shaking his head. "You know, I got me a little thought, but I dunno. Probably wrong anyway."

"What?" Tina said, curious by the troubled expression on his face and the mystery in his tone.

He shook his head again, as if trying to convince himself what he was thinking was beyond reason. "Nah, couldn't be. Most likely not anyway."

"What?" she demanded impatiently.

"Well, I dunno, Princess, but are you sure this Ryan fella ain't some relation to Jake Blaggette? Like a cousin, maybe? Brother? Something like that?"

The thought sliced through her like ice through warm water, chilling her to the bone. Memories, sensations, incidents flashed through her mind. The sense of familiarity she'd felt instantly upon meeting Mitch, and had experienced again several times since. The way he'd touched his finger to her lips, just as Jake had always done. The feelings Mitch stirred in her when he drew her into his arms. They'd made her wonder about him, but she'd always dismissed those feelings, told herself she was just being ridiculous, or fanciful. Now they made sense, but... She struggled against her uncle's speculation. "No." Tina rubbed a hand over her eyes and shook her head. "It can't be anything like that, Uncle Deano. It can't. They don't look a thing alike.

They're different. Jake's eyes were blue, and his hair was…''

Deano nodded. ''Yeah, I know, Princess, but think. Your papa and me, we didn't look alike either, remember? I got me this dark, curly hair. Marcus, his hair was brown and straight as a board. I'm tall, and as your Aunt Marge would say, stout as a beer bottle, while your papa was as thin as a bayou reed and almost as short as your mama. But we were brothers, Princess. We were brothers.''

Her mind whirled at the mere thought her uncle could be right. Jake's cousin. Or brother. She tried to discount the idea, but it refused to leave her mind now that it had been put there. But why would any of Jake's relatives come to Reimour Crossings? And why would he seek her out? She thought of Mitch, and in her mind, saw Jake. Tina's hands began to tremble as her thoughts spun wildly out of control. The fire of panic took root in the base of her stomach. Why would one of Jake's relatives come to Reimour Crossings—unless it was because of Jimmy and Joey?

Did they want her sons? Suddenly she remembered another stranger who'd come to Reimour Crossings—about two years ago. He'd looked a little like Jake, but she'd put that down to her imagination.

Deano saw the fear that came into Tina's eyes and knew he'd made a real blunder voicing his contemplations. ''Hey, don't pay attention to me, Princess,'' he said, and laughed, though even to his ears it was evident the effort was little more than halfhearted. ''I'm just an old man making up stories. What if this…what if that.'' He threw up his hands, as if in exasperation. ''Anyway, you said this Ryan fella and Jake had different color eyes, right? And hair?''

She nodded, but the fear didn't subside.

''Well, I ain't never heard of brothers having different color eyes. All you girls got blue eyes. My kids, they all got blue eyes." He shook his head. "Nope, just don't happen like that."

Mitch Ryan didn't have to be Jake's brother. He could be his cousin. He could be a friend. He could... The thought froze in her mind, and brought terror with it. He could be another FBI agent.

"Yeah," she said weakly, turning away and pulling a crate from beneath the sink, and saying what she knew her uncle wanted to hear. "You're probably right. It's just my imagination working overtime."

Who was Mitch really? What did he want? The question nagged at her. "Uncle Deano," she said, turning toward the office, "I have a phone call to make. Can you keep an eye on the kids?"

"Sure, Princess, take your time."

Tina closed the door behind her, hurried to her desk and pulled her address book from one of its drawers. When her brother was growing up, he'd had two best friends, Ben Dubois and Travis Manning. Her father had always jokingly called them the three musketeers. She hadn't seen Travis since shortly after Ben's funeral, and she didn't know if he could help her, but she had to ask.

"Savannah Police Department," a voice droned into her ear.

"Detective Travis Manning, please," Tina said.

The woman told her to hold on, and transferred the call. "Manning."

"Travis? This is Tina Peychaud. Dubois," she added hastily, having never gotten used to using Ben's last name.

"Tina, hi. I was just thinking about you."

The comment startled her, and she stood abruptly, her chair toppling over. Did he know something she didn't? Had Mitch already talked to him? "You were?"

"Yeah. I saw Lianne when she was in town a couple of days ago and we kind of rehashed old times, you know?"

"Oh." Now she remembered Lianne mentioning it.

"She was telling me how well you're running the café, and how big your kids have gotten. So, when are you going to pack them up and come down to Savannah and see me? I'll take you all out on the town."

The relief that sped through her was almost enough to buckle her knees. Hurriedly, she righted the chair and nearly collapsed into it. She hadn't been sure he'd help, since the break-up between him and Dee had been an angry one, to say the least. "Travis, I need to ask you a favor."

"Sure, what do you need?"

Tina felt like a fool as she hung up. She had rattled off what she knew about Mitch, and Travis promised to get back to her as soon as he could. What if the check she'd asked Travis to do came back okay, and Mitch was who and what he said he was? But what if it came back differently? What if what her uncle had proposed was true?

Tina prayed she'd done the right thing, knowing she'd had no choice. She folded her arms on the desk and laid her head down on them, and closed her eyes.

"Tina, I think you got company," her uncle called out, his booming voice reverberating off the building's ancient walls.

Her head shot up. Company?

"Better come on out here, Princess."

She rose hastily and hurried out to the main room of the café, hoping it wasn't Dack. She didn't need that at the moment. No one was there but her uncle. She threw a puzzled glance at him and he nodded toward the window. Tina turned. Mitch's black Thunderbird sat in the parking lot, its windows setting off a brilliant reflection of the late-afternoon sun.

Her mind whirled in a mixture of hope and fear, like a trapped animal seeing the hunter approach. She heard his footsteps on the stairs, saw him through the glass of the entry door, then watched him turn upon hearing the yells of the children out back.

"Hey, what are you guys doing?" he called, laughing as he saw Jimmy and Joey running around the jungle gym set up within the trees behind the café. Lily was sitting on a nearby bench, reading. He walked to the end of the veranda.

"I'm a airplane," Joey yelled, his arms stretched out straight. He ran crookedly, zigzagging this way and that and making a guttural noise in his throat that Mitch assumed was supposed to be the sound of the plane's engine.

Jimmy followed in his brother's footsteps, though the way he was flapping his arms, Mitch figured his airplane was a little more bird than jet. A swell of pride, and a feeling of need filled Mitch as he watched them.

What would Tina do once she knew the truth? If his suspicions of the past two years were right, there wouldn't be anything she could do. He would take his sons, and she would go to prison. The thought of her behind bars failed to give him the satisfaction it once had.

But if she was innocent—and more and more he was finding himself hoping that she was—what would she do then? Deny that they were his sons? Refuse to let him be a part of their lives?

There were things he could do if she did, but would he want to drag his children through a court battle? He remembered the constant arguments between his parents before they'd died, how each had seemed to get uglier and uglier, and he knew he didn't want that for his sons. He shrugged the thought aside for the moment. That was a bridge he'd cross when and if he came to it.

Mitch threw a leg over the veranda's railing and jumped

to the ground, then walked toward the boys, paused and hunkered down. "Looks like fun, guys. Got room for any more airplanes in that sky?"

"Yeah, yeah, yeah," both boys yelled, turning to run toward him.

Tina stepped outside and walked quietly to the end of the veranda to watch, her gaze quickly taking in the situation. How many times had she wished this for them? "Boys. Lily," she called a minute later.

Lily looked up from her book, and the boys' airplanes instantly sputtered to a standstill.

"You need to come inside now," she said coolly, keeping her eyes from meeting Mitch's. He was a stranger, and one she wasn't sure about anymore. Until she was, there was no room in their lives for him.

"We wanna play airplane with Mitch," Joey whined, though it came out more like "weanna pay airpane w'Mikch."

"Yeah, weanna..."

Tina shot both boys a not-another-word glare.

Jimmy scuffed the toe of his shoe in the dirt and stared down at the ground. Joey mumbled "Pooey" and kicked a clump of grass, then, as if knowing they'd pushed their luck as far as it would go, both boys charged past her and into the café, screaming for Unkie Deano.

Lily gathered up her book and notepad and followed the boys inside. "Can I get us some ice cream?" she asked quietly as she neared Tina.

Tina nodded and Lily disappeared inside.

Mitch looked at Tina, puzzled. "Did I do something wrong here?"

She shook her head, straining to hang on to her composure, which was dangerously close to slipping away from her. Lord, why had she called Travis? And why hadn't he called back yet? She wondered, knowing not enough time had gone by for him to have found out anything.

She'd already decided she had to have nothing to do with Mitch until she knew if he was really who and what he claimed to be. At the same time, she had to admit to herself that, at this moment, she wanted nothing more than to feel his arms around her again. She rubbed nervously at her bare arm. "It's just time for them to come in now, that's all," she said. "They've been out here playing all day and if they don't take a short nap soon they'll be monsters this evening and too tired to even go to sleep. That kind of evening is murder and..." She was babbling, yet she couldn't seem to stop herself.

"We could all go out for pizza, and maybe between us we'd wear them out," Mitch offered.

Tina shook her head. She couldn't afford to be around him, to let her feelings veer any more out of control than they already were. "Thanks, but the boys don't really like pizza, and—"

"Then how about hamburgers? Or I bring over some fast food? Chinese? Fried chicken?"

She shook her head again.

Mitch tried to hide his disappointment, and told himself it wasn't personal. He needed to be with her. There were no other leads, no other trails to follow toward the truth. "Okay. So how about tomorrow night?"

"I don't think so, Mitch. First day back at work, I'm usually exhausted by five. But thank you." She turned away and walked back inside before he could say anything else. It was just about the hardest thing she'd done in years, but she knew it was the only way. He might leave Reimour Crossings before Travis called her back, and if Mitch was who and what he claimed, she would probably regret this move for the rest of her life.

On the other hand, she couldn't discount her suspicions, and she couldn't let herself fall for a man only to have him walk out of her life again. This time it wasn't just her feelings that would be hurt. She had to think about her children. Lily liked Mitch, and Jimmy and Joey had accepted him instantly.

Tina quietly closed the café's door behind her as she entered. Almost from the day she'd discovered she was pregnant she'd had one priority, to protect her baby. It was why she'd married Ben, so her child would have a name, so no one in town would look down on him as illegitimate, or whisper that his father had left him. After the twins were born, that protectiveness had grown even stronger, and now it included Lily. She couldn't ignore it now, even if it meant saying goodbye to Mitch Ryan. She only prayed she was doing the right thing.

"Chocolate!" Joey screamed from the kitchen.

Tina smiled and walked toward the swinging doors, knowing any moment Jimmy was going to yell strawberry, and all Lily was going to find in the freezer was vanilla.

Mitch stared at the closed back door, feeling a sudden sense of loss. He turned away and walked to his car, angry with himself for once again letting his feelings get in the way of his objectivity, of his investigation. He'd trusted her with his life once and almost lost it. But was it her fault? That was the question he couldn't get away from, the one he had to have an answer to before he could hope for anything else. If there was anything else.

He swore viciously beneath his breath and climbed back into his car. This tangled web of lies he'd spun was beginning to get to him.

Once he could have pulled off this investigation without even blinking, without feeling anything more than the satisfaction he'd derive from playing her until he found out whatever he wanted to know.

So what had happened to him? Was he no longer any good as an agent? Or had he only been fooling himself that his feelings for Tina now were only physical?

Chapter 10

"It's as if McAllreaux didn't exist before he moved to Reimour Crossings," Raskin said.

Mitch sat on his bed, leaning against the headboard and cradling the phone between ear and shoulder. Everything about Raskin's time away from the office had checked out, which had left Mitch considerably relieved. He doodled aimlessly upon a notepad sitting on the nightstand as Raskin kept talking, then stared at his scribbles.

Laren McAllreaux. Laren McAllreaux. Laren McAllreaux.

The fact that the Agency hadn't been able to come up with anything on the man who lived in Chancellor Oaks and owned a corporation called Brigand bothered Mitch. But there was something about the man's name alone that bothered him too. He stared at it long and hard, as if by doing that, the reason behind the feeling niggling at the back of his neck would come into focus. He rolled it about in his head, rearranging the emphasis on pronunciation,

M*Callreaux*—Mc*ALLreaux*—Mcall*REAUX*. He cursed silently, positive there was something he was missing.

"Mitch, do you hear me?" Raskin demanded, when he didn't respond.

"Huh? Oh, yeah, just thinking about something. Listen," he went on, before Raskin could say anything else, "what about the company, Brigand? Anything there?"

"We're still checking," Raskin said. "It's a shell, we know that. There is something else I felt you'd better be aware of, though. Just came up."

Mitch heard the change in his tone and instantly sat up, his senses instantly alert. He'd worked with Raskin long enough to know when the man was worried about something, and he definitely sounded worried now. "What?"

He heard Raskin sigh.

"Dammit, Ivor, what?" Mitch demanded impatiently.

"We've learned that she contacted a friend in Savannah, with the police department. Detective Travis Manning. He was an old friend of her brother's and husband's. Ran together during high school. Anyway, he's started an investigation into the background of Mitch Ryan."

Mitch swore softly. "And?"

"And what?" Raskin nearly bellowed through the phone. "She's having someone investigate you, Mitch. Isn't that enough?"

"No," he snapped. It was enough to make him uneasy. It was enough to make him wonder. It was even enough to stir his anger, and leave him wondering why she was doing it. But it was not enough to make her guilty of betrayal and murder. "She's just being cautious," he said.

"Or suspicious," Ivor Raskin countered. "And you can't afford for her to be suspicious, Mitch. You can't afford for her or any of her friends to be poking around in your past."

"My cover's good."

"The sheriff checked on you too," Ivor said.

"They won't find anything."

"There's always something to find," Raskin snarled. "And you know it. There's only so much we can do to make up a person, Mitch."

"I don't think she's guilty," he said, surprising even himself with the announcement.

"Good. Terrific. But what if you're wrong?" Raskin challenged. "What if you're wrong and she finds out the truth, my friend? Whoever attacked you the first time will not let you survive again."

Flames—heat—fists—pain. The sensations instantly filled Mitch's mind. Unconsciously, he flexed a hand into a fist as pain assaulted his right knee, and the nagging throbs of a headache began to softly reverberate just behind his restructured nose.

"And don't forget," Raskin said, cutting into his thoughts, "whoever is behind this scheme, whatever it is, murdered your brother when he got too close to uncovering them."

The man's words were like a knife to Mitch's heart. Perry. He'd been trying to help Jake. Trying to find out what had happened in an effort to bring him out of his coma, and his assailants to justice.

Memories, feelings and the kind of pain his anger and long-honed physical defenses were useless against, assaulted Mitch.

"Give me the money, or we'll beat you to a pulp and leave you here for the vultures to feed on."

With tears streaming down his face, Perry clutched his lunch money in a tightly fisted hand pressed to his chest and covered by his other hand, and glared at the bigger kids. "It's my lunch money," he said bravely. "My grandma gave it to me, and you can't have it."

The four bigger kids began to close in on him, ugly, snickering scowls on their faces.

Jake stepped from the bushes, his own four friends right behind him. "Leave him alone, Larry, or you guys will be the ones getting beat to a pulp."

The leader of the other kids turned and sneered at Jake. "Oh, yeah?"

Jake raised his fists and squinted his eyes. "Go ahead," he said, in his best imitation of Clint Eastwood's Dirty Harry, "make my day."

The four boys threw quick glances at one another, then the leader looked back at Jake. "Ah, hell, orphans ain't probably got but a few pennies for lunch anyway. Not enough to waste our time on." The four laughed and started to turn away. Then their leader stopped and looked back. "Hey, Jake, you and that weenie brother of yours gonna be like your old man and try to kill off your whole family when you grow up?" The boys laughed loudly then, slapping Larry on the back as they turned and walked down the sidewalk toward their own neighborhood.

"It was an accident," Jake screamed after them, but they only laughed louder.

The memories pummeled Mitch, hard, cold and merciless, like snow, breaking away from its mountaintop perch and racing, crashing its way downhill, destroying everything in its path and, finally, burying its victims.

They'd lost their parents only a few months before that day, and had gone to live with their maternal grandparents, who had tried to shield the children from the truth. But they couldn't stop the kids at school from talking. Blake and Melinda Blaggette had been on the verge of divorce, their arguments having escalated beyond words. The police labeled the car wreck an accident, even though there was a multitude of unanswered questions that went along with that verdict. Like why was there no evidence Blake had even tried to put on the brakes before the car plummeted over the edge of that cliff?

Mitch shook off the unpleasant memories. He hadn't let himself think about his parents since that day, and he wasn't about to start now. But not thinking about his brother wasn't something he'd learned how to do yet.

Being two years older than Perry, Jake had always been the one to protect him. With the deaths of their parents, the job just grew more demanding.

But he'd been unconscious in a hospital when Perry had taken on a case he never should have been involved with. He hadn't been there to help Perry then, and now his brother was dead.

"He might have been close," Mitch said finally, "or might even have unmasked the whole thing, but my brother obviously didn't have time to write whatever he'd discovered in his notes, because I haven't come across a damned thing that points directly to anyone."

"Well, don't forget our two most important points."

Mitch inhaled deeply. He knew exactly what those points were. They'd belabored them endlessly before he'd left to come back to Reimour Crossings. But he let Raskin voice them anyway.

"Perry was centering his investigation in Reimour Crossings, and had not notified me or anyone else that he was going to Savannah, and there was no field notebook on him when he was discovered."

Mitch nodded. Perry had always followed procedure. It had been a real thing with him. Like a religion. If he had been going to Savannah, for any reason, he would have contacted Raskin and informed him. And he would never have gone anywhere without his field notebook, yet it was

missing. Mitch knew that could mean only one thing: whoever had killed Perry had taken his notebook from him first.

Which meant Perry had incriminated them in it.

"We know he was killed somewhere else and then his
body was dumped in that city park in Savannah," Raskin
said, drawing Mitch's attention back from his musing.
"And the coroner claims he hadn't been dead for more than
three or four hours when he was found a little after two
a.m."

"Yeah, I know," Mitch said, feeling especially weary
now as Raskin went over the same ground they'd covered
for hours on end while Mitch had been recuperating. "And
the patrolman who found him swears Perry's body wasn't
there when he made his regular rounds through the park at
midnight."

"Which means," Raskin said, rather smugly, "either he
lay dead somewhere for three to four hours before being
taken to the park, or he was being transported during that
time."

"And it's two hours and change from here to Savannah," Mitch said, knowing that was the point Raskin was
heading toward making. The same point they'd agreed
upon long before Mitch had come back to Reimour Crossings.

"No one there knew who you really were except Tina
Peychaud," Raskin continued. "Maybe, after you told her,
she told someone else, or maybe she just slipped up and
gave you away by accident."

Mitch opened his mouth to respond.

"And maybe there is some reason we haven't come
across yet that she'd have for wanting you dead once she
found out you were with the FBI."

"No," Mitch said. He didn't want to believe that anymore. "I know that's what we've thought all along, but I don't think so anymore. It's too pat."

"Don't go getting sentimental on me now, Mitch," Raskin snarled. "I don't want to bury another Blaggette, understand?"

Mitch sighed. Whatever he wanted to believe, he had to stay focused on the facts. Raskin was right. He'd been attacked, Perry had been murdered, and Tina was still the only one they knew for a fact had known who and what he really was.

After hanging up with Raskin, Mitch had a pizza delivered and tried to concentrate of reading through all of Perry's notes again. Halfway through, Mitch rubbed his eyes and shut the computer down. There was nothing there. Perry had been suspicious of several people who knew Tina, including her father and Ben Dubois, but he'd come up with nothing concrete in any of their backgrounds or business dealings that confirmed they were anything more than what they'd seemed.

And now both those men were dead.

He hadn't liked the sheriff either, but nothing had come up that made the man look anything but the arrogant SOB that he was.

Mitch opened his e-mail and clicked on Raskin's URL.

Recheck the circumstances of death for Ben Dubois and Marcus Peychaud.

Mitch stared at what he'd just typed.

He went back to reading Perry's notes. Twenty minutes later he felt as frustrated as when he'd started. There was nothing there. Perry had come up with no new suspects. Mitch scanned the list of names Raskin's secretary had made up of all the people in Perry's notes that he'd come into contact with when in Reimour Crossings. McAllreaux and Harlon Gates weren't on it. Sheriff Dack Brenaud was.

Mitch sighed in frustration. McAllreaux could have been on vacation, and Perry would naturally have consulted with the sheriff's office—if not by confessing the truth of who he was and why he was really in town, then at least by feeling out the man and his staff. "This is useless," Mitch snapped a few minutes later, and flicked off the computer. He got up and began to pace the small room, clenching and unclenching his fists with each step, as if preparing for a fight. He was missing something. He could feel it in his bones. Feel the instinctive certainty in his gut. There was something staring him in the face that would give him the answers he needed. He knew it, and he knew he was missing it.

Tina was the only one he'd told, the only person in town three years ago who'd known he was an agent with a secret branch of the FBI. No matter how he looked at the situation, he couldn't get away from that fact.

Grabbing his jacket, Mitch jerked the entry door open, then slammed it behind him and stalked to his car. Something about McAllreaux wasn't right. Instinct told him that. And she'd gone to McAllreaux's house, then denied it. If he was going to find out the truth, dammit, he was going to have to confront her. He didn't know how he was going to do it, he just knew it had to be done. And right now, because if he waited much longer, he was going to drive himself crazy.

The patience he'd possessed three years ago was gone. He had once staked out a suspect for forty-six hours straight, and had been prepared to go another forty-six if necessary to get what he was after. He'd worked undercover with the sleaziest of the sleazy for six months to get his man, and had worked a case for almost four years before gathering enough evidence on his suspect for an arrest.

Now he couldn't wait one more minute to find out the truth about Tina and McAllreaux. The easiest way to cut through all the questions and confusion was to go right to the source, and that was exactly what he intended to do.

Approaching Tina's house, he noticed her car sitting in the drive with its lights on. Telling himself he was being ridiculous, Mitch drove past nevertheless, and pulled off to the side of the road. A moment later, the car honked and Tina came running out of the house.

"I'm coming, I'm coming," she called, then waved to the kids, standing in the doorway with a woman Mitch assumed must be a baby-sitter.

Mitch watched Tina walk toward the car, the black cocktail dress she was wearing hugging her body seductively, the split up one side of the skirt revealing just enough of her thigh to tantalize a viewer.

She was beautiful, he thought begrudgingly, not wanting to notice, and unable to help himself.

Her arms were bare, and the dress's neckline demurely high, but as she turned to open the car's passenger door, Mitch saw that the back of the gown's décolletage plunged dramatically.

As the car's interior light went on he also noticed something else: it was her sister Lianne sitting behind the wheel.

They pulled onto the road and headed toward town. Mitch waited a minute, not wanting them to realize they were being followed, then turned his lights back on and swung the car around.

Fifteen minutes and a stop at the drugstore later, Mitch watched as Tina's red Chevy pulled past the gates of the McAllreaux mansion.

"Damn." He'd been hoping... One glance toward the

house told Mitch there was a party in full progress. Torch-lights lined each side of the drive, their flames dancing merrily upon the ends of the poles rooted in the ground and cutting into the darkness of the night dramatically. If it weren't for the cars parked alongside the drive, quite a few of which were limos, the sight might have been one from a hundred plus years ago.

Mitch rolled down his window, and the faint hum of soft music and laughter floated in upon the sultry night air. He looked down at his jeans and T-shirt, obviously not the right attire to crash a black-tie party. But that wasn't going to stop him from taking a surreptitious look around. Leaving his car parked several hundred yards down the road from the main entrance to the house, he checked the gun clipped to the back of his belt, then quietly moved past the bushes, following the fence line toward the river that bordered the mansion's rear property line. With all these guests milling about, he seriously doubted McAllreaux had any guard dogs loose on the property.

Praying he was right, he quickly climbed over the wrought-iron fence and dropped silently to the ground, crouching low and looking around hastily to make certain no one had noticed him. The house was to his right, the Ogeechee River to his left. He stood still, getting his bearings and the lay of the land. The outer gardens were left to grow in their natural state, while those closer to the house were manicured to perfection, and a lush green lawn swept from the house to the river, where Mitch thought he could make out the shadows of a small dock. A brilliance of light poured out from the huge windows at the rear of the old antebellum mansion, obviously a modern-day renovation. They gave view of the spacious gallery and deck, as well as the yard and river, and offered Mitch what he knew would be his best chance of seeing just exactly who was inside other than Tina and her sister Lianne.

He stayed within the shadows of the tall oaks at the outer perimeter of the manicured yard, and moved cautiously toward the house.

The sharp bark of a dog brought him to an abrupt standstill. He looked around quickly, expecting any second to see sharp white fangs flying toward his face. Instead, he saw a standard poodle standing a few yards away, his head reaching to about Mitch's waist, a glistening collar of rhinestones and rubies around his neck, his curly hair chestnut, and his deep brown eyes curious. He was panting heavily, and his tongue dropped from a mouth that looked more like it was smiling than snarling. Mitch knelt and held out a hand. "Hey, fella," he said softly, "what are you doing out here all alone? Guarding the place, huh?"

The dog wagged his tail and took a hesitant step toward Mitch.

"Angel?" a male voice called from the front of the house. "Angel? Where are you?"

The dog barked, then whirled around, tail wagging, and bounded toward the house.

Mitch waited, every muscle in his body tensed and ready, but no one came his way. Finally, he rose and moved toward the rear of the house. It was built on a slope so that, though the main floor was on the ground at the front of the house, at the rear it was not. A twin set of curving brick stairs, their handrails white wrought iron, led to the main floor, while beneath it, set far back from the stairs, was a series of doors that Mitch assumed probably led to be storage rooms.

He couldn't chance using the stairs. They didn't offer any cover. Mitch climbed a trellis at the gallery's side, carefully avoiding the rosebush that twined itself around the wooden support. Once he was on the gallery, there would be nowhere to hide. The thought pounded at him, but he ignored it. He grabbed a balustrade and swung over the railing, then flattened himself against the house's exterior wall.

So far so good.

The sounds from inside seemed to vibrate through the wall and slip under his skin now. Laughter. The tinkling of glass against glass. Soft music.

Mitch remained still, fighting his own anxieties.

Flames—heat—fists—pain. The sensations and memories suddenly flashed through his mind, taunting him. A veil of perspiration broke out on his forehead. He exerted all his will to push the feelings away. Now was not the time. Continuing to hug the wall, he waited until he felt he had control of his nerves, then moved cautiously toward the window, and peeked around its frame.

The spacious room beyond the tall windows was filled with people. Women in dazzling evening gowns, men in tuxedos, servants moving through the crowd holding trays laden with flutes of champagne.

In stark contrast to the restored, antebellum style of the exterior of the house, at least in the front, which obviously was demanded by the historic registry that had tagged this place a monument, the decor of the room reflected the more modern tastes of its owner, like the tall windows and deck. The dominant color of the room was white—walls, overstuffed furnishings, rug, fireplace, drapes. Crystal-encased sconces were positioned about the walls, while track lighting shone from overhead. A vase of red roses, at least three dozen, supplying the only color in the room's furnishings, sat on a glass-topped coffee table, and a huge mirror hung above the fireplace mantel, reflecting everything and everyone in the room.

Mitch's gaze scanned the guests in search of Tina, and finally found her. She was standing on a raised step he assumed led to the foyer, and talking with a man whose back was to him.

She laughed, clinking her glass against his, then raised it to her lips.

Mitch swore softly as a searing jolt of jealousy tore through him.

Lianne joined them then, touching the man's arm intimately and saying something to him. He nodded, then turned to walk away from them.

"Son of a..." The same shock that brought the epithet to Mitch's lips left it there unfinished as he caught a glimpse of the face of the man Tina had been talking to. He felt as if the world had suddenly tilted off its axis and turned reality into a nightmare. And it was a nightmare worse than the one he'd already been living.

He swallowed hard, moved away from the window and stood with his back pressed against the wall. Mitch closed his eyes, fighting for composure, and sucked in several deep breaths. This couldn't be happening. His eyes were lying to him. He took another deep breath, trying to steady his jangled nerves, turned and looked around the frame of the window again, searching for the man who had been talking to Tina. He was standing by the fireplace now, his image reflected within the glistening mirror.

There was no mistake. It was Lawrence D'eillmoreaux.

Mitch shot away from the window, bolted from the gallery and ran toward the trees. Hopefully no one had seen him, but at the moment all he could think about was getting away, back to the trees, back to his car, back to the cabin.

D'eillmoreaux was dead. At least, everyone thought he was. He should have been.

The words repeated through Mitch's mind. Dead. Dead. Dead.

He didn't know how he got back to the cabin, or how he got Raskin on the phone.

"What in the hell do you mean D'eillmoreaux is in Reimour Crossings? The man's dead."

"Then he's got an identical twin brother we didn't know about," Mitch said, as much fury, shock and sarcasm lacing his tone as had his boss's.

"Blast," was all Raskin muttered for several seconds.

Silence hung black between them as each tried to think of how this could have happened, and of its most likely implications.

"Somehow he escaped us," Raskin said finally.

"No. You think?" Mitch snarled.

Lawrence D'eillmoreaux had been the head of the largest crime syndicate in Louisiana until Jake Blaggette infiltrated it six years ago.

"How in the hell did he escape that explosion?" Raskin wondered aloud.

Mitch thought back on the bust. D'eillmoreaux had left his men to fend for themselves when it was apparent they were outmanned and outgunned. He'd taken off in his cabin cruiser, heading downriver toward the gulf. Seconds before Jake had been about to overtake him in a helicopter, D'eillmoreaux's boat swerved, as if out of control, and crashed into the side of an oil tanker on its way upriver to New Orleans.

The cruiser exploded instantly.

"We never found his body," Mitch said.

"Hell, we never found much of anything," Raskin said. "That boat exploded into splinters.

"Yeah, well, D'eillmoreaux managed to survive." A hell

of a lot better than Jake had, Mitch thought. At least
Lawrence D'eillmoreaux still had his own life, and his own
face.

"Okay, now we know. Laren McAllreaux is really
Lawrence D'eillmoreaux."

Laren—Lawrence. McAllreaux—D'eillmoreaux. The
names weren't the same, but similar enough that Larry
could operate comfortably with his new one. Mitch
slammed a fist against the wall. Stupid. It had been in front
of him the whole time, taunting him, and he hadn't been
able to put it together.

"He's the one behind this," Raskin said. "But how?
Why? Did he see you three years ago and panic? Or did
she tell him? Is there something between them?"

"I don't know," Mitch said softly, knowing he wasn't
ready to tell Raskin that he'd seen Tina go to the party at
the mansion that night. Part of him felt a new hope, while
another part felt as if all the hopes and dreams he'd been
afraid to acknowledge were still within him were being
bludgeoned to death again.

"Then go find out," Raskin ordered. "Unless you want
me to send someone else in to do it."

"No."

Mitch drove back to the mansion. The pieces of the puz-
zle were finally coming together, and he didn't like the way
they were starting to fit.

Was McAllreaux a.k.a D'eillmoreaux Tina's lover?
Mitch remembered how she'd looked at the man, laughed
and touched her champagne flute to his. Toasting another
conquest? Had her friend on the Savannah Police Department gotten back to her with some information Mitch didn't
know about? Were they, even now, plotting Mitch's death?

The questions nagged at him, cold and cruel. He parked

outside the mansion and waited. Two hours later, he saw her red Chevy pull past the gates of D'eillmoreaux's mansion and head out of town.

Mitch followed at a discreet distance, his hands wrapped around the steering wheel so tightly his knuckles had turned white. Fury roared through his veins—at her, at himself, at Lawrence D'eillmoreaux.

He should never have assumed D'eillmoreaux was dead. Not without a body. He'd known how cunning the man could be. He'd had a reputation—the fox who'd always managed to escape from the trap and get away. Except, as far back as he could remember, Jake had always considered D'eillmoreaux to be more like a snake than a fox—slippery, cold and evil.

After parking in the drive of the Peychaud house, Tina and Lianne disappeared inside.

Mitch pulled off the road, far enough away not to be seen, but close enough so that he had a clear view of the house, and settled down to wait. He wanted to confront Tina alone, not with her sister and baby-sitter present.

The minutes ticked by with torturing slowness. Mitch drummed his fingers upon the steering wheel, shifted position and wished for a cigarette. He hadn't had one since before the attack, but the craving was still there. Sometimes he figured it was always going to be there, but it was times like this that it bothered him the most.

Finally, the front door opened and Lianne stepped outside, followed by the older woman. Both waved after getting into Tina's car, and drove away.

"Show time," Mitch whispered to himself, straightening and turning the key in the car's ignition.

Chapter 11

Tina's hand froze on the light switch as she heard the car pull into her drive. Frowning, she glanced around the living room, looking for whatever it was Mrs. Stimple or Lianne had forgotten. She didn't see anything.

Footsteps sounded on the porch.

Tina's heart skipped a beat. They were too heavy sounding to be a woman's steps. She instantly remembered all the times Lianne had admonished her for hanging on to the old family house. It was several miles from town, set back from the road, surrounded by forest and the river at its rear, with no neighbors within a mile.

"You used to have Papa," Lianne harped constantly. "But he's gone now. You're alone out there with three children. Anything can happen, Tina, and no one would ever know until it was too late."

She'd always scoffed. She loved the old house. It was home. Where she'd grown up, and she couldn't picture herself ever living anywhere else. But she had to admit, since

Ben's and her father's deaths, the remoteness of the house, the loneliness of its location, did bother her every once in a while. Mostly at night, when the kids were asleep, when the house's ancient beams and walls began to settle with the sinking of the sun, their creaking sounds like soft footsteps in whatever room was just beyond where she was, their groaning like the cries of its past residents wanting back into her world.

She took a step toward the study.

A knock on her front door nearly sent her nerves into overdrive and brought a scream to her throat. She slapped a hand over her mouth, stifling the scream just before it made it past her lips and filled the old house, and whirled to stare at the door.

"Tina? It's Mitch," he called out, suddenly realizing that at this late hour he most likely had frightened her. The last thing he needed at the moment was for her to call the sheriff...or worse, D'eillmoreaux. Mitch wasn't prepared just yet for that type of confrontation.

Tina stared at the door as relief surged through her, so sudden and hot the sensation left her weak in the knees. It was the first time since her father's death that she'd been frightened enough in the old house to think of his guns. Steadying herself by holding onto the back of the sofa, she took a deep breath and sought to quiet her scrambled nerves. Mitch. She said a prayer of thanks that it was he, then instantly wondered why he was at her door at this hour?

"Tina?" Mitch called again.

Her icy fingers slid around the ancient silver doorknob, but instead of turning it, she laid her forehead against the century-old cypress and closed her eyes. Her insides were still quivering.

Whatever he wanted, she had to send him away. Travis

hadn't called her back yet. She didn't know anything more about Mitch Ryan than what he'd told her, and that wasn't enough. Not for the way she'd started to feel toward him.

Jake's image flashed through her mind, melding with that of Mitch Ryan's. His kiss suddenly seemed to burn upon her lips. Tina's shoulders shook as another shiver slipped up her spine. "Not now," she whispered softly, trying to push the images from her mind. "Please, not now." She needed answers, needed to be sure Mitch was who and what he said before she could trust her emotions with him any further. Drawing her shoulders back, Tina straightened. She'd loved and trusted a man once and he'd left her. She wouldn't do that again. It had been a hard lesson to learn, but three years ago she'd had no choice, and she wasn't going to forget that lesson now. She would open the door, see what Mitch wanted, then politely send him away. If it turned out to be a mistake, she would face that, and try to correct it when the time came.

Unless it's too late, that little voice in the back of her mind whispered, *like with Jake*.

The fact that Jake had been an FBI agent had deeply troubled Tina. She remembered when Jake had told her he was an agent, only minutes before he asked her to marry him.

She'd been nearly devastated.

Sleep that night had eluded her, and she had vowed to tell him the next morning that his job didn't matter, only the fact that they loved each other. But when he'd come to the café the next morning he'd seemed in such a good mood that she'd figured he had forgotten about her anxieties over his job, or decided to ignore them, so she didn't bring it up.

He'd kissed her long and hard as they stood on the café's steps, said he loved her more than anything in the world and promised to be back in plenty of time to take her to dinner. Then he'd driven away and never came back.

Tina straightened. Not again, she promised herself. She would not go through that kind of pain and worry and devastation again. She drew back her shoulders and opened the door. "Mitch, what are you doing here this late?" she said, smiling and trying to sound cheery.

His fist was in midair, ready to knock on the door again. He dropped it to his side and smiled at her. "I couldn't sleep and decided to go for a drive. I saw your lights still on, figured you were still up...well, actually, I didn't see your car and..." This wasn't going quite as he'd planned. She wasn't saying anything. "But I hoped if you were home, and still up, we could talk."

Tina stared at him, past and present coming together right before her eyes, blending and becoming one. With the moonlight at his back, and only the pale light from her living room filtering onto the porch from behind her, his face was left mostly in a contrast of dark and light shadows. The waves of his hair seemed softer, longer, the curves of his facial bones more classically smooth, and for the briefest of moments his eyes appeared blue.

A soft gasp caught in her throat, her breath stalled in her lungs, and her heart fluttered past an entire beat, tripping and threatening to stop altogether as she stared at Mitch Ryan, and saw Jake Blaggette.

"I'm sorry," Mitch said, seeing the color instantly drain from her face. "I know it's late, and I didn't mean to frighten you." He cursed his own stupidity and reached out for her, afraid she was about to faint and meaning only to steady her by lightly grasping her arm.

Tina jerked away, then stared at him, long and hard, her eyes narrowed, mistrust emanating from her.

Apprehension seized Mitch as he realized she was staring

at him as if trying to decide if she knew him—if she recognized him.

"I'm sorry, I shouldn't have come," he said quickly, knowing it was true. He'd made a mistake. He didn't know what it was, but he saw it on her face, in her eyes, and knew it could very well be a deadly one. But he also knew it was too late to do anything more about it than leave.

She shook herself then, the veil that had momentarily clouded her blue eyes lifting, the hard look that had been on her face disappearing. "Mitch?"

He merely stared at her, confused, and maybe a little bit frightened himself. What had she seen when she'd looked at him?

Tina laughed weakly. "I'm sorry, I was a little rattled by the late-night footsteps on my porch. Anyway, I was, ah, just on my way to bed." She blushed at hearing her own words, picturing them together, naked in her bed. Was that what she wanted? Her fingers tightened around the doorknob, pressing down relentlessly. It didn't matter, because it wasn't going to happen. "Why don't you come by the café tomorrow? We can talk there, if you want." She needed him to leave. Now. "Come by around ten and I'll buy you breakfast and take a break."

He was about to agree, when he remembered why he'd come in the first place. "Tina, I need to talk to you now," Mitch said, more soberly this time. "Tonight. Please?"

Tina looked at him, as an old ditty flashed into her mind. *Come in, said the spider to the fly.* Only in this case, he was the one who wanted to come in, and she was the one who felt like the helpless fly.

She pushed the silly thought away and told herself she was being ridiculous. It was Mitch Ryan standing on her porch, not Jake. Her mind was playing tricks on her, and she was just getting carried away by her emotions because of a loneliness she hadn't even been aware of until Mitch came to town. It was merely that unexplainable familiarity she felt toward him that had her spooked. Even if he was a relative of Jake's, he still wasn't Jake.

And she wasn't helpless. Nevertheless, she grappled with her indecision, with the feelings she'd been battling since the first moment she'd seen him. The struggle not to call him had been tearing at her ever since she'd sent him away from the café that afternoon. Regardless of who or what he was, she cared about him, most likely more than she should, and definitely more than she wanted to admit. Knowing she should refuse to invite him in, that she should send him away, close the door and go to bed, she stepped back instead, and opened the door wider. "Of course, if it's important. Come in," she said softly.

Mitch smiled and stepped into the house. "So, where's your car?" he asked innocently. Even though he knew the answer. "Not at Quattman's garage, I hope?"

Tina turned instantly, needing to put some distance between them, and walked toward the kitchen. "Oh, no, my sister's borrowing it. Hers is the one in the shop. Come on in here," she said over her shoulder. "We can talk in the kitchen without waking the kids."

Mitch watched her as he followed her, appreciating the sight and drinking it in like a man who'd been starving for one glimpse of this woman his whole life. She was still dressed in the little black cocktail dress she'd worn to the mansion, its sheer material draping her body gracefully, yet with enough teasing snugness to seductively delineate every line and curve. The high heels she wore, along with the skirt's slit running up one thigh, aided the illusion that her legs were as long as forever, while the low-cut back dared the viewer to even wonder whether or not she was wearing a bra, let alone anything else under the dress.

Tina pulled a pan from a cupboard beside the stove. "I'll make us some hot chocolate."

Mitch nearly crinkled his nose in distaste, but caught himself just in time. He hated hot chocolate. Suspicion clouded his thoughts as he remembered the incident in the café, with the syrup. Was she testing him? Or was he just paranoid?

She glanced over her shoulder toward him. "Do you like it straight, or with whipped cream on it?"

He didn't like "it" at all, but he was going to grin and drink the damned stuff anyway.

A few minutes later she brought their steaming cups to the table and sat down across from him.

"Okay, what did you need to talk to me about that couldn't wait until tomorrow?" she asked, her gaze meeting his.

For a brief moment, Mitch became lost within her eyes. Why did all of this have to happen? Resentment flared in him.

"Mitch?"

He shook off the self-pity that had momentarily invaded his thoughts and focused his gaze on Tina again. "Sorry," he mumbled. "I was just thinking about how beautiful you look tonight."

She smiled. "Thank you, but I doubt that's what brought you knocking on my door at one in the morning."

"It's part of it," he said, knowing it was the truth.

"And the other part?" she persisted, sipping her chocolate.

Mitch picked up his own cup and wrapped his fingers around it, but didn't lift it to his mouth. Instead, he slowly rolled the hot ceramic between his hands. "I've been wondering why you sent me away today, at the café? Obviously I must have said or done something to offend you and I..."

She shook her head. "No, you didn't do anything, really. I was just having a bad afternoon, that's all. Inventory day is never a good day," Tina lied. She couldn't tell him about Jake, about the feelings of familiarity that were growing stronger and stronger every time she was around Mitch. And she certainly couldn't tell him about calling Travis to check up on him. Ever since she'd made that call she'd been admonishing herself, furious one moment that she'd done it, but seconds later knowing she'd had no choice and wishing he'd get back to her with something. If she were the only one involved in this situation maybe she wouldn't have done it. Maybe she would have relegated those feelings of familiarity to the absurd and just braved it out and hoped that Mitch wouldn't do what Jake had done. But she wasn't the only one involved this time. She had the boys and Lily to think about now. She had to protect them, even if she wasn't sure exactly what it was she was trying to protect them from.

Mitch nodded, knowing she wasn't being truthful with him. She'd sent him away, and she called her policeman friend in Savannah, because she was suspicious. But was it because having the man she'd loved "walk out on her" had made her suspect of any man that came into her life? Or did she suspect the truth about him?

"Well, I'm glad I didn't do anything wrong. I was worried." He smiled and attempted a change of subject. "So, you look like you belong on the cover of a magazine. Did you go to a party tonight?"

"Yes." Her brows rose slightly, as if she'd suddenly remembered something. "Actually, it was at the mansion we talked about. Remember? Chancellor Oaks. The one at the edge of town?"

He nodded.

"My sisters, Lianne and Dee, have an interior decorating

business, and the owner is thinking of hiring them to redo a portion of the house.''

''And you're helping?''

Tina laughed. ''Oh, heavens no. If I tried to decorate one of those old antebellum homes it would probably end up looking like a country inn rather than an elegant mansion. Crystal chandeliers, satin drapes and marble-top tables are just not my thing.''

''Well, I prefer your style,'' he said. ''It's more comfortable.''

Tina laughed. ''Actually, comfortable is about all you can hope for around kids.''

''So, do you go there often?'' Mitch asked, hoping he wasn't coming off sounding too nosy. ''To the owner's parties?''

She shook her head. ''Actually, it was my first time there since Mr. McAllreaux bought the place. Remember? I told you that when you asked before.'' She rose and walked to the stove to pour herself more hot chocolate.

Mitch watched her, trying to decide if he thought she was lying.

''More?'' she asked, turning to glance over her shoulder at his cup.

''No, I'm fine,'' he said.

Tina resumed her seat across from him. ''Actually, Dee couldn't go to the party, she wasn't feeling well. And Lianne didn't want to go alone.'' She smiled. ''For all my sister's independence, she still hates to go out anywhere alone. For any reason. So she roped me into going with her.''

It suddenly occurred to Mitch that if she was telling the truth now, then she'd been telling the truth the other day. It hadn't been her that he'd seen going to the mansion, it had been Lianne, driving Tina's car.

Did it matter? His eyes bored into hers. He wanted it to. He suddenly realized he really did want to believe her innocent. Memories surged up from the recesses of his mind before he could stop them. Tina in his arms, her lips capturing his, pressing her naked hot body to his length, telling him how much she loved him.

Mitch rose suddenly, pushing his chair back with such force it skidded on the tile floor.

Tina looked up, surprised at the abrupt move.

He walked to the back door and stared past its window toward the dark, hulking shadow of the barn, and the ragged-edged silhouette of trees just beyond.

Could he believe her? Or had he somehow been made? Was this some story cooked up between her and D'eillmoreaux to throw him off guard?

Tina moved to stand beside him. "Mitch?"

He turned and stared down at her. She had the most beautiful eyes he'd ever seen. The blue always different, changing color depending on the reflecting light, the black aureole that surrounded them like the shadow of night, continually threatening to close in. A hint of moonlight touched her hair, causing the long tendrils to glisten as if strands of gold were hidden within the dark waves. An ache of want seared through him. In spite of all his suspicions, she was still the embodiment of every dream he'd ever had, the incarnation of all his fantasies. Her face had haunted his thoughts for three years, calling to him, beckoning him to come home.

He reached up, unaware of his own actions, only knowing that he could no longer deny what he wanted most in the world. His fingers caressed the side of her cheek, ran slowly, and ever so lightly, along the delicate curve of her jaw, until pausing upon her lips and pressing tenderly.

A sense of déjà vu swept over Tina, and once again, as

she stared at Mitch, it was Jake's face she saw, his eyes she stared into. She could feel the heat of his body warming the air around her, smell the faint aroma of the cologne he'd always worn, hear the sensual tone of his voice as he whispered her name.

The room swam out of focus, blurring into nothingness, as the man standing before her became the only reality in Tina's world. Emotions, feelings and desires she'd struggled to keep under tight rein, surged forth, breaking the bonds she'd enforced upon them for so long.

As his fingers touched her lips, and their gazes met, Mitch knew he could not turn away from her this time. He was as lost to her now as he had been three years ago.

Tina's eyes held his, and she unconsciously leaned into his touch.

Her slight acquiescence ripped away whatever self-control Mitch still possessed, what little restraint he still held over himself. In spite of all his denials, in spite of all the anger and resentment and suspicion, he had never stopped wanting her. She was the only woman whose mere presence could tease his senses, whose touch could soothe away the scars of his soul, whose kiss could inflame his deepest and most secret desires.

Almost without thinking, he slid his arms around her slender waist and dragged her body toward his almost savagely, until there was nothing left between them, no space, light or air existing to separate them, and he could feel every line and curve of her length pressed to his. Need rose within him like a volcanic surge, hot and fierce, destroying any thread of rational thought left to him and leaving him nothing but the basic hungers of desire.

Tina's hands slid over his shoulders, her fingers slipped within the soft tendrils of hair at his nape.

An agonized groan of need rumbled deep within Mitch's

throat as he felt her hands upon him like ribbons of fire, searing into his flesh. His head lowered toward hers as she looked up at him. She felt his arms tighten around her, felt his hands splayed, hot and tight, upon her back, and turned a deaf ear to the frantic whispers of caution that raced through her mind. Nothing could make her give up this moment. She had been waiting too long to be held in his arms again, too long to feel his love wrap around her again.

Mitch knew, somewhere deep down, somewhere far in the back of his mind, that what he was about to do was wrong. But he also knew it was too late to stop, too late to deny the passion that had been building in him from the first moment he'd seen her on the road with her horse.

His mouth closed over hers, in a kiss that was hard and demanding, meant to command her surrender, ignite her passions and satisfy the burning need sweeping through his blood.

Right or wrong, good or evil, innocent or guilty…it didn't matter to him anymore. She was his, and that was all he cared about, all he could let himself care about.

Her lips parted in invitation and, as Mitch's tongue thrust deeply into her mouth, all the loneliness, the need, the urgency of the past three years swept over him, then disappeared.

Tina clutched him to her, afraid to accept him, terrified of letting him go. His kiss devastated her senses, and turned her insides to an inferno that threatened to consume her. He had kissed her before, aroused her desire, but this time was different. This time his kiss seemed to touch the very essence of what made up her being. Or maybe it was merely that she had finally admitted to herself that no matter who or what Mitch Ryan was, she wanted him, if only for a little while.

She slipped her tongue between his lips, pressed against

him, clutched him to her. A moan of pleasure and endless need tore from Mitch's throat, and a thrill of satisfaction rippled through Tina, and intensified her hungers. All her fears and uncertainties were gone, all the passion and need she'd thought never to feel again, engulfed her.

"Tina," Mitch whispered, over and over, her name like a long-denied love song upon his lips. Caution continued to nag at his conscience, begging him to listen, pleading with him to understand that what he was doing was wrong, that it was dangerous, that it could lead to the same deadly situation he'd faced three years ago. But he refused to pay any heed. He'd listened and denied himself for too long.

Whatever was to come later was a reality he would face then. Now all he wanted was to make love to Tina one more time.

The world slipped from her reality. His kiss, his embrace, were the dark magic that had been missing from her life for so long, the mysterious seduction that made her universe complete. Without conscious thought, only knowing what she wanted, what she needed, Tina's hands slid from around his neck. Her fingers released the buttons that secured the front of his shirt.

Mitch's breath sharpened as her hands slid beneath the fabric and, with a touch as burning and indelible as smoldering steel, moved sensuously over his flesh, teasing his passions, stoking his needs. It was an ecstasy he'd thought never to feel again, an ecstasy he knew he didn't want to live without again.

Tearing his lips from hers, Mitch swept Tina up and into his arms, turning and striding from the room into the foyer.

"There," she whispered, clinging to him and directing him to her bedroom with her eyes when he hesitated.

Pausing beside the large bed that dominated the room, Mitch looked deeply into Tina's eyes, then captured her lips with his again. His hands moved the zipper at the back of her dress downward; his fingers brushed it from her shoulders. The fragile black crepe fluttered softly, silently, to the floor, along with a flimsy, lace-trimmed slip.

Her skin was burning. Caution was something of another world. He was all she needed. All she wanted. She pressed against him, and Mitch lowered them both to the bed.

In spite of the gnawing, urgent need to lose himself within her, Mitch moved slowly, savoring each caress of his hands over the gentle lines of her body, each pause of his fingers upon her curves. With each touch, the need within him to take her intensified. Instead, his hands moved with infinite tenderness, a sweet torture that fed both their passions as his lips ravaged hers and drew them both into the darkly mystical world of their past, where everything was beautiful, and anything was possible.

She writhed beneath him, her body responding to every touch, and pleading for more. Then suddenly he was gone. Tina's eyes shot open as a feeling of desertion swept over her.

"You are so beautiful," he said, the heavy emotion in his tone turning the words to little more than a ragged breath.

She reached for him, but he evaded her arms. She felt his fingers, warm and teasing, send a shiver of need slicing through her as they slipped between her breasts and released the hook of her brassiere. Then he bent over her and his lips touched first one nipple, then the other, as if paying homage. Her fingers clutched at the sheets, twisting them in her grasp as a shudder of pleasure swept through her, leaving her trembling and weak, and wanting so much more.

He rose away from her then and gently slid the sheer

black panty hose from her hips, her legs, her feet, and with a devilish smile, tossed them over his shoulder.

His fingers moved lightly over the silk triangle of her underpants, caressing the lace.

She felt his touch through the thin threads, felt the heat of his hand, the fire of his eyes upon her. "Come here," Tina said, her voice breathless as she held her hands out to him. "Please."

Instead he gently pulled her panties over her legs and dropped them to the floor.

She lay before him, naked, and feeling more wanton and alive than she had in years.

He shrugged out of his shirt, then reached down to the belt at his waist.

Tina watched, mesmerized, as moonlight filtering softly through the lace-covered windows bathed him in its soft, amber glow.

His belt fell open, he pushed the zipper of his jeans down, forced them over his hips, then stood and let them fall to the floor.

Tina's eyes devoured him, drinking in the sight she had ached for so long to see again. His shoulders were broad, each arm a ropy length of muscle that she knew could be all strength and hardness one moment, soft and tender the next. Her gaze fell to a pale, ragged scar that sliced horizontally across one rib, but before she had time to think about it, to wonder why she'd never seen it before, he slid back onto the bed and pulled her into his arms again.

His lips descended upon hers and the touch of his hands on her body ignited a fire that swept over her flesh and sent desire to invade her blood. A physical hunger deeper, stronger, than any she'd ever known, coiled like a hot knife between her thighs.

She arched her body toward him, pressing against his

mouth, against his length, needing every touch, every caress, every kiss, just as much as she needed breath in her lungs.

His hands were everywhere upon her, yet her every thought was that she needed more...more...more.

She opened her mouth to cry his name, but his lips caught hers and his mouth swallowed the sound as her body filled with his. The mind-shattering ecstasy of their union was almost more than she could bear, and tears fell from the corners of her eyes as she clung to him, kissed him and moved with him. She had no inhibitions, no more hesitations, no more questions. He had come back to her, the only man she had ever loved with all of her heart, and that was all she cared about. All she would ever care about.

"I love you," she whispered then, as delicious currents of euphoria suddenly sliced through her, one rumbling wave after another.

Upon hearing her words, a deep rending tore at Mitch's heart, like the torturous knives of a hundred assailants. At the same time, trembling waves of the deepest, most soul-wrenching pleasure ripped through his body.

Agony and pleasure, guilt and duty. They sliced through him, cutting him in two, shredding his senses, devastating his emotions.

Even as the last, trembling shivers of ecstasy slowly deserted their bodies, Mitch was unable to let her go. He held her in his arms, pressed his lips to the curve of her neck and buried his fingers within the rich, dark tendrils of her hair.

Tina lay contented within the circle of his arms, having no desire to ever move away from them, and fighting the desire to be possessed by him again. Finally, long moments later, she could fight no more, and gave in to the deliciously hot hungers growing so rapidly within her again. Turning toward him, she pressed her lips to his cheek, and trailed her hands down the hard length of his body, feeling him tremble beneath her touch.

"Make love to me again," she whispered boldly.

Without waiting for her to change her mind, his mouth and body covered hers, and the outside world once again disappeared.

Chapter 12

He stood at her bedroom window, looking past the sheer lace curtain and out at the night. But it wasn't the moonlight-touched landscape that held his attention, or even the woman asleep on the bed behind him.

Who was he? The question had been nagging at him for hours. Part of him was still Jake Blaggette. But only part, because part of him now was Mitch Ryan. The gnawing need for revenge still burned within him, but not as strong as before. He glanced over his shoulder at her. Part of him wanted to just forget the whole thing. Pick up where he'd left off three years ago, and go on with his life.

But that was the problem. Which life? Jake's? Or Mitch Ryan's? If Tina was innocent, if she hadn't betrayed him, did she need to know the truth?

He turned back to stare past the window, and a long, shuddering sigh shook his frame. What did he want? he asked himself again, but the answer was the same as it had been all the other times he'd asked himself that question. He didn't know anymore.

He stood like that for more than an hour, letting his mind wander, asking himself questions, tearing at his conscience for answers, and finally he came back to where he had started.

It shouldn't have happened. Whatever else he'd intended, he should never have let this thing between him and Tina go this far. The conviction tore at his gut, while guilt hammered at his very soul. Everything he'd told her was a lie. And for all he knew so far, everything she'd told him was a lie.

Lawrence D'eillmoreaux was as cunning and cold as any criminal he'd ever come up against, maybe more so. It would only stand to reason that any woman he was involved with could be the same way. There had been rumors floating around for several years that he'd killed his own father to get control of the organization, and Mitch had no doubt those rumors were based on fact. Though most likely anyone who knew the truth other than D'eillmoreaux himself, had probably been working on Satan's chain gang since about five minutes after helping the cherished son pull the trigger.

Mitch rolled his shoulders, trying to push the knots away, but they merely tightened. He didn't want to believe Tina could be involved with a man like that. Yet he couldn't totally dispel the possibility, had found no reason, no evidence, to dispel it.

Tina moaned softly and he glanced back at her. She rolled over, snuggling deeper into her pillow, her dark hair splayed out around her on the white bed covering like a dark halo. Moonlight caressed the golden hue of her skin, touching one bare shoulder, and softly shimmered along the rumpled sheet that covered her body, creating tantalizing shadows that beckoned him to come explore their hidden secrets.

He steeled himself against the temptation. How well did he really know Tina Peychaud? It was a question he'd been asking himself from the moment he'd opened his eyes in the hospital room two years ago and Raskin had filled him in on everything that had happened.

"Jake. Ummm. Where..."

Mitch's thoughts froze and he whipped around to stare at her, but she seemed to still be asleep. Or was she? He watched her for several long minutes—time that seemed an eternity—but she didn't stir again. She'd called out for Jake, not Mitch. It shouldn't have mattered to him, but it did.

He cursed her for making him still want her. But he knew it was his own weakness that was his real enemy—an enemy that could get him killed if he didn't control it. Get them both killed if she was innocent.

If she was innocent. The words echoed endlessly, cruelly, through his mind, taunting him without the slightest mercy. His hands closed into fists.

An urge to grab her and shake the truth from her lips seized him, but he fought it off. That was not the way. Determination burned in his chest, forcing out every other emotion, every other thought. No, trying to force her to tell him what she knew, if anything, wasn't the way, but he was going to uncover the truth. No matter what he had to do, no matter whom he had to walk over, he was going to find the person who'd stolen his life and murdered his brother, and he sure as hell wasn't going to die while doing it.

Turning abruptly, Mitch grabbed his clothes and hastily jerked them on. He didn't trust himself here anymore, not in her bedroom, with nothing between them but the thin threads of a sheet, because in spite of everything, he still wanted to slip under that cover and make love to her again.

Slut. That was what she was. What they all were. His breath struggled raggedly past his lips, as rage, impotent and fiery, swelled within his chest. She was doing it again, about to ruin everything.

He watched Mitch's car pull out of her driveway. Didn't she see that this one was no good? Just like that other one, three years ago?

He flexed his gloved fists and pounded them on the steering wheel. Was he going to have to "fix" things again, as he'd done then?

He'd forgive her for what she'd done. Again. It was only right. After all, she was just a woman. This time, however, when the time was right, he'd make certain that she understood the way it was supposed to be. That was all that was wrong. She just didn't understand.

Mitch drove almost automatically. Jake, not Mitch. The thought hammered at him, like a club, slamming down repeatedly at every emotion he possessed. Why did it bother him so much that she'd called out for Jake? It wasn't as if it was another man.

Rancor, at himself, at D'eillmoreaux, at Tina, threatened to overtake him. What was the truth? If she was guilty, he was a fool, because only a fool would give his assailant a second chance to kill him. If she was innocent, he was still a fool, because he'd let himself get involved with her again. There was no sense trying to lose himself within the lie anymore. It was more than physical.

The car swerved around a curve in the road, its weight pulling to the outside. The passenger-side tires slid off the pavement.

Mitch gripped the wheel tightly, cursing as the sounds of dirt and gravel flying up against the undercarriage yanked him from his musing, and the sensations of that other time his car had left the road overtook his thoughts. He fought to get the car back onto the pavement. Relief left him weak as the car straightened and cruised along the smooth blacktop.

He glanced into the rearview mirror and tensed, seeing headlights there. But then they were gone. He slowed and watched, but they didn't reappear.

He was halfway back to town before he relaxed enough for his thoughts to return to Tina. Whatever happened, it was no good for them. Their time had come and gone. Anyway, why would she want anything to do with a man who couldn't give her his trust? Mitch almost laughed aloud. The people he'd given his trust to during his entire lifetime could be counted on fewer than the fingers of one hand. He'd trusted his father, and he'd killed himself and taken Mitch's mother with him. He'd trusted his grandfather, and he'd died on him too. He should have trusted his brother, and he had, but not enough. He'd gotten too used to being Perry's protector, and protectors had to be strong. That meant holding back, letting no one near enough to find a vulnerable spot, and that meant refusing to trust. He had never totally trusted Ivor Raskin either, but then Raskin didn't ask for his trust, had told him to keep it in fact.

He had, however, given both his heart and his trust to Tina three years ago, without question or reservation. For that, he'd ended up almost dead, and his brother had been murdered.

Nothing good came of trust. "Highly overrated," Mitch said beneath his breath. Like love.

He glanced into his rearview mirror and again noticed

headlights behind him. Narrowing his eyes, he squinted into the mirror, trying to make out the car.

Dack smiled and flipped two switches on the dashboard of his patrol car. The red and blue lights on his roof instantly went on, as did his siren, its loud wail cutting through the dusky morning silence.

Mitch swore. He was on a lonely stretch of highway, with no one else around, and the man behind him didn't like him. He hurriedly pulled his gun out from under the seat where he'd tucked it just before going into Tina's house. Leaning forward, he clipped it to the back of his belt, then pulled the car over to the side of the road.

The sheriff pulled in directly behind him and shut the siren off, but left the lights flashing as he climbed from his patrol car and walked toward Mitch.

Mitch forced a smile to his lips, hoping it didn't look as stiff as it felt. "Good morning, Sheriff. What seems to be the problem?"

"See you ain't got that busted taillight fixed yet," Dack said. He folded his arms across his burly chest and stared down his nose at Mitch, returning the smile.

The taillight. Mitch damned his forgetfulness. It had totally slipped his mind. "No, I was actually going to have that done today. Think your local garage will have a replacement lens for a T-bird?"

"Maybe. Ain't my place to know what Quattman's got or ain't got." He unfolded his arms and began to write in his ticket book.

Mitch frowned. "You're not ticketing me for the taillight again?"

"Nope. Speeding."

Mitch's jaw nearly dropped into his lap. A curt response popped into his mind, but he left it there. In spite of the affable, good-ol'-boy facade the sheriff presented at the café, when other people were around, Mitch had long ago pegged him for an arrogant SOB who was obviously spoiling for a fight with him. He'd have loved nothing more than to oblige the man, but knew better. It was a risk he couldn't take.

Ending up on a southern chain gang for the rest of his life was not in Mitch's plans. He suspected whatever Brenaud's problem with him was, it had to do with Tina. The way he had been making eyes at her at the café, it was apparent to him, if not Tina, that the sheriff wanted Tina Peychaud for himself, and that meant Mitch was in the way.

"Speeding?" he said finally. "Really? I thought I was…"

"You were doing thirty-eight in a thirty-five mile-an-hour zone, Mr. Ryan." The sheriff handed him the ticket book and his pen. "We don't allow speeding of any kind in Reimour Crossings."

Mitch signed the ticket, then folded and placed his copy into the console's glove box after the sheriff handed it to him.

"Kind of early for a drive in the country, ain't it?" Dack said.

Mitch smiled and shook his head. "Most beautiful time of the day, Sheriff."

After offering little more than a grunt as reply, Dack stalked back to his car.

Mitch waited until the sheriff's patrol car was well out of sight before he pulled back onto the road. Dack Brenaud's being on this road, at this time of the morning, directly behind Mitch, hadn't been a coincidence. He was as sure of that as he was that his eyes were starting to burn from leaving his contact lenses in too long without a break.

When Tina woke the bedroom was flooded with the bright rays of the morning sun, and she was alone. She lay perfectly still and stared at the ceiling, waiting for sleep to fully desert her body, and wakefulness to take over. For some reason her legs ached a little, yet she felt so warm and snuggly, so unusually contented.

Jake.

His name slammed into her mind with the force of a two-by-four across the forehead. Tina bolted upright, her heart suddenly thudding furiously. She jerked the sheet to her breasts as memory brought a hot tingle of sensation to her nipples.

He had been here last night, with her. He'd come back. Made love to her. She twisted around and stared down at the empty space of bed beside her. A lone dark hair, short and nearly black, lay on the pillow. She stared at it. Mitch, not Jake. She closed her eyes, but it was Jake she saw lying beside her on the bed, Jake kissing her, making love to her. She looked at the pillow again, still indented where his head had lain. Her hand trembled as she reached out and touched the lone strand of hair with the tip of her fingers.

Mitch, not Jake.

But no matter how many times she repeated the names to herself, the impression that she'd been with Jake Blaggette was so strong it frightened her. She rammed the back of her curled fist into her mouth to keep a whimper of fear from escaping. Mitch, not Jake, she told herself again, frantically.

Then she remembered it all; looking into his face as he'd held her, as they made love, and seeing his blue eyes, the aquiline curve of his features, the long, silky strands of his brown hair. How could she have imagined that? The question pounded at her. Could she have made love to one man, while pretending, even subconsciously, that he was someone else? Had she pretended that Mitch was Jake?

The mere thought sickened and frightened her. She was

losing her mind. There was no other explanation. Throwing the sheet aside, Tina scrambled from the bed and ran into the bathroom. She jerked on the faucet and splashed cold water onto her face, once, twice, three times. But the feeling persisted.

She stared at herself in the mirror. Jake. She remembered the way he'd drawn his fingers lightly across her cheek, then along the line of her jaw, until coming to her lips, where he gently pressed, as if to draw the impression of her lips onto his fingers. A kiss he could keep with him forever.

Coincidence. That's all it was, Tina told herself. Jake had left her. He'd said he loved her, promised to love her forever, and then he'd just walked away. She had to remember that. She wasn't in love with him anymore, merely his memory, merely the ideal of the life they'd once planned on having together. A plan that she'd learned, too late, had only been hers.

But what if Mitch was related to Jake, as her uncle had speculated? Tina grabbed her clothes from the closet. No. It couldn't be. She couldn't let herself think that. Not yet. Her hands trembled and she dropped her jeans. She had to call Travis. Tears filled her eyes as she scooped the jeans up from the floor and fought to get into her clothes. Travis had to have found out something by now. He probably just hadn't had time to call her. Maybe there had been an emergency in town, or at the police department. Maybe he'd had to pull a double shift or something. Her thoughts spun. If Mitch was who and what he said he was, Travis would know by now. It should only have taken a few official phone calls for him to verify the things Mitch had told Tina. Unless…

Chapter 13

"**D**ack Brenaud's got a bank account in Statesboro that's a hell of a lot heftier than he could have saved off the salary he's making as sheriff," Raskin said, his tone laced with disgust. "And we haven't come up with anything that says he inherited it from any childless, old, rich aunt."

"You think he's on D'eillmoreaux's payroll?" Mitch asked, knowing what Raskin's answer would be.

"He's on somebody's payroll other than the city's, and our old friend D'eillmoreaux seems to be a prime suspect, wouldn't you say? What about the woman? Got anything there?"

Mitch felt every muscle in his body tense. The woman. Tina Peychaud. If Raskin knew what Mitch had done only hours ago, he'd have his head on a platter and his rear roasting over a fire pit. "She went to a party at D'eillmoreaux's place," he mumbled. "Her sisters have been consulted about doing some redecorating at the mansion, and Tina went along to the party because one of them couldn't make it.''

''So she says,'' Raskin snapped. Disbelief hung in his tone. ''Look, as soon as I come up with anything here, I'll get it to you. Meanwhile, watch your back. And watch D'eillmoreaux. But stay away from him.''

Mitch heard a click, and the connection went dead. He set the phone receiver back onto its cradle, typed a couple of notes into his laptop, then closed it and slid it into the narrow space between the rear of the desk and the wall. He picked up a pencil from the desk and began to play it absently between his fingers as his thoughts drifted and he stared past the window.

In the old days he'd have chain-smoked half a pack of cigarettes in the three hours between the time he'd gotten up and now. But the ''old days'' were another lifetime ago. He was another person now, and he didn't smoke. But he did feel the walls closing in on him, and he needed to act.

Mitch left the cabin. He was going to stake out the mansion, but first he had to stop by the café. He wasn't looking forward to facing her. He'd made love to her, then walked out on her this morning without a word. She'd wonder why, and most likely ask him, and he had no answer other than the truth.

Because you called out for Jake in your sleep.

Because I'm still not convinced you didn't set me up to die.

Because I think you might be responsible for murdering my brother.

Disappointment weighed down on him. He should have been able to uncover the truth by now. The café came into view. If he was lucky, his libido would behave this morning when he saw Tina, and not get the better of his brains as it had last night. And if he was real lucky, he'd get a line on whatever it was Lawrence D'eillmoreaux was up to in Reimour Crossings.

Tina set the Coke Harlon had ordered down in front of him, then refilled Dack's coffee cup. "The fair sounds nice," she said, "but I'll really have to let you know, Dack. Since taking over the café, I just don't seem to have much time for anything anymore, and…"

He reached for her free hand and caught it before she had a chance to draw away from him with any degree of casualness. "You know how I've always felt about you, Tina," Dack said, his voice low but husky with emotion. "You don't have to try and do things alone."

She nodded and pulled away from him, not wanting to say anything to encourage him, yet knowing better than to make life even more difficult for herself by flatly refusing him, by telling him there was never going to be anything between them.

"Maybe she just likes making things difficult," Harlon said, sneering.

Tina didn't mind letting him see that she didn't like him. The man made her skin crawl. She turned and walked into her office.

She was still on the telephone with the secretary of Travis's department at the Savannah Police Department when she heard the bell over the entry door tinkle again. She looked up, expecting to see one of her regulars, hoping to see Mitch and dreading the idea of seeing him.

Their eyes met and the intangible bond between them locked into place. Everything in Tina told her to be angry with him. He'd come to her home, made love to her in her bed, then left without a word.

Like Jake, a little voice in the back of her mind whispered again, as it had been doing all morning. Just like Jake.

"So when will he return?" she asked, forcing her attention back to the woman on the other end of the phone.

"We're not certain, Mrs. Dubois. It was a special duty call. Unscheduled."

Tina thanked the woman and hung up, more suspicious now than ever. She'd asked Travis to check on Mitch's background. Now Travis had been yanked from his normal duties and assigned to some "special duty call" with another agency. Coincidence?

Deano exchanged a few words of greeting with Mitch, set a cup of coffee and a pastry roll down on the counter in front of him, then walked toward the office, stopping at the open door and poking his head in. "Hey, Princess, someone here wants to say good-morning and apologize for something—" his brows soared and he eyed her questioningly, but when she didn't explain, he went on "—before he takes off for a hike in the woods. Want me to call Marge and have her come in for a while so you can go with him?"

"Thanks," Tina said, "but no."

"Sure?"

She glared at him mockingly. "Will you just go back to your kitchen?"

Tina drew in a deep breath, stalling and looking for the courage to face Mitch. How should she act? Angry? Insulted? Nonchalant? She opted to try for the latter and left the office. "Good morning. I hear you're going for a hike in the woods," she said, pouring herself a cup of coffee as she paused across the counter from him. She fiddled with the sugar, which she normally didn't use, then reached for a cream pitcher, keeping her gaze averted from his. If she met his eyes he would work his magic of seduction on her, and she knew all thoughts of caution would be lost to her again.

"Want to join me?" Mitch said, forcing himself to play the game. He'd thought he had himself under control again, but from the moment he'd stepped into the café and seen her, his emotions had gone to war against one another.

How could she have made love to him, told Jake she loved him, and be in collusion with Lawrence D'eillmoreaux?

The questions and feelings tore at him like claws of torture, ripping his emotions to shreds, leaving him feeling raw and vulnerable, more uncertain, more in need of answers than breath to fill his lungs.

"We could take a picnic lunch," Mitch said, reaching out to touch her hand, running his fingers lightly along the length of hers. "Find a secluded spot, talk, and do—" he smiled wickedly, a devilish gleam sparking from his eyes "—whatever."

"I'd love to," Tina said, smiling, "but I can't. Work, you know?" She laughed lightly, hoping she sounded as cheerful as she was trying to be. "Only some of us around here are on vacation."

"I didn't have the heart to wake you this morning," he said, knowing he needed to offer her something for walking out. "You were sleeping too peacefully."

She merely stared at him.

"I forgot I had to make some early calls to the office."

"Um. I hope everything's okay."

He nodded. "Fine. But I want to make up for not serving you breakfast." He smiled wickedly again, letting her make of his words what she would. "How about dinner tonight? Pizza? The Lamp Post?"

She busied herself wiping a towel across a portion of the counter. Say no, her conscience urged. "Stop by when you get back from your hike,'' she said, ''and we'll decide then.'' And maybe by then, she prayed, she would have talked to Travis.

''Tina, it's Travis.''

She sank into the chair beside her desk. Thank heavens. ''Travis, is everything okay?'' she asked anxiously. ''I tried to call, but…''

''Listen, I don't have much time here. I don't know who Mitch Ryan is, Tina, but there's definitely something funny going on.''

Jake. His name came to her mind instantly. No, it wasn't possible. Tina's hand tightened around the receiver, bearing down on the plastic with such force her fingers began to ache. But she didn't notice, aware only of her own apprehension, and waiting for Travis to tell her she was wrong.

''Everything checked out, birth certificate, his company, address, ownership, social security number, driver's license, the whole bit.''

He wasn't Jake. He was Mitch Ryan, not Jake. Her mind swam in confusion. ''Then what's…?''

''It all checked out, but something's wrong,'' Travis said again.

''I don't understand. What's wrong?'' Tina said, sitting on the edge of her chair now. Tremors rippled through her body. She didn't want anything to be wrong. He was Mitch. Her feelings of familiarity had only been fantasy. He was who and what he said he was.

''You tell me,'' Travis said on a frustrated sigh. ''I don't know.''

She heard the worry and confusion that colored his deep tone.

''Look, I was about to call you and tell you the guy was who and what he claimed,'' Travis said, ''when I got a call

from a friend of mine at Quantico. He's owed me a favor
from way back and I decided to call it in, which, considering where I'm at now, may have been a mistake. Anyway,
he wouldn't give me specifics and swore if I told anyone
we'd even spoken he'd deny it. He said I should never have
put that inquiry out, or called him, and if I knew what was
good for me I'd keep my nose glued to my own hometown
affairs and forget I ever heard of Mitch Ryan.''

"He threatened you?'' Tina nearly shrieked, her heart
fluttering to a near faint.

"No. He's a friend, he was warning me. But two hours
later I got called into my captain's office and told, in no
uncertain terms, I was being assigned to a special detail,
working a case with the FBI in Beaulieu.''

FBI. She felt as if her senses were suddenly spinning.
Jake had been an FBI agent. The man Travis had called a
"friend,'' had been at Quantico, the location of the FBI's
main training facility. And now Travis was assigned to
work on a case with the FBI.

"It doesn't make sense,'' Travis was saying when Tina
finally refocused on his words.

Images of Jake and Mitch kept floating through her mind,
melding, becoming one. She tried to shake them away.
"Maybe it doesn't mean anything,'' Tina said, feeling as
if she were hoping against hope. "Maybe your assignment
doesn't have anything to do with the inquiry.''

"Yeah, and maybe gators fly, but I've never seen one
do it.''

Five minutes later, after promising, several times, to be
careful and call him back if she needed anything, Tina hung
up and sat back in her chair, staring at the calendar on the
wall and not seeing it. She didn't know what to think, or
how to feel. Her thoughts were a blur, her mind moving
from one possibility to another so quickly she barely reg-

istered one before it changed. Her emotions were just as bad. She was more confused now than ever.

Travis's initial background check had proved Mitch to be exactly who and what he claimed, yet someone was making certain Travis didn't look any deeper. And he'd been warned away by a so-called friend.

Was it possible? Could Mitch be...? She shook her head, then dropped it into her hands as Jake's image once again filled her mind. No. Mitch and Jake didn't look alike. They didn't sound alike. Didn't even move alike. And she'd know. If anyone would recognize Jake Blaggette, she would.

But you did, didn't you? a little voice in the back of her mind whispered.

The question taunted her, flaring over and over again through her mind. Persistent. Relentless. She couldn't deny that from the first moment she'd seen Mitch, she'd thought of Jake. When he'd kissed her, when he'd made love to her, she'd thought of Jake. Not purposely, but it didn't matter. Jake's image, his presence, had been there.

Tina stood and began to pace the room. Was it possible? Could Mitch be Jake? The thought turned her emotions inside out. But how? And why? Why would he come back and pretend to be someone else?

She thought of the twins, and a moment of panic coursed through her, but as quickly as the thought came to her, she dismissed it. Jake didn't know about the boys. Her father and Ben had known who the twins' real father was, but they were dead. Now, no one knew except her sisters, and they would never tell anyone.

Tina returned to the café, moving around in a daze, picking things up, cleaning, rearranging, all the while her emotions in a turmoil, her thoughts tumbling from one possibility to the next.

Relief...anger...panic...fear...joy...fury...hope. She felt them all, but confusion kept her from knowing which she should really be feeling.

She had to talk to him.

Tina pulled into the inn's driveway. Parking under a wide-spreading oak tree, she walked up the path toward what had once been the town house of one of the area's richest antebellum planters.

"Hello, honey, what can I help you with?" the day manager asked, as Tina stepped past the front door.

"You have a guest," Tina said, wishing there were some other way to do this and knowing there wasn't. "Mitch Ryan. I need to know which room he's in."

"He's in one of our cabins, honey." She wrote down the number and handed it to Tina, as if trying to be discreet. "Just go back outside and on down the drive. You can't miss them. The first two were the old *garonnières*, and the third was—"

"I'll find it," Tina said, and hurried out before the woman could go on. Moments later she stood in front of the door to Mitch's cabin, having left her car parked back by the main inn. She knocked, but there was no answer and a quick peek in the large window showed no one inside. If anyone was watching, they were about to get an eyeful. She glanced over her shoulder in both directions, then stared down at the doorknob. It had been a long time since she and her brother had broken into school lockers, but picking one lock was about the same as picking another. If she hadn't lost her touch.

Tina removed her mother's brooch from the collar of her blouse and, holding out the long pin, knelt down and inserted it into the door's keyhole. A minute later the tumblers fell into place, the knob turned, and she was inside.

It was almost identical, but it wasn't the same cabin that Jake had stayed in three years ago. She'd known that while still outside. His had been farther up the drive. Even so, memories crashed down around her as she stood in the doorway and looked around. An image of herself and Jake, naked, lying on the bed, loving each other passionately, filled her mind's eye. A bottle of champagne had sat on the desk. The lone rose he'd brought her that night lay beside the bottle. Their clothes were on the floor. The window was open to the night's breeze. Soft music from the radio filled the room.

Tina closed her eyes and willed the images to go away, then stepped inside and closed the door behind her. She drew the drapes across the window, said a prayer she was doing the right thing and began to search the room, trying not to disturb anything.

Within less than half an hour she was through. There was nothing in the cabin to indicate Mitch Ryan was anything other than what he claimed—a man on vacation. Except for the clip of bullets she'd found in the nightstand's drawer. But in and of itself, that didn't mean much either. A lot of people carried guns. Especially when traveling.

Tina felt suddenly filled with guilt. Maybe he was telling the truth, and she was letting her imagination get the better of her. It wouldn't be the first time, and she had no doubt it wouldn't be the last. But before the guilt overrode her better senses and made her do something foolish, like leave him a note of apology for searching his room, she remembered her phone conversation with Travis, the mysterious call from his friend at Quantico, his reassignment and her need to protect her children.

She turned to go and was just reaching for the doorknob when she tripped and fell against the desk. The tin of pencils sitting on its edge fell off, bounced on something be-

hind the desk, then clattered to the floor and rolled toward
the bathroom door. Tina hurried to pick up the pencils and
saw the leather case wedged between the wall and the rear
of the desk. She knew immediately she was looking at a
computer bag. Pulling it from its hiding place, she set it on
the desk, and, unzipping the case, removed the computer
and turned it on. The small machine buzzed and whirred,
lights flashed, and the screen came to life.

Tina stared at it as it blinked at her, demanding a password to proceed further. A password. She grappled with
the idea, then typed in the word *agent*. The computer denied her access. She tried the name he'd given her for his
company: Ryan Security. The machine denied her access
again. Tina sighed, her fingers trembling now. What if he
came back and caught her? What if she got past the password? What if she found out something she didn't want to
know? She tried several more times to no avail. "Oh, this
is hopeless," she snapped at herself, slapping a hand onto
the desk. She glared at the screen as it continued to demand
a password.

Did she really want to see his files? The question wasn't
worth answering. She had to see his files, because she had
to know the truth. She had to put her fears to rest, to convince herself that she was reading things into circumstances, into her feelings, that were ridiculous.

Tina sat for several seconds, staring at the computer
while trying to think of what word or phrase Mitch might
use as a password. Her eyes suddenly blurred with tears
and she shook her head at the idea that had formed in her
mind. "No," she murmured softly, trying to deny it. "No."

But the thought wouldn't go away. Taking a deep breath,
she typed in the one word Jake had always used to describe
the future: Someday.

The screen suddenly went blank.

Tina jumped in surprise. Terror, unreasonable, unexplainable and more basic than anything she'd ever felt swept through her. It tore at every cell in her body and seized her heart in a cruel grasp that seemed to tighten further with each passing millisecond.

A buzzer beeped, the computer's drive whirred, and a list of files appeared on the screen.

Tina's hands flew to her mouth, stifling a scream as she stared in disbelief. "My God," she whispered, unaware she'd even spoken. She thought she'd been prepared for whatever would happen. Thought she knew what she was doing. But she'd been wrong. She scrambled to her feet, and pushed away from the desk, knocking the small tin of pencils from the desk again. Her entire body shook from the shock and fear threatening to consume her as her gaze remained riveted upon the computer.

It couldn't be. There had to be some other explanation. The thought kept playing over and over through her mind. But there was no other explanation, at least not one she could think of. But maybe...

Tina directed the cursor to the first file in the list, labeled Tina.

Chapter 14

Mitch was exhausted. He'd watched the mansion all day and come up with absolutely nothing, except for the fact that he had a hard time concentrating solely on what he was doing with thoughts of Tina constantly invading his mind.

Groceries had been delivered to the mansion, a maintenance man had worked on the pool for more than an hour, two gardeners spent most of the afternoon puttering around cutting this and trimming that, and the mail was picked up from the box set into one of the gate's brick pillars before it had even lain there five minutes. But D'eillmoreaux never left the house.

Mitch pulled his car up beside the cabin and, after turning off the engine, let his head fall back against the headrest and closed his eyes.

How in the hell had his life turned into such a mess? All he'd done was fall in love and ask a woman to marry him. An image of Tina, smiling up at him, filled his mind. Then the image changed, and it wasn't him she was smiling up at anymore, it was Lawrence D'eillmoreaux, as she touched her champagne flute to his, and laughed.

Apathy and exhaustion instantly deserted him, replaced with a fury beyond rage, a resolve beyond determination. He bolted from the car and stalked toward the cabin.

He hadn't stopped by the café to see if she'd go to dinner with him, so he'd just have to hope she would. If she said no, he'd find a way to change her mind. He had to, because he was running out of patience, and that meant he was running out of time.

He remembered the way she'd felt in his arms, how right it had felt to make love to her again. "Dammit," he swore at himself. "Stop it." Tonight, he'd get at the truth one way or another. Mitch slid his key into the door lock, and froze. It was unlocked. He stared at it, knowing he'd locked it when he'd left that morning. The hairs on the back of his neck stood on end, and every cell in his body jumped to full alert. Reaching behind him, he pulled his gun from its holster, stepped to the side of the door and pushed it open.

Nothing happened. No one fired, no one ran out.

But they could be waiting inside for him.

He took another deep breath and, crouching, wheeled around the door frame and charged into the room.

It was empty.

But it had been searched…again. His computer sat on the desk, its screen saver playing. Mitch reholstered his gun, and stared down at the tiny figure skiing across the monitor, then touched one of the computer's buttons. The man disappeared and a list of files took its place. Only one showed that it had been opened.

Mitch pressed a button and the file opened onto the screen. He knew every word that was on it, every suspicion and thought he'd written down about her, but he stared at it anyway.

Tina Peychaud.

The only one in Reimour Crossings who knew JB was an FBI agent.

Two hours after telling her, JB was attacked and left for dead.

Married Ben Dubois less than three months later.

Gave birth to twins. JB's sons.

Perry Blaggette murdered after questioning her.

Is a friend of Lawrence D'eillmoreaux. Or more?

Is suspicious of Mitch Ryan. Has background check being done.

Believe she senses the truth. Made several mistakes. Said I missed her. Touched her lips the way I used to. Caught myself just in time.

Did make love to her.

She called out for Jake.

Conclusions: None yet.

If guilty, seek custody of twins.

Mitch's gaze remained captured for several seconds by one of the comments he'd typed into his notes that morning. "Did make love to her. She called out for Jake." The last had been eating at him all day.

He turned away from the computer and looked around the rest of the room, going over it slowly, methodically. Was whoever searched it the same one who'd done it before? Maybe, but he didn't think so. Whoever had searched his room before hadn't wanted him to know they'd been there. This person hadn't cared. Mitch directed the computer to download his e-mail, then turned toward the bathroom. If he hurried, he had just enough time to take a quick shower and get to the café before Tina left.

He felt something beneath his foot as he took a step. Pausing, Mitch looked down. A small yellow tassel lay on the thick, burgundy-colored carpet. He bent and picked it up, then rolled it slowly, thoughtfully, between his fingers as he remembered the colored tassels on the tennis shoes Tina always wore when working at the café.

He looked back at the computer. It had been Tina. She knew the truth now, and that changed everything. He felt a twinge of disappointment as his suspicions darkened. She had searched his room. Did that mean D'eillmoreaux knew about him now, too? Was there already someone on their way here to kill him?

Mitch stepped away from the window and reached for his gun again, then paused. No. His old enemy was more careful than that. He'd wait until Mitch was alone again. Alone and far from town, like the last time, where there would be no chance of anyone seeing.

Or was that what he wanted Mitch to think now, so that he could surprise him by taking the opposite tack? He let his mind go, and tried to think like D'eillmoreaux. It had worked once, back in New Orleans. Maybe he could do it again.

The phone rang, startling him. Turning, he snatched the receiver from its cradle. "Yeah?" he growled, angry at being interrupted.

"Where in the hell have you been?" Raskin bellowed. "I've been trying to reach you for hours."

Mitch pulled his cell phone from his pocket. Off. He cursed silently. He'd turned it off when he'd gone sneaking around the perimeter of the mansion, not wanting to alert anyone to his presence by getting a phone call. Obviously he'd neglected to turn it back on.

"We've got a lead," Raskin said, not waiting for a response.

Mitch felt his pulse leap. "What?"

"We've discovered several calls have been made from the Agency to the Chancellor Oaks mansion in Reimour Crossings over the past four years."

"What?" Disbelief and fury swept through Mitch like water bursting from a dam. "Someone in the Agency's been calling D'eillmoreaux's place for the past four years and your people are just now noticing that?"

"Dammit, Mitch, we're just now noticing that because we just now found out D'eillmoreaux is the man at the other end of the calls," Raskin snapped. "You think if we'd known that McAllreaux was Lawrence D'eillmoreaux we would have just been sitting here…"

"Okay, okay," Mitch said, knowing he'd been wrong. "Have you been able to trace the extension? Pinpoint who's been placing the calls?"

"Yes," Raskin said, sounding even unhappier.

Mitch waited.

"Evelyn."

Shock ripped through him. "Evelyn? Evelyn Trayner? Your secretary?"

"Yes."

He felt dumbstruck. Evelyn Trayner had been with the Agency for years, and everyone half suspected she'd been in love with Ivor Raskin since long before she'd been assigned to him when he came in from the field. It was almost too much to believe. "Are you sure?" Mitch said, knowing even as he asked the question that Raskin would never have identified Evelyn as the caller if he wasn't sure.

"Yes. She's been taking money from D'eillmoreaux for almost ten years. We had a full financial investigation done, and we've searched her home. She's the one who betrayed you three years ago, Mitch.''

A weight, like a ton of steel, suddenly lifted from Mitch's heart. It hadn't been Tina. ''You're sure?'' he asked again, almost afraid to give up the suspicions he'd lived with for the past two years only to wake up and find this whole conversation nothing but a dream.

''Dammit, Mitch, yes, I'm sure,'' Raskin snarled. ''Evelyn betrayed you for a nice, fat sum of money from D'eillmoreaux, and she's done it again.''

Raskin's last words made it through the rainbow of joy and hope that Mitch had let nearly consume him. ''Done it again? She's told D'eillmoreaux about me? But how?''

''She managed to break into the file where your new identity had been sealed. Don't ask me how,'' Raskin growled. ''Obviously the woman has developed some talents none of us here knew about. She broke in, that's all there is to it, and we're pretty damned certain she's already informed D'eillmoreaux about you. There was a call to his place registered on her phone an hour ago.''

''D'eillmoreaux knows I'm Jake Blaggette,'' Mitch said to himself, mulling the possible consequences of that betrayal through his mind.

''Yes,'' Raskin said, thinking Mitch was talking to him. ''That's why you've got to get out of there.''

Fear, such as he'd never known in his life, gripped Mitch's heart. Tina. D'eillmoreaux knew who he was, and the man was vengeful if nothing else. He would be furious Jake was still alive, but he wouldn't risk coming directly after him again, which meant he might use Tina to draw Mitch to him. But D'eillmoreaux would have to kill an innocent person, because he wouldn't be able to let her live after he used her for bait. It was crazy, and that was why

Mitch knew he was right. He dropped the receiver and pulled out his cell phone, quickly dialing the café's number.

"I'll send someone else in undercover," Raskin said, not realizing Mitch had stopped listening. "We'll get him. But I want you out of that town now."

Mitch listened to the café's phone ring. Answer Tina, he prayed. Please, answer.

Tina eased the Malibu out of the parking lot and headed for home, thankful Lianne had finally returned her car. But she didn't know how she'd gotten through the dinner crowd. Thankfully, it had been light. A few people had teased her when she'd confused their orders, or dropped something, and it had been all she could do to hold herself together.

She'd seen her uncle watching her, wondering what was wrong, waiting for her to come to him, talk to him, as she usually did. But this time she couldn't. At least not yet. She was too terrified. All she could think of was what she'd seen on Mitch's laptop. Mitch was Jake. It explained so much, and it explained nothing. Now she knew why she'd had those feelings of familiarity whenever around him. Now she knew that when he'd touched his finger to her lips, as Jake always had, her imagination wasn't getting the better of her. Now she knew she wasn't crazy because when Mitch had been making love to her, she'd thought it was Jake. But it was still almost impossible for her to accept. Mitch didn't look anything like Jake. He didn't sound like him, or even walk like him. And his eyes were brown instead of blue.

Yet she'd always known. Somewhere deep down inside of her, somehow she'd known. But it still didn't make sense, and she had even more questions now than she had before. She just wasn't certain she was ready for the answers. And she wasn't certain how she should feel. Jake had come back, but he wasn't Jake anymore. He'd come back as someone else. He'd lied to her, and he'd seduced her. Why?

Tina turned the car onto the road that led to her house. She was grateful to her uncle for taking the kids for burgers and video games when she'd gotten back to the café and he'd seen she was upset. He'd offered to keep them all night, but she'd said no, she only needed a few hours to herself. It might have been better if she'd let the kids stay at Deano's, but she didn't want to be in the house alone all night, with her thoughts, with her ghosts.

She was surprised and more than a little disconcerted to see Dack's patrol car sitting in her driveway when she pulled in, the sheriff leaning casually against its rear bumper. Parking to one side of the drive, as she always did, Tina climbed from the car, stifling a sigh. "Dack, what are you doing here? Something wrong?"

He waited until she crossed the drive and paused near him before answering. "You need to come with me, Tina." He took her by the arm and steered her around the patrol car toward the passenger door.

Fear clutched at her. "Did something happen to the kids?" She turned and grabbed his arm. "Dack?"

He shook his head. "No. Nothing."

"My sisters?"

"Ain't nothing happened to no one," he said gruffly, and yanked open the passenger door.

Tina stared into his car, suddenly overcome by an intense sense of wariness and not knowing exactly why. She looked back up at him. "What's wrong? Where are we going?"

His pale brown-green eyes met hers and there was a sadness behind the hard glare that sent a shiver racing over her skin, turning it to gooseflesh. "I just wanted to take care of you, Tina. That's all I ever wanted. You knew that."

"But…" She stared at him, not understanding what he was saying, what he was doing, only knowing that her fear was mounting. He sounded calmly insane.

"Why couldn't you just let me take care of you like I wanted, huh, Tina? That's all I wanted, but you had to keep ruining things."

"Dack," Tina said, trying desperately to control her fear. "What's going on? Why are you saying these things?" She tried to yank free of him, but his grasp on her arm tightened, and his fingers dug into her flesh. She cringed in pain. "Dack. Please, you're hurting me."

"You shoulda just let me take care of you, Tina. I've wanted that forever, you know? Just me and you." He shoved her toward the seat without waiting to see if she'd climb in on her own, then glared down at her, the look on his face a mixture of anger and pain. "Don't try to get out. You have to come with me." He slammed the door, turned and walked toward the front of the car.

Terror threatened to strangle her. She didn't know what was happening, but she knew she didn't want to go with him. She waited until he was almost on the other side, then yanked the door open and bolted out.

Dack was on her within seconds, grabbing her arm and nearly jerking her from her feet. He dragged her back to the car.

"Dack, stop it," Tina screamed. "Why are you doing this?"

He forced her back into her seat. "I don't want to hurt you, Tina," he said, staring down at her with eyes that seemed to have turned as cold as ice, "but I will if you make me." He slammed the door again, stalked around the front of the car, and climbed in behind the steering wheel.

Tina stared at him, suddenly remembering the other times she'd glimpsed a darkness in Dack Brenaud. Like when he'd purposely goaded Jake into a near fist fight at the fair... Sometimes over the years she'd tried to tell herself she had imagined it, but she knew she hadn't. The laughing, affable, good-ol'-boy charm of the man she'd known was only a facade. This was the real Dack Brenaud, and she was suddenly more frightened than she'd ever been in her life.

Mitch glanced at his speedometer. Ninety. His headlights cut through the darkness that had descended while he'd been talking to Raskin. He looked into his rearview mirror, surprised not to see Dack Brenaud's patrol car hugging his bumper, red and blue lights flashing wildly, siren shrieking through the night.

His wheels squealed in protest and the tires on one side of the car left the pavement as he took a curve in the road without slowing down. Seconds later he swerved into Tina's driveway, the T-bird momentarily fishtailing on the loose gravel. He saw the Malibu parked to one side of the drive, doors shut, lights off. Mitch slammed on the brakes and skidded to a stop near the path that led to the house. Instinct told him instantly that something was wrong. The porch light was on, but the windows remained dark, the curtains drawn back. He remembered she'd said she had a timer for the porch light because she was always forgetting to turn it on and off. But she wouldn't be in the house with all the lights off at seven-thirty. Especially with the kids.

He drew his gun, threw open his car door and ran up to the porch. "Tina?" He banged his fist on the door. "Tina?" Then he saw the note. The blood in his veins froze as he stared at it.

Jake,
   Come alone, or Tina will be killed.

It could still be a trap. He could be wrong. His suspicions could still be right. But he knew they weren't.

There was no signature on the note, no named place where he was supposed to go, but he didn't need either. He knew exactly who'd taken Tina. He knew where they'd gone, and he knew why. He had no doubt, however, that if he just walked into the place, neither one of them would make it out alive, and he couldn't let her die. It was his fault she was in this situation. She hadn't done anything wrong. She hadn't betrayed him.

All she'd ever done was love him.

Agony tore at Mitch's gut. He'd been such a fool. If only he'd trusted her, and told her the truth. If he'd just called her when he'd come out of that coma, given her the benefit of the doubt, her life wouldn't be in danger now.

Hatred, dark and seething, filled his mind as he thought of Tina being held by Lawrence D'eillmoreaux.

Ripping the note from the tack that held it in place, he turned and ran back toward his car. If D'eillmoreaux or any of his goons harmed her in any way, he'd kill them. He wouldn't care if they were armed, he wouldn't care if they surrendered. He wouldn't even care if they begged for their lives. If they'd harmed Tina, he would kill them all.

Halfway to his car headlights pierced the darkness and pinned him in their glare. An RV that looked more like an ancient box on wheels pulled into the drive and Mitch stopped.

"Hey, Ryan," Deano Peychaud yelled from the driver's window. A minute later he climbed out of a side door. "You two going somewhere? Need me and the missus to keep the kids for the night?"

Mitch looked at the older man, trying to think of an answer, but before he could, Deano's eyes shot to the house, saw the lights were out and looked back at Mitch. He told the kids and his wife to stay put, closed the door, and walked toward Mitch.

"What's wrong?" Deano asked softly, a deep frown pulling at his brow.

Mitch made an instant decision. He needed help, and there was no one else he could trust. The Agency couldn't get anyone here for at least an hour, even if they flew out of Savannah by chopper. And the sheriff wasn't even a consideration. He held out the note to Tina's uncle.

Deano took the scrap of paper and read the short note. His eyes, suddenly hard and cold, turned back to Mitch. "Who wrote this?" he asked, his tone murderous.

"I don't know who wrote it," Mitch said, "but I know who's responsible for it, and where she's at. I'm going to need help to get her out alive though."

Deano nodded. "Then you've got it." He turned, but Mitch grabbed his arm.

"Are you sure, Deano? This is going to be dangerous," he warned.

Deano met Mitch's eyes square on. "Son, it can't be any more dangerous than wrestling with a gator, or holding your own against the Vietcong, and I've done both."

He opened the RV's door and the kids piled out, all chattering excitedly.

"Marge," Deano said softly as he helped her step down, "we got trouble. Stay here with the kids. Lock the doors, and don't let anybody in, you understand?"

She looked at him, concern in her eyes. "Be careful," she said, then turned and walked toward the house, ushering the kids up the walkway before her.

Deano went back into the RV and rummaged around in a closet.

Another set of headlights pulled into the drive, and Mitch swore as Deputy Harlon Gates climbed from his patrol car. "What the hell's going on?" Gates demanded.

Mitch frowned, crumpling the note in his fist. "Nothing. Why?"

"The sheriff's not answering his radio."

"So? What are you doing here?" Mitch asked, suspicious.

Gates drew a wallet from his back pocket and flipped it open. His ID card said FBI, Internal Affairs.

"You're FBI?" Mitch snapped, fury nearly overtaking him. "What the hell is this?"

"I was assigned here to watch the sheriff. A case we had down here a while back had too many unanswered questions and coincidences. And they all seemed to point toward Brenaud."

Deano joined them.

Mitch made another instant decision, hurriedly filled Gates in on what was happening, and told him to follow them, lights and sirens off.

Once in the T-bird, Mitch headed toward town. He pulled out his cell phone and called Raskin.

"I need backup," he said, the minute Raskin answered the phone.

"Where the hell are you?"

"On my way to D'eillmoreaux's."

"No," Raskin thundered. "You are not. I want you out of there."

"I'm going in. You've got twenty minutes."

"Dammit," Raskin bellowed, "you know I can't have backup there that fast. Your sheriff's crooked, which means I can't trust the rest of the department. Don't do this."

"I have to. Twenty minutes." Mitch cut the connection.

He knew by the time the Feds got to the mansion it would all be over one way or another, and he was going to do his best to make it over his way.

"So is it true?" Deano said, his voice hard as he stared at Mitch. "You're Jake? The one who left her three years ago?"

"I'm Jake," Mitch said, "but I didn't leave her. I was attacked on my way to Savannah to buy her an engagement ring. I managed to call the Agency after they left me for dead, then I lost consciousness. I didn't wake up from the coma for a year."

"So, why didn't you call her then? Why this charade?"

"Because I was a fool," Mitch said. He pulled the car up across the street from the Chancellor Oaks mansion. No one was at the gates, which stood open, and he didn't see anyone on the grounds. But he knew they were there, waiting, and the damned house was lit up like a Christmas tree. He turned to Deano. "The man in there is the one responsible for the attack on me three years ago. He also murdered my brother, and now he's holding Tina so that I'll come to him. Whatever happens, I won't let him kill her."

The older man nodded. "Good. Then you won't mind if I kill the SOB if he's hurt my niece."

"You'll have to beat me to him."

They climbed quietly from the car and hurried across the street. Mitch waved at Gates to go to the left. They went to the right.

"We need to get around back," Mitch whispered as they stood within the shadows of a tall oak at the far perimeter of the property. He motioned for Deano to follow him and ran along the fence line.

Mitch stared at the row of tall windows at the rear of the house. Light poured from them onto the deck and sloping lawn. The other night he'd looked through those windows, filled with rage and jealousy as he'd watched Tina smile at D'eillmoreaux and touch her champagne glass to his. God, how could he have been so stupid?

Everything he'd thought about her in the past two years, every suspicion and doubt was wrong, and he should have known better.

Deano nudged him and pointed to a guard standing in the shadows at the corner of the house.

Mitch nodded and started to move, but the older man stopped him and indicated he'd do it. Before Mitch could argue, Deano slipped into the shadows and was gone. Seconds later, he was back, a smile on his face. "All done," he said softly.

They moved toward the house, then froze as another guard came around the far corner.

Deano indicated this one was Mitch's.

Mitch moved stealthily forward, hugging the wall of the house. The man heard him coming when he was just a yard away. He grabbed for the gun at his waist, but it was too late. Mitch's fist connected with his jaw, then the side of his other hand crashed down on the man's neck.

A faint grunt escaped his lips and he dropped to the ground.

Climbing onto the deck, Mitch peeked through the window. Every ugly curse he'd ever known moved through his head as he saw Tina sitting on the white couch, Lawrence D'eillmoreaux standing before her, smiling smugly and saying something Mitch couldn't make out. He was about to turn and make his way back to Deano, when a movement across the room caught his attention.

Dack Brenaud walked through the archway that led from the room, a drink in one hand, his gun in the other, an unhappy scowl on his face.

Mitch jumped to the ground and ran to where Deano was waiting. "She's in there," he said softly. "So is D'eillmoreaux."

"Who?" Deano said.

"Laren McAllreaux. It's an alias. He was the head of a crime organization I busted in New Orleans six years ago. We thought he was dead."

Deano nodded. "So this is all about revenge."

"Yes. Your sheriff's in there, too."

"Brenaud?" Deano shook his head, but didn't look too surprised. "Well, I'll be. I always could spot a snake a mile away. Just didn't know how low his belly really was to the ground."

"Now you do," Mitch said. "It's draggin'. But I don't know how many more of D'eillmoreaux's goons are in there."

"How do you want to do this?" Deano asked, pulling a gun from his pocket.

Mitch glanced at the weapon, surprised, then at the older man.

Deano smiled. "Keep it tucked away in the RV. Never know when you'll need a little protection."

Mitch nodded. "You work your way around and come in the front with Gates. I'll go in the back. Let me make the first move."

Deano disappeared into the shadows even before Mitch was through talking. He waited ten seconds, then climbed back onto the deck and made his way toward the windows and the sliding glass door next to them. Once beside it, he pushed slightly on the handle, testing it. It moved, indicating it was unlocked.

Mitch inhaled deeply, drew his own gun, and counted to three. "Show time," he whispered softly, and pushed open the door.

Chapter 15

Lawrence D'eillmoreaux turned toward Mitch as he stepped casually into the room. "Ah, Jake Blaggette, I presume?" He swept out an arm in exaggerated welcome. "Please, come in. We've been waiting for you."

Mitch nodded. "D'eillmoreaux." The man didn't look any different than he had six years ago, on the night Mitch thought had been D'eillmoreaux's last.

Dack leveled his gun at Mitch, who ignored him. He glanced at Tina, who sat on the white sofa. She wasn't hurt, and Mitch tried to reassure her with his eyes that everything was going to be all right. He hoped it was the truth.

Lawrence smiled coldly. "Welcome to my humble home, Jake," he said, drawing Mitch's gaze and attention again. "It's been a long time."

"Too long," Mitch said, watching the other man with cool appraisal.

D'eillmoreaux smiled. "But you've, ah, changed since our last little encounter."

"I didn't have a choice. But then, you know that, don't you?"

D'eillmoreaux shrugged. "Do I? Hmm." A smile that looked almost innocent curved his lips. "Oh well. But I'm glad you decided to accept my invitation."

"It was so gracious," Mitch said, sarcasm dripping from his tone as their eyes met and he took several steps farther into the room. "How could I refuse?"

"Yes—" he glanced at Tina, beside him "—how could you?"

She looked from one man to the other, still terrified, but no longer confused. Dack had angrily explained everything on the way to the mansion, thinking she would believe and understand that he'd done it all because he loved her. She tried to catch Mitch's eye now, but he kept his gaze coldly focused on the man beside her.

Mitch was furious. She could almost feel the heat of his rage emanating from him. Her captor was obviously arrogantly amused. He had been the epitome of charming since the moment Dack dragged her into the mansion, just as he had been the night of the party, but this time she'd been able to see the evil that lay just beneath the boyishly handsome face and cultivated charm. Cruelty played upon the almost effeminate curves of his full lips now, while the warmth in his brown eyes when he looked at her, the classic lines of his features and the expensively tailored clothes, were no longer enough to hide the ruthless thug that he really was.

"Let her go," Mitch said.

There was a silken thread of warning to his voice that Tina had never heard before and she wasn't sure whether she found it comforting or disturbing.

"Let her go?" Lawrence D'eillmoreaux chuckled softly, slapping a hand against the silk lapel of his smoking jacket.

"Oh, I don't think so, Jake. You know I try never to leave any loose ends, and—" he bent and reached into an elegant porcelain box on the coffee table, drew out a cigarette, straightened and looked back at Mitch "—well, she'd be a loose end. Don't you think?"

"She won't talk," Dack Brenaud said, stepping forward. "I told you I'll—"

D'eillmoreaux glanced at the sheriff, the look in his eyes becoming murderous. "You'll what?"

Stains of scarlet instantly appeared on Dack's cheeks and he seemed to nearly wither under the man's glare. "I, ah, told you, I'd take care of her."

"Like you took care of Jake three years ago?"

Mitch's gaze moved to the sheriff, and anger singed at the edge of his control. He should have known.

"I thought he was dead," Dack said. "He should have been, after what we did to him."

Why hadn't she ever guessed? Tina's gaze darted from one man to the other.

"Well, you obviously thought wrong," D'eillmoreaux snapped, the cool facade breaking for a moment.

"Guess you didn't get your money's worth, did you, Larry?" Mitch goaded, knowing his opponent hated losing money almost as much as he hated being called Larry.

D'eillmoreaux turned back to Mitch and smiled coldly. "You shouldn't have come back here, Jake."

"I had to."

"Really?" His gaze slid to Tina, and a look of appreciative lust came into his eyes. "Well, I guess I can understand that, but..."

"You killed my brother, Larry," Mitch said, trying to get the man's attention off Tina. "That was a bad mistake."

"Actually," he said, smiling, "I thought it was rather a coup. First you, then your brother. But—" he threw Dack a sneering glance "—I thought you were dead." He smiled again as he looked back at Mitch. "It's all right though, because now you've given the sheriff a second chance, and I'm sure this time he'll do it right."

"No." Tina bolted from the couch.

D'eillmoreaux grabbed her, nearly jerking her from her feet, and dragged her up against him. "She is beautiful, Jake." He ran one hand slowly, intimately, down Tina's side, over her hip, down the length of her thigh, but never took his eyes from Mitch. "I'm looking forward to finding out if she's as good in bed as she looks."

"Hey, wait a minute," the sheriff said, his eyes narrowing with anger.

"Shut up," D'eillmoreaux snapped.

Mitch's gaze never left his opponent's.

Mitch felt a hot knot of fire in his gut, felt his hatred for the man in front of him flare to new depths. Everything in him suddenly ached to wrap his hands around D'eillmoreaux's neck and strangle the life from him.

Just then Mitch saw Deano look through the arch into the large living room. He nodded to Mitch, then glanced toward the windows, gauging whether or not his reflection would show in them if he tried to enter the room. Less than ten feet separated him from Dack Brenaud, who stood with his back to the archway. Deano slid his gun back into his pocket and, crouching low, crept around the corner toward his prey.

At the last second Dack sensed someone behind him and started to turn.

Deano straightened instantly, swung his hand into the air and brought it down in a forceful blow at the base of Dack's neck.

A grunt of surprise and pain escaped Dack's lips. The gun flew from his hand and crashed onto a glass end table.

Startled, D'eillmoreaux spun and fired wildly, then spun again and aimed at Mitch.

"No!" Tina screamed and threw herself at D'eillmoreaux, knocking him off balance.

Mitch lunged across the coffee table and tackled D'eillmoreaux. They fell onto the sofa, grappling over the gun, limbs tangled. Suddenly D'eillmoreaux jerked away from Mitch and jumped to his feet, the gun in his hand. An ugly smile creased his face as he pointed the weapon at Mitch, who leapt at him.

The sound of another gunshot filled the cavernous room, echoing off the high ceiling.

Tina stared at them, too terrified to scream, to move or even take a breath. What seemed endless seconds of silence passed. Time froze. No one moved, and the only sound she could hear was her own hammering heartbeat, echoing in her ears. Tears filled her eyes.

Mitch kept his grip on the gun, even as he felt the blood beneath his hand, warm and spreading. Death was near. He could feel it. He looked into Lawrence D'eillmoreaux's eyes. Hatred blazed from their dark depths, along with fear. Mitch had seen enough death to know that both would be extinguished forever within a matter of seconds.

A minute later he pulled away and pushed himself to his feet. It was finally over.

"I would have rather seen him stand trial," Harlon said, staring down at D'eillmoreaux. "But he didn't leave me much choice." He slid his gun back into his holster.

Tina started, Harlon's movement and words jerking her from the mesmerizing spell of fear that had momentarily frozen her reactions and thoughts. "Jake?" she said haltingly, her voice barely above a whisper as relief and joy filled her heart, rushing through in hot, delicious waves.

He turned. "Tina. Are you all right? He didn't hurt you?"

She shook her head and ran into his arms, throwing her own around him. Jake. He had come back to her. The words kept echoing through her mind.

"I called the state troopers," Gates said, as he helped Deano finish tying Dack's hands with a cord he'd ripped off the drapes. The sheriff had taken a bullet in the shoulder when D'eillmoreaux fired blindly, and now seemed in no mood to do anything more than lie on the floor and moan.

Mitch held Tina tightly, drinking in the fact that she was all right, that she wasn't hurt, that she was in his arms, her body pressed to his, that she was holding him, that it was finally over.

The sound of approaching sirens filled the air.

"Guess I'll go out and greet them," Deano mumbled, realizing that his presence wasn't needed anymore.

Mitch looked down at Tina. "I'm sorry," he said softly. He brushed a hand tenderly over her cheek, swept back the hair from her face. "I'm so sorry." He glanced toward D'eillmoreaux, lying lifeless on the floor, then back at Tina. "I never thought...we never knew..." He shook his head. They'd suspected all the wrong people, for all the wrong reasons.

She looked up at him, into those dark, fathomless eyes that were brown instead of blue, at the face that was supposed to be Jake's, but wasn't, and remembered the notes she'd read on his computer, remembered everything that had happened over the past few days, over the past few years. Suddenly all her joy and relief and hopes deserted her, overtaken by a fury beyond any she'd ever felt. Tina jerked herself out of his arms and took a step away from him, needing to put some distance between them. "Sorry?"

she said coldly. Her entire body began to tremble with her rage. "Sorry?"

Before he could respond, she spun about and ran from the house.

"Tina, wait," Mitch called.

"Let her go," Deano said, coming back into the room, a state trooper behind him. "Ain't no reasoning with her when she's mad."

Mitch glanced at the older man, then turned and followed Tina onto the deck. She stood at its edge, looking out at the river, her arms wrapped tightly around herself. "Tina," he said, moving to stand beside her. "I am sorry. I..."

She turned then, and anything else he'd thought to say died on his lips at the hard reproach he saw glistening in her eyes.

"You're sorry?" she said, her words clipped with frost. "For what? Lying to me? Using me? What? What are you sorry for, *Mitch?*"

"Tina, it's me," he said, pushing the words past a throat threatening to close with the emotion crowding in on him, and grasping her upper arms. "Jake."

She jerked away from him again and stepped back. "I know who you are, and I know what happened three years ago. What I don't know, what I don't understand is why no one notified me about what happened to you. We were supposed to have been engaged, we'd planned to get married. Why didn't your brother or that precious Agency of yours call me? Why didn't you call when you came out of the coma? But even more important," she continued, her voice becoming as shrill as her nerves, "why did you come back and lie to me? Why did you pretend you were someone else?"

Tears fell from her eyes as she stared at him, waiting for him to answer, waiting for an excuse she could accept, and knowing there wasn't any. Anger and hurt and frustration tore at her insides like claws, mauling her emotions, shredding her memories and destroying her heart.

"I couldn't tell you, Tina. We weren't sure..." He saw the look that came into her eyes and knew he'd started to say the wrong thing.

"Oh, yes, *the Agency,*" Tina said, her voice full of distaste. "Can't you even think without them?"

"You don't understand," Mitch said. "I trusted you then, but afterward, everything seemed to point..."

"To me. And you didn't trust me enough, you didn't love me enough, to know I could have never done that."

He reached out for her again. "I was wrong, but..."

She pulled away from him. "Yes, you were. And there really isn't anything more to say." She couldn't bring herself to call him Jake, yet he wasn't Mitch to her anymore either. "I loved you, and you thought I'd betrayed you." Her eyes narrowed slightly. "I don't understand how you could believe I would ever have done that."

"I didn't want to." At that moment he would have given anything to erase the hurt and disappointment he saw in her eyes. "I swear I didn't want to believe that, but you were the only one I told here that I was an agent, Tina. We didn't know about D'eillmoreaux. We thought he was dead. Then Perry was murdered and..." He shrugged, knowing there was no reason to go on, no excuse she would ever accept, because there was no excuse he could accept.

"And naturally you thought I had something to do with that, too."

The guilt he felt was like the weight of the world on his heart, but the pain he knew he'd caused her—over the past few years, over the past few days, was almost more than he could bear. "Tina, maybe if we..."

She slapped his hand away as he tried to take hers, his

touch a hot caress that could still affect her, but that she
didn't want to feel anymore. Her thoughts whirled between
the past and present as she stared at him. He had accused
her of betraying him and he'd been wrong, but with his
accusation and suspicions he had betrayed her. Squaring
her shoulders, she drew herself up stiffly and pulled on a
mantle of hard, cold composure that she was far from really
feeling. "Goodbye, Jake," she said. "Or Mitch. Or whoever you decide to be next." Turning, she walked back into
the house, past her uncle, and toward the front door, knowing this time it really was the final goodbye.

Three hours later, Mitch pulled the T-bird up beside his
cabin at the Magnolia Inn, killed the engine and sat staring
past the windshield at the night. Through the half-open window beside him he could hear the soft sounds of the night
creatures in the woods just a few yards away. A nearly
starless sky blanketed the earth like a drape of black velvet,
while the barest sliver of moon hung cradled within that
darkness, just above the ragged silhouette of nearby treetops.

Everything seemed so peaceful, yet peace was the farthest thing from what he was feeling. Loss. Emptiness. Anger. Guilt. Those were the feelings that filled him, gnawed
at him, threatened never to leave him.

*Goodbye, Jake. Or Mitch. Or whoever you decide to be
next.*

Her words echoed mercilessly through his mind. He
threw open the car door and stalked into the cabin, slamming its door behind him and throwing his jacket and gun
on the bed. The message light on the phone was flashing.
He glanced at the computer, which he hadn't put away
earlier. *You have mail,* the little e-mail icon flashed. He
wasn't interested.

He turned to the mirror hanging on the wall over the bureau and stared at himself. A man with a face he had yet to get used to stared back at him, looking tired and beaten. Mitch ran a hand through his coarse, dark hair, then walked toward the mirror. Who was he?

Mitch Ryan stared back at him.

He pulled the brown contact lenses from his eyes, grasped the edges of the bureau tightly and looked back into the mirror.

Jake Blaggette's eyes stared back at him—but it was still Mitch Ryan's face.

Who was he? The question played through his mind like an endless recording. Who was he?

He spun away from the mirror and crossed the room, pausing to stare out at the night, yet not actually seeing it.

Jake would never even have considered leaving the Agency, not even for Tina. Mitch would, in a minute. Jake had never thought twice about killing a man in the line of duty. Mitch had felt an overwhelming sense of regret as he'd watched Lawrence D'eillmoreaux die, in spite of the fact the man had been responsible for the attack on him three years ago, for the destruction of his life, and Perry's death. He dropped onto the bed and stared at the ceiling. And he would have killed Tina.

He closed his eyes. Loss. Emptiness. Anger. Guilt. The sensations filled him, hammered at him, threatened to consume him. Was that how he was going to feel for the rest of his life?

He sat up, jerked the phone receiver from its cradle and pushed the message button.

"Call me, dammit."

Mitch swore. Didn't the man ever sleep? He rose and walked to the desk, pulling up his messages on the computer. They were both from Raskin, saying the same thing his phone message had said. Mitch walked back to the phone and punched out Raskin's cell number.

He answered on the second ring, and from the sound of his voice he hadn't been asleep.

"It's me," Mitch said. "It's over."

"Good, but I ought to have you brought up on charges for disobeying me and going in when I ordered you not to. Are you okay?"

That was the question of the century, and he didn't have an answer.

"Evelyn's been arrested," Raskin went on, not waiting for Mitch to respond, "and she's been talking her head off. Obviously she figures if she's going down, it isn't going to be alone."

"Why'd she do it?" Mitch asked, figuring he already knew the answer.

"Money, what else is there?"

What else is there? Mitch didn't know anymore.

"Evidently D'eillmoreaux wanted to make sure we didn't come anywhere near his new operation after he ditched us in New Orleans. He set his sights on getting an informant established in our office, and at the time Evelyn was the perfect target. Her mother was in the hospital dying of cancer, and her insurance had quit paying. The bill collectors were banging on Evelyn's door, the bank was threatening to take the family house, and a repo grunt had already tried to grab her car. D'eillmoreaux's offer was too good to refuse. All she had to do was keep him informed on your whereabouts, and what the Agency was up to."

"So she warned him when I came to Reimour Crossings three years ago," Mitch said, his voice flat, a statement rather than a question.

"Well, since your vacation destination was a secret, technically no, she didn't warn him, though she obviously would have. D'eillmoreaux spotted you. Evelyn said it was just dumb luck. He was returning home from a trip abroad earlier than expected and was being driven home in his limo. The car has blacked-out windows so he was able to see you, but you couldn't see him."

"Dumb luck," Mitch repeated.

"Yeah. Evelyn claims he called her and sounded ready to kill her for not warning him you were there."

"She was lucky he didn't just send one of his goons for a little social call."

"He didn't want to lose his informant," Raskin said. "Even if she had screwed up. Anyway, he knew you were still alive the whole time. She did tell him that. But she had to do a lot of fancy-stepping to find your new identity and destination, since I locked those papers in my private safe." Raskin sighed deeply. "It was all a damned coincidence, Mitch. You taking a vacation in the same place where D'eillmoreaux had set up his new operation, and him spotting you. One chance in a million."

"Yeah," Mitch said, one chance in a million that had totally changed and destroyed his life, and gotten his brother murdered. He hung up and lay back on the bed. "One chance in a million," he mumbled softly. One damned, lousy chance in a million, and it had been all his.

For the next couple of hours he paced, cursed, broke a half dozen of the inn's pencils between his hands, beat his fists into a pillow in frustration and thought about all the mistakes he'd made over the past two years. He pondered the question of who he was, looked in the mirror, then, for the first time in longer than he could remember, he looked into his heart. It was filled with shadows.

Memories hammered at him. He thought of the past, of the future, of what he should have done and what he had done. But most of all, he thought about Tina.

He'd trusted her once, then thought she'd betrayed him. He had come back to confront her, not giving her the benefit of the doubt, refusing to believe he could ever trust anyone again, especially her, and she'd saved his life.

By the time the sun began creeping over the treetops in the distance, Mitch knew what he had to do. He wasn't sure if it would work, figured it most likely wouldn't, but he had to try. After a quick shower and shave, he donned a clean pair of jeans and a shirt, ran a brush through his hair and left the cabin. Five minutes later he slowed the Thunderbird slightly as he neared the café. He saw her Malibu in the parking lot. Then, in the split instant just before his view inside the café was gone, he spotted Tina at the cash register.

She turned toward him then, as if feeling his gaze upon her, realizing he was there, and Mitch pressed down harder on the accelerator and headed out of town.

Chapter 16

Tina moved through the morning like a zombie; waiting on customers, ringing up orders, taking money and paying attention to none of it. She'd felt this way three years ago, and she had hoped it was a feeling she would never have the misfortune to experience again. Her plan had been to never give her heart to anyone again, but she hadn't counted on losing it all over again to Jake.

She'd gotten little sleep after the fiasco at the mansion, but then she hadn't expected to get any. She had spent the night tossing and turning, staring up through the darkness and hurting worse than she'd ever thought she could hurt. Her thoughts had blurred with her memories until she hadn't known what to think anymore. She'd hated Jake for leaving her, and knew she would always love him. She had cursed him to the blackest depths of hell, and secretly hoped he would come back to her someday. He was the man of her heart, and yet he wasn't that man at all. There were so many things about Mitch Ryan that reminded her of Jake, and yet there were so many differences that at times, while she'd lain in bed trying to sleep and losing the battle, she'd wondered if she had just dreamed up this whole situation in her mind as some kind of twisted torment.

Jake and Mitch. They looked nothing alike, sounded nothing alike, yet when Mitch held her in his arms, when his lips ravaged hers and his body pressed against her own…

A headache began to throb at her temples.

Was Mitch Jake? she asked herself for the hundredth time. Or was Jake Mitch? She didn't know. Did it matter? She didn't know that either. What she did know was that she was finding it almost impossible to accept that both men were one and the same.

A long sigh of frustration slipped past her lips. She grabbed the order Deano slid onto the serving counter, turned and dropped it. The plate shattered on the floor, along with fried sausage, scrambled eggs and Deano's special home potatoes. No one looked up. No one said anything. It wasn't her first accident of the morning, and it most likely wouldn't be her last.

Kneeling, she mopped up the spilled food. Whoever he was, Jake Blaggette or Mitch Ryan, she hated him—and she loved him desperately. She needed him and cursed him, yearned to be in his arms again and wished he had never come back to Reimour Crossings. Tossing the food in the garbage, along with the broken plate shards, Tina turned toward the back window and looked out at the kids. Joey and Jimmy were building a fort in the sandbox, while Lily sat nearby, her nose in a book, as always. Tina smiled to herself. They were such good kids. She'd always hoped, always prayed…. But it wasn't meant to be. The thought brought a surge of fresh tears to her eyes, and she hurriedly blinked them back.

He'd thought she had betrayed him.

He *had* betrayed her.

A flash of black in the mirror on the wall beside the window caught her eye, reflecting whatever was behind her on the main street. Tina turned, emotions raw and on edge, hoping it was him, damning him for coming.

But there was nothing there.

As the car neared the spot where it had happened, Mitch eased his foot slightly off the accelerator, and the Thunderbird slowed. His gaze involuntarily went to the rearview mirror, every muscle in his body tensing as his mind half expected his eyes to see a black pickup truck racing toward the rear of his car.

But the highway behind him was empty.

He looked toward the edge of the road and the copse of young trees where there had once been entrance to a small clearing. There was no evidence of a car ever having been forced off the pavement. There were no skid marks, no broken bushes or toppled trees. The wild grasses alongside the road stood tall, the bushes full. He drove on without stopping. That was one memory he could do without, one place he didn't care to visit again.

For the next two hours he drove the winding old highway, but his mind wasn't on the scenery. He drove automatically, his eyes guiding his control of the car, while his thoughts ambled through the past—not just Jake Blaggette's past, but also Mitch Ryan's, because both were entwined with his memories of, his desires for, Tina.

He made it to Savannah by midday, avoiding a backup on the parkway by turning off long before he was near downtown. The city was one that cherished its history and never changed, so it wasn't hard to find his way around the business district to the older section of town, even though he'd only been here once before, for a few days before he'd gone to Reimour Crossings, three years ago.

He drove slowly down West Oglethorpe Avenue. Passing Colonial Park Cemetery, he turned left and parked the car. He'd avoided doing this for two years, but now he had to confront the last of his past. It was the only way he could go on. The only hope he had. Climbing from the car, he walked across the street and entered Columbia Square. It was one of many sprawling parks set about the old city, but this was the only one Mitch was interested in.

Mitch's gaze wandered the grounds as his mind's eye turned the peaceful park sinister with darkness. Night could be beautiful in a place like this, but he knew it could also be deadly. He looked back at the fountain. This was where they'd found his brother's body.

A long sigh rumbled through his frame, settled upon his lips, then slipped away. This was where Perry's body had been left, the last place he'd been, but it wasn't where he'd died. Mitch hunkered down and touched the cool slate of the fountain's bordering edge. An image of himself and Perry as kids slowly formed in Mitch's mind. "I miss you, little brother," he said softly, not bothering to even try to stop the tears that filled his eyes. A few minutes later Mitch stood, but instead of walking back to his car, he turned toward the river.

Factors Walk, the pre-Civil War warehouses and office buildings that lined the river's edge and had been converted into restaurants and shops, was buzzing with tourists. A few of the shops had changed hands since the last time he'd been here, but most were the same. He pushed open the door of the same one he'd intended to visit three years ago.

* * *

The dinner rush was nearly over. Tina set the twins and Lily at a table near the office. Marge, who'd come to the café to pick up Deano for their weekly bridge night tournament, began serving them dinner.

"You sure you don't mind closing up by yourself tonight?" Deano asked, setting a T-bone steak dinner down on the counter in front of Fred Gateau, who hadn't eaten a meal away from the café since his wife died, a year earlier.

Tina smiled. "Uncle Deano, you ask me that same question every week."

"Well," he said, laughing, "one of these times you might do me a favor and say yes."

Marge threw him a mocking glare. "You give up poker, old man, and I'll give up bridge."

Tina chuckled softly and stifled a yawn. She was exhausted, both mentally and physically. Black clouds had been hanging over her mood all day and she'd done her best to battle them off, but it seemed she was losing the war.

From the moment she'd walked away from Mitch... Jake... Tina sighed in frustration. She couldn't decide how to think of him anymore, so she told herself not to think of him at all. And that didn't work either.

Now all she wanted to do was close up the café, go home, put the kids to bed and submerge herself for several hours in a very hot tub of water and softly scented bubbles.

The bell over the door tinkled merrily as someone entered.

Tina nearly groaned aloud, having been hopeful they'd seen their last dinner customer for the evening. She looked up from the slice of apple pie she was lifting onto a plate, and her heart nearly stopped.

Mitch's gaze caught hers instantly and refused to let her look away.

Tina watched him approach. Part of her wanted to flee. Another part wanted to run into his arms. She hated him. She loved him.

He crossed the room, his steps slow and deliberate, then paused in front of her.

Everyone in the room turned to see who had entered. Movements instantly stilled, conversation died, and the room became deathly quiet. Some patrons sneered, some smiled, all prepared to jump to Tina's aid or defense, if needed.

"I need to talk to you," he said softly, his deep voice wrapping around her and sending delicious chills racing up her back.

Tina trembled. Suddenly talk was the last thing she felt capable of doing. She shook her head, feeling the tension-filled silence in the room bearing down on her, his gaze boring into hers. "I have customers," she finally said through stiff lips. She tried to ignore the now hammering beat of her heart, the way her anger and resentment toward him had all but disappeared the moment he'd walked into the room, the way her pulse wouldn't slow down, and how she couldn't quite catch a normal breath. "I have to close the café, take the kids home and—"

"Please?"

She looked into his eyes, those fathomless dark brown eyes that seemed capable of seeing straight through her, that were so familiar, yet so strange. Her resolve weakened further, and she struggled to hang on to it. "I'm sorry, maybe tomorrow. I'm too…"

He could feel everyone watching, listening, but he didn't care. The woman standing in front of him, the one he'd lost three years ago, the one he knew he might have lost again, was the only thing in his life that mattered anymore. "I was a fool, Tina," Mitch said, cutting her off. "My grandmother always used to tell me I had to learn to trust people, but I couldn't do it. After my parents died—'' he shook his head, as if he himself didn't even understand why he was the way he was ''—the only person I could relate to was my grandfather. Then he died too, and that was it for me. I couldn't trust anyone or anything. Not my grandmother, or even my own brother, at least not the way I should have. I've never trusted another agent, or even my boss. Only myself, Tina.''

His gaze probed hers, as if trying to see into her soul, to touch her heart, to make her understand what his words might fail to do.

"Then I fell in love with you, and suddenly I trusted you with my life.''

Tears filled her eyes. "But…''

He pressed a finger lightly to her lips to stop her words, the touch burning into her flesh.

"I did trust you—with my life, and I should have known you wouldn't betray me. I should have known, but when I came out of the coma and discovered you'd married someone else, and my brother had been murdered while trying to find out what had happened to me…'' He tore his gaze from her then, and stared toward the window, but the scene he saw was a montage of the past playing through his memory.

Flames—heat—fists—pain. His father, screaming at his mother, then purposely turning the steering wheel of the car toward the cliff. Perry crying because he'd broken their grandmother's favorite candy dish, but letting Jake take the blame. His grandfather lying sick in his hospital bed, saying goodbye, even as Jake begged him not to leave. His first partner, sneaking money off a bust, then implicating Jake. Tina saying she loved him, but couldn't accept his job.

"All I could think of then was that you were the only

one in Reimour Crossings who'd known I was an FBI agent. The Agency suspected you, so I did too."

He looked back at her then, the inner torment of the mistakes he'd made concerning her tearing into him. "But I never stopped loving you, Tina. I denied it, I tried to convince myself that all I felt for you was physical attraction, a lust that could be satisfied easily, then forgotten. But I knew, when I got to your house last night and found that D'eillmoreaux had taken you, that all I had been doing was lying to myself."

He reached out and took her hand, a spark of hope igniting within him when she didn't pull away. "I know there's probably a part of you that will never understand how I could have doubted you, and I don't know if you can forgive me, or if you even want to..."

As a silver stream of tears trickled from her eyes, Tina raised her free hand to his face, a featherlight touch of her fingertips across the rugged curve that had once been classically smooth and aquiline straight.

Emotions she'd tried to bury in the past and forever ignore and forget swept through her.

"I need you, Tina," Mitch said, his voice so husky with the feelings surging through him that his words were barely above a whisper. Dropping to one knee, he grabbed both her hands in his and looked up at her. "Three years ago you said you couldn't marry me." His own eyes filled with tears as he thought of how much he stood to gain...or lose, in the next few seconds. "Marry me now, Tina. Marry me now, and let me spend the rest of my life loving you and making up for all the hurt I've caused you."

Everything in Tina urged her to throw her arms around him and say yes, to shout it to the world, but she hesitated, though not because she was uncertain of her feelings. She knew now that she loved him as much, maybe even more, than she ever had.

He saw the hesitation in her eyes, and his hopes fell. He'd tried to tell himself all morning that she might say no, that she would most likely say no, but he'd known he had to try. And he wasn't ready to give up yet. "I love you."

This time it was Tina who pressed her fingers to his lips, silencing his words. "Three years ago I had misgivings about your job."

He nodded and stood.

"I still do," she said softly. Her heart was breaking. She was sending away the only man she'd ever loved, the only man she ever would love, again. But she had no more choice now than she'd had then. She couldn't live with the daily threat to his life, and even if she could find it in herself to do it, she wouldn't put her sons and Lily in that kind of jeopardy.

Mitch smiled. "It doesn't matter."

"Maybe it wouldn't if this only concerned me, but it doesn't." She sighed deeply and drew one of his hands between both of hers. Her heart contracted painfully as she stared up at him, her gaze taking in the powerful contours of his face, the ruggedly cut cheekbones, the flinty brown eyes. It was a face that would haunt her dreams for the rest of her life, just as Jake's had for the past three years. "I have to think of Lily and the twins," she said softly.

Mitch drew her into his arms then, crushing her against his body. "We'll think of them together," he said, brushing his lips across hers. "I'll quit the Agency. I'll wash cars, wrestle gators or pick cotton. I don't care, as long as you'll marry me."

She wanted so badly to stay in his embrace, to believe what he was saying. But she couldn't help but remember that this man was really two men. Mitch Ryan and Jake Blaggette. Which one loved her? Which one was asking her to marry him? The questions and doubts tore at her.

Mitch felt her hesitation, saw the skepticism in her eyes. "Marry me," he said again, his voice deep with the emotion raging through him. "Marry me, Tina."

Everything in her wanted to say yes. "But who are you?" she whispered instead, unaware she'd even said the words aloud until a frown drew Mitch's brow.

"I'm the man who loves you," he said, pressing his fingertips to her lips, then brushing his lips lightly across them.

A shiver of desire moved through her, slow and tantalizing.

"I'm the man who wants to feel your body next to mine every night as I sleep, then wake every morning and feel your kiss on my lips. I'm the man who wants to share your joy and your pain, and help you raise our children. I want to grow old with you, Tina, and I want my body to lie in its grave beside yours, while our spirits walk into eternity together.

"I'm the man who never stopped loving you, Tina," Mitch whispered finally. "And never will."

She looked into his eyes and suddenly knew that all the pain and the hurt of the past didn't matter anymore.

Epilogue

He stared at the computer screen, unable to believe the message he'd just read. Raskin had refused to accept his resignation.

"We're ready," Tina said, walking into the room.

Lily scooted past them and ushered the twins out to the car.

"I've got a problem I..." The words died on his lips as he turned and his gaze fell on Tina. The sight of her nearly brought his heartbeat to a stop and stole the breath from his lungs.

She had chosen to wear her mother's wedding gown, a figure hugging drape of ivory silk and lace that, on Tina, was both Victorian innocence and provocative seduction. Her dark hair had been pinned up, but soft, wispy curls fell about her temples, ears, and down the slender curve of her neck. A string of pearls was woven within the cascading waves and shone brilliantly as the sun filtering in through the nearby window touched them. But they could not rival the spark of happiness he saw in her eyes.

"Isn't it..." He found it difficult to speak for the emotion threatening to consume him, and cleared his throat. "Isn't it bad luck for the groom to see the bride in her dress before the wedding?"

She closed the distance between them, and slipped her arms over his shoulders, her fingers sliding into his hair. "All the 'bad' for us is in the past," she said huskily. "And—" she brushed her lips lightly across his "—I believe it's only bad luck for the groom to see the bride in her gown if he isn't sure about what he's doing."

He gripped her hips with his hands and pressed her against him. "Then you're right, my love, because I've never been more sure of anything in my life."

Mitch would have sworn that every citizen in Reimour Crossings was packed into the tiny church.

Half of them were there to wish him and Tina well. The other half, he was sure, were there to make certain he didn't disappear on her again.

He stood by the altar and his gaze moved over the room and guests. Any minute the music would start and Tina would appear at the door, then walk down the aisle toward him.

It had been two weeks since she had said she'd marry him. He glanced down at Jimmy and Joey, dressed in tuxedos and sitting on the floor at his feet, playing with several tiny trucks. Since his brother was dead, and he had no real friends, he'd decided his sons would be his best men at the altar, even if they weren't quite sure what was going on. He smiled, his heart swelling with pride as he watched them play.

Another guest slid into one of the rear pews. In the first

row, to his right, his aunt sat beside Marge Peychaud. He winked at her, and Sarah Blaggette's smile widened. She'd come down for the wedding, and to get to know her great-grandnephews, whom she was going to stay with and take care of while he took Tina on a honeymoon he hoped she'd never forget.

When they returned he had two things he intended to do: talk his aunt into moving permanently to Reimour Crossings, and find himself a job.

A shadow at the door caught his attention, and he turned, expecting to see Tina. Instead, he was shocked to see Ivor Raskin and his wife walk down the aisle, then move off to one side to take a seat.

The blood in his veins suddenly went cold. What was Raskin doing here? Bringing him bad news? Was someone from his past looking for him? He remembered the e-mail message he'd received that morning.

Resignation declined. Talk at five o'clock. New assignment pending.

He felt one of the boys bang into his calf, glanced down, then back at his supervisor. Raskin and the Agency were not going to ruin this for him. He stepped over to his grandmother and bent to whisper in her ear. "Nona," he said softly, "would you keep an eye on the boys for a minute?"

She looked up questioningly, but nodded and went over and knelt beside the twins.

He hurried down the aisle, avoiding the curious stares of several guests. Raskin and his wife had taken a seat in the rear and were exchanging pleasantries with Fred Gateau and his nephew.

"What's going on?" he demanded, his voice low but harsh as he reached the pew where they were seated.

The old Russian smiled. "Well, my boy," he said, and smiled, "I guess congratulations are in order."

"What's going on, Ivor?" he demanded again, glaring at the man now.

"I believe you're getting married," he said, and laughed softly.

Mrs. Raskin smiled knowingly.

He felt his temper rising and glanced toward the rear door, then back at Raskin, one dark brow soaring contemptuously. "I'm not coming back, Ivor."

"Oh?" Raskin's eyes widened in surprise. "I'd rather thought, after talking with your fiancée..."

"You talked to Tina?"

"Well, yes, I..."

Mitch spun on his heel and walked out of the church. An image of Tina, packing her bags and running from him, kept flitting through his mind. In the lobby, he strode to the door of the small room she had disappeared into an hour earlier to "do a few last-minute things." He knocked loudly. "Tina?"

"Just a minute," someone called out.

He pushed the door open and entered, deciding another minute was too long to wait.

"You can't come in here," Lianne said.

Tina, standing before a full-length mirror, adjusting her veil, turned as he strode across the room toward her. "What's wrong?"

He grasped her shoulders, the feel of her confirming to his panicked senses that she was still there. "What's Ivor Raskin doing here?"

"I invited him."

"Why? I told you I quit the Agency. I know how you feel about it. He can't make me work for them, Tina. I won't. I'll find another—"

"I told him you'd stay," she said softly.

He looked down into her eyes, totally confused. "You told him I'd stay?"

She nodded. "He promised he wouldn't send you on assignment anymore, he'd only use you for research and training."

"No." He shook his head. "I know how your family feels, how you feel about them. I told you I'd quit and I meant it."

She smiled and touched a finger to his lips. "It's all right. The family's okay with it, my brother's okay with it, and I want you to stay with the Agency. It's part of you, part of the man I fell in love with."

His eyes bored into hers, those dark, brown fathomless eyes that she now knew so well.

"Which man?" he asked seriously.

It was the first time he'd asked her that, but she didn't hesitate. "Both of them."

"Are you sure?"

"That I want you to stay with the Agency? Yes. That I love you both, Jake and Mitch?" She smiled wickedly. "As sure as I am that they've just started playing the wedding march, and neither of you are standing at the altar where you should be."

He brushed his lips quickly over hers. "Have I ever told you how much I love you?"

"Yes," she said, as a tingle of desire rippled through her, "but please don't ever stop."

"Do you, Jacob Mitchell Ryan Blaggette, take this woman, Christina Marie Peychaud Dubois, to be your lawfully wedded wife, to have and to hold her from this day forward, in sickness or health, for richer or poorer, until death do you part?"

Jake's hand closed around Tina's as he looked down at her. "I do," he said softly.

"Then you may kiss the bride," the minister said.

"Welcome home, Jake," Tina said, as his lips captured hers in a kiss that promised her an eternity of tomorrows.

*   *   *   *   *

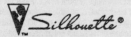

If you enjoyed what you just read,
then we've got an offer you can't resist!

Take 2 bestselling love stories FREE!
Plus get a FREE surprise gift!